FBI agents are trained to delve deep into the minds of the most dangerous predators. So when the tables are turned and the hunter becomes the prey, they can trust their instincts—and their hearts—to keep each other from harm . . .

FBI Special Agent Hannah Cambridge is trying to rebuild her life after the death of her partner. But Jack Benton wasn't just a fellow agent. He was her lover—and the father of her newborn baby. Now Hannah is in Boston, heading a task force to catch a serial killer. It's a case that could make or break her career. Until the madman turns his twisted sights on her . . .

When Jack Benton went deep undercover, he thought it was a way out of a relationship that was spiraling beyond his control. He never knew Hannah wouldn't be told about his "death"—or that she was pregnant. Turning up in Boston in the flesh, and looking better than ever, will send Hannah into a tailspin. But both will need to keep their wits about them to keep her alive—and to survive the truth about the passion that binds them . . .

Visit us at www.kensingtonbooks.com

Books by Kris Rafferty

Secret Agents
Caught By You
Catch A Killer

Published by Kensington Publishing Corporation

Catch A Killer

Secret Agents

Kris Rafferty

LYRICAL PRESS
Kensington Publishing Corp.
www.kensingtonbooks.com

First Electronic Edition: June 2018
eISBN-13: 978-1-5161-0814-5
eISBN-10: 1-5161-0814-0

First Print Edition: June 2018
ISBN-13: 978-1-5161-0817-6
ISBN-10: 1-5161-0817-5

Printed in the United States of America

For my smart, beautiful, funny mother. I love you, Mom.

Chapter 1

FBI Special Agent Hannah Cambridge was in a strange city juggling work and motherhood, and failing miserably. As was her habit, she woke with a start, heart racing and feeling confused, blinking at the unopened moving boxes in her beige-walled bedroom. She was alone.

It took a moment to realize her cell phone had woken her, and when she did, Hannah untangled her arm from the sheets and slapped at the device on her bedside table, accepting the incoming call without reading the caller ID. It was summer, and though her brownstone had central air, she felt hot and sweaty as dreams lingered and reality scratched at her consciousness.

Work. Check. The baby needed to be fed and changed. Check, check. Jack was dead...check.

Anxiety clutched her belly and worked its way up, pressing at the back of her throat until she could barely breathe. Hannah squeezed her eyes shut, clutching the phone as she grimaced through the familiar wave of grief. Jack died last September, and his murder still threatened to cripple her with sorrow almost a year later.

Hannah pushed dark blond bangs from her eyes, blinking past tears as she struggled to speak without revealing she was upset. "Cambridge here."

"It's Ferguson. I wanted to call you sooner, but..." She could hear the detective suck in a breath as he paused.

"What? What's going on?"

Detective Padraic Ferguson—tall, sexy, ex-military—after long hours and lots of legwork, was the one who had discovered Boston had an active serial killer on its hands for at least four months now. In her new role as FBI liaison for the task force, its team leader, Hannah heavily relied on Ferguson, even more than normal. She was just back from maternity leave, a new mom, and needed all the help she could get with the transition. There were rumors he was crushing on her big-time. Sometimes Hannah didn't mind.

"I've conferred with Lieutenant Pepperidge and the DA's office," he said. "I wanted to call you earlier, but you were exhausted, and really, there was nothing you could do, so—"

"Talk to me." She sat, swinging her legs over the bed's edge, wiping her tears.

"Hannah, there's been movement in the case. The bureau felt the need to send more personnel. They're here at the office. You need to come in. Now."

"Okay." She stood, disabled her alarm clock, and stretched out her aches and pains. Ellen had cried most of the night, so yeah, she was *still* exhausted.

"And Hannah?" Ferguson still sounded hesitant. "I sent a protective detail to your apartment last night."

Hannah's eyes glazed over as she turned her head toward her bedroom door, visualizing the baby's bedroom down the hall. Protective detail meant she was in danger. Her four-month-old, Ellen, was in danger. "What happened?"

"Your computer was on when I left the precinct around midnight." He paused, as if asking a question, but before she could decipher what information he was seeking, he continued. "Hannah, our killer sent you one of his emails. You're his next target."

Her legs gave out and she found herself sitting on the edge of the bed with a strange buzzing in her ears. "I'll be right in."

She hung up before she revealed her panic and triggered the detective's protective streak. Hannah had already lost so much. She refused to lose control over her life, too. Given a chance, she knew Ferguson would use this threat as an excuse to put her in bubble wrap and hide her away. He couldn't know she had other responsibilities that made that impossible. He didn't know about Ellen. None of her co-workers did.

The baby cooed from the other room as Hannah fought for composure. Clenching and then shaking out her hands, she struggled to slow her racing heart, hating her weakness, hating that her job put Ellen at risk. And most of all, she hated that Jack had been murdered and left her in this precarious position.

After his death last fall, Hannah had left the D.C. office and transferred to Boston, taking a desk job that allowed her to work from home. Pregnant, hoping to avoid the inevitable questions from her superiors, the transfer also allowed Hannah to put needed distance between herself and the Murtagh case; the one that got Jack killed. Now, she had a new life—back in the field, new city, a healthy, happy baby—but Jack's killer was still out there.

Eventually, Hannah would learn to trust people again, to tell them about her daughter, but...not today.

Hannah dialed Natalie, a fellow agent and friend, one of the few who knew about the baby, and that Jack was Ellen's father. At call's end, Natalie promised to grab the first flight to Boston and be at Hannah's apartment by nightfall.

Hurrying past the moving boxes lining the hall's edges, she stepped to her daughter's crib and found her fine, if disgruntled. Unlike the rest of the apartment, Ellen's room was decorated. Framed pictures of sunflowers hung neatly on pale yellow walls. The white eyelet drapes and bedding were new, and chosen with care. As was the new baby furniture—solid wood crib, bureau, changing table—which gave the room a cheerful vibe as morning sunlight streamed in from its two large windows.

Baby smell fragranced the air. As did wet diaper.

Ellen was on her back, shaking her drool-covered fists and kicking her feet. Blinking and scowling at her lamb mobile, Ellen saw Hannah approach and quieted, smacking her lips. The baby was hungry and their morning routine had begun.

"Hey, sweetie." Lifting Ellen, she kissed her cheek. "Yuck," she teased, wiping her mouth on her nightgown's sleeve. "You're a yucky girl, aren't you?" She laid the baby on the changing table, irrationally afraid of dropping her. Hannah's confidence was still shaky when it came to caring for her daughter. Without warning, she felt a pang of worry that she'd gone back to work too soon, but after that month-long stay in the hospital, and then three months of maternity leave... "Mommy's got to work early today."

Putting the phone on speaker, she multitasked, changing Ellen and calling Mrs. Branaghan, a retired nurse and now Ellen's babysitter, who lived downstairs. The line connected immediately. "Mrs. Branaghan, I need a favor." She explained the situation, afraid the woman would refuse given the target on Hannah's back.

"I'll be right there," she said. A wave of gratitude swamped Hannah. Mrs. Branaghan sounded concerned. She cared, and that mattered more than Hannah could possibly express. She and Ellen were alone in the world, so they relied on their friends, and Mrs. Branaghan was once again proving she was a true friend.

"I'll make sure the police stay until Natalie arrives tonight," Hannah said. "She's an FBI special agent who specializes in this sort of thing." Another friend.

Their conversation ended quickly, and Mrs. Branaghan's prompt arrival made it possible for Hannah to leave the apartment fifteen minutes later, despite growing agitation, fumbling with zippers, and a frantic search for clean socks and Hannah's left shoe. Hair wet and clipped back, no makeup to hide her pallor...*her composure fried...* Hannah still counted it a win that she got out the door.

Sergeant Patrick O'Neil met Hannah downstairs. In his late fifties, he was New Sudbury precinct's street supervisor for the day shift. Shaved head, blue eyes, sexy as hell, O'Neil was the real deal. He handed her a paper cup filled with scalding coffee, then explained the two hovering policemen's assignments. One would watch the apartment at the front stoop, and now that Hannah had left her apartment, the other would watch her door.

O'Neil escorted Hannah to his cruiser at the curb. "You got somewhere to go, Special Agent Cambridge, you call me. Got it? I'll assign one of my guys to escort you to where you need to be."

"You're too good to me, Sergeant." She saw a dimple crease his cheek, but it was short-lived.

He pointed at her just before he got behind the wheel. "I'm serious."

Hannah nodded, lifting her coffee cup in salute. "Thanks." And she was grateful, because she was afraid. Not so much for herself, but for Ellen. Her baby had already lost one parent. Hannah refused to allow her to grow up an orphan.

Cruiser lights on, the sergeant got her through rush hour traffic to the precinct office in fifteen minutes flat. She was through security with a flash of her badge after the minor inconvenience of putting her gun and personal effects into a bin for screening. Heels clicking on the polished tile, keeping time with her anxiety-fueled heartbeat, she stepped on to the elevator, then hit the sixth-floor button. A feminine, well-manicured hand stopped the doors from closing.

"Mrs. Pepperidge, hello." Hannah forced herself to shelve her worries and dredge up a smile.

Mrs. Jolene Pepperidge, the wife of New Sudbury precinct's patrol commander, Lieutenant Cooper Pepperidge, was a regular visitor to the homicide department. Always perfectly coiffed, her roots were routinely bleached to a honey-blond, her blunt cut blown out and curved just under her chin. Rumor said she came from money and that she'd been a model in her youth. Hannah believed it. Tall, muscular in a cosmetic way, she looked stunning in her blue sheath dress and heels, towering over Hannah's five feet four inches.

"Special Agent Cambridge, I've brought muffins and doughnuts." She opened the Dunkin' Donuts box and urged Hannah to indulge. "Cooper keeps telling me I spoil his troops, but I can't seem to help myself. Food is love, right? I must be overcompensating for something." Her brown eyes twinkled with self-deprecating humor. "Does it seem as if I'm buying affection?"

"No one's complained yet." Mrs. Pepperidge was the type of person who made you feel calm by virtue of their proximity, so Hannah's tension settled more comfortably on her shoulders. She grabbed a muffin and was chewing before she remembered muffins and her nervous stomach didn't mesh.

"Well, Cooper complains," Mrs. Pepperidge said. "He blames his expanding waistline on me. *The bugger.*" She snorted, and it clashed with her ladylike appearance.

Hannah knew from late-night confidences with her team that Mrs. Pepperidge and the lieutenant had lost at least four children to stillbirth, one just recently. The news didn't come as a surprise to Hannah. During her month-long hospital stay last spring, Hannah had lived in fear of suffering a stillbirth, too. One quiet night, when she couldn't sleep, Hannah had glimpsed Mrs. Pepperidge wandering the maternity ward in a hospital gown. She hadn't known the lieutenant's wife at the time, but the woman's striking looks made her impossible to forget. Hannah never mentioned the incident to anyone, not even Mrs. Pepperidge, because she didn't want to pry. They weren't friends. Not really. And Hannah didn't want to raise questions that might force her to expose Ellen's existence. Hannah's daughter was a secret for a reason.

The elevator door opened. "Here we go," Mrs. Pepperidge said. "The start of another day." Tucking her hair behind her ear, the lieutenant's wife squared her shoulders and was the first to step into the hall.

Then life intruded by way of 7:00 a.m. at New Sudbury precinct. The floor was already loud and still filled with the overnight crowd. Sleepy prostitutes lined the halls or were cuffed to benches. Detectives sat at file-covered desks, writing up reports, taking statements, answering one of the many incoming calls ringing and ringing. Hannah and Mrs. Pepperidge walked past the activity, down the hall to the homicide department. When they stepped through the door, all eyes focused on the Dunkin' Donuts box, which Mrs. Pepperidge set on Detective Ferguson's desk, off to the left.

The lieutenant's wife waved everyone over. "You're welcome!" she said, in response to the many ardent thank-yous. Then she disappeared into her husband's office, leaving a heavy silence in her wake.

The team focused on Hannah as Ferguson, brawny and brooding, his green eyes pinning her in place, stood before her and waited. The detective exuded strength. It was strength she envied, because Hannah wasn't feeling it this morning. She was a FBI task force leader, on the hunt for a deadly serial killer, the full might of the United States government at her fingertips, but…she felt more like Ellen's mom, afraid, looking for someone to tell her everything would be all right. Be that as it may, it was her responsibility to set the tone for the day, and to make a statement about the case's latest development.

Hannah made a big show of rolling her eyes and grimacing. "Everyone needs to relax. This is good news. We finally have a break in the case."

Vivian O'Grady, the homicide department's IT specialist, stepped forward. She seemed uncertain, standing there in her prim skirt and suit jacket, her hands nervously clasped. The woman opened her mouth to speak, but stopped herself when Lieutenant Pepperidge—black uniform pressed, his silver badge shiny—stepped from his office.

"Let's be clear, Special Agent Cambridge. This new lead is not good," the lieutenant said.

"I would say not." Mrs. Pepperidge followed him out of his office. "This is horrible. Cooper just told me. I can't believe you didn't tell me while I was chattering away in the elevator. I feel so foolish!"

"Jolene." Lieutenant Pepperidge gave his wife a look, which she interpreted as *not now.*

"Fine." She kissed her husband. "We have reservations at Jimmy's Restaurant tonight. Don't be late."

"I'll see you later." Pepperidge smiled at his retreating wife. When he turned back to Hannah, the smile was gone. "You're our perp's next target and this guy is three for three. As of *now* your safety is our primary concern." In his late forties, sharp features, Lieutenant Pepperidge glared at Hannah. She was feeling the love.

The lieutenant stepped to the murder board and taped something next to pictures of the three victims in their case. It was another picture. Hannah's.

"Lieutenant." Ferguson's eyes widened as he raked his black hair off his forehead. "She's not dead yet."

"And we're going to keep it that way," the lieutenant said. "The district attorney and bureau chief had a confab in the small hours of the morning, and then made a few calls. Special Agent Cambridge's replacement has already arrived with his team."

Replacement? The news felt like a punch to her gut. Why hadn't Hannah seen that coming? It made sense, followed protocol, but damn…she was losing control of this case.

Pepperidge indicated the door, and the man walking into the room. "Cambridge, I was told you know Special Agent Jack Benton."

Her first impression was a lean and muscular man. Sexy. Familiar. Then she locked eyes with him and things got fuzzy. *Jack.* Her mind told her not to believe it. She was seeing things. The man wasn't smiling. In fact, he looked as if he feared she'd faint. He knew her too well. *Jack.* Or *had* known her…before he'd *died* eleven months ago and gave her a September from hell.

She still couldn't believe it. *Special Agent Jack Benton.* Her partner in the bureau. Her secret lover. Ellen's father.

Jack stepped toward her, extending his hand for a shake. The moment was surreal. Automatically, she took his proffered hand, felt his familiar calluses scratch her palm, unearthing memories of his hands on her skin, of him making love to her more times than she could count. Solid. Strong. Towering over her. His touch galvanized her and forced her to accept the truth. This wasn't a dream.

Jack is alive. This is real. This is happening.

She shivered, felt her face flush, and knew there was no hiding her shock. Now everyone was staring at her as if they feared she'd faint. Well, she wanted to faint. She wanted to curl into a ball and cry. She waited for the euphoria, for the relief that he was alive, but it refused to come.

He'd betrayed her. He'd allowed her to believe he'd been murdered. She squeezed his hand tighter. He'd allowed her to suffer such grief and pain it had killed the woman she'd been, and replaced her with someone she still didn't recognize. Someone *less*, someone weaker, someone she'd come to despise.

Tugging sharply on his hand, Hannah pulled him toward her and lifted her knee to strike his groin. Jack stopped it with a palm heel to her thigh, and then quickly clasped her into a restrictive hug, deftly disguising that she'd just attacked a fellow officer, a firing offense.

"I'll explain," he whispered into her ear. His breath sent a shiver through her body, leaving her trembling. *This was happening. How could this be happening?* "Really, Hannah. I'm not the ass you think I am. I can explain." Then he loosened his grip.

Hannah pushed him aside, struggling to find her composure, to find her breath.

She'd mourned him.

"That's right, Lieutenant." Hannah hated that her words sounded breathy, and weak. "I know *Jack.*"

Blindly, she stepped to the refreshment table, and with shaking hands, she poured a cup of coffee and then sipped, scalding her tongue. The brew was bitter…and painful.

Chapter 2

"Special Agent Cambridge." FBI Special Agent Jack Benton didn't know how to say his next words without sounding like the ass he'd promised Hannah he wasn't, but they had to be said. He couldn't allow her to take risks with her life. The bureau rightly had stepped in and given him this case. On his insistence, of course, but she didn't have to know that. "I'm here to relieve you of your post and place you in protective custody."

She kept her back to him, sipping her coffee, so Jack glanced at Pepperidge, hoping he'd take over the explanation. Would she have a meltdown? She deserved one, but it would be a lot easier if she gave him the benefit of the doubt and rolled with this change of command. She had to know there was a reasonable explanation for what'd happened last year. Right?

Pepperidge held up a fax from the bureau, and another from the district attorney's office. "Special Agent Cambridge, you know protocol as well as we do."

"I don't want protective custody." Hannah's tone brooked no argument as she kept her back to the room. "I've made other arrangements."

"You have no choice." Jack would protect her whether she liked it or not. A serial killer—an extremely successful serial killer—had targeted her. Protective custody was a no-brainer. "I have authority to relieve you of duty."

"Relieve me all you like." Hannah glanced at him over her shoulder. "But you can't put me in protective custody without my consent. To do that, you'll have to arrest me."

"Don't tempt me." From the looks he was getting from the team, Jack could see where their loyalty lay, and he didn't blame them. Hannah was one of the good guys. She could be oppositional, like now, but she was relentlessly by the book. Which was why it made no sense that she didn't see what had to be done.

Hannah belonged in protective custody.

Heading a task force to track down a serial killer was a coup, sure, and it had to be hard to give up the lead role in such a high-profile case. He understood her resistance. He did. Hell, Jack was only hours back from a job he took *knowing* it was dangerous, but he took it anyway for the same reasons: high-profile, lead role.

Hannah's life was more important than any promotion, though. She had to know that. She wasn't *Jack*. People cared about her. Why didn't she see that?

Hannah turned toward the room, and leaned against the refreshment table, sipping. She scanned the faces in the incident room, probably gauging the likelihood of her team supporting a mutiny. It was a reminder that she'd never been good at admitting defeat. He suspected it was why they'd stayed together so long in D.C., despite their shaky relationship; a shaky relationship that nudged him into taking the undercover assignment in New Jersey.

It had happened fast. Overnight, in fact, and then he was deeply embedded, under radio silence, cut off from all who knew him. Did he regret the decision? Not really. Sure, Jack took the easy out and allowed his superior, Special Agent in Charge Goodwin, to break the news to Hannah. Only Goodwin didn't break the news. Jack's boss made an executive decision to withhold pertinent information from Hannah—that Jack *wasn't*, in fact, *dead*—fearing snitches in the FBI's ranks. Goodwin didn't know he and Hannah were lovers, but still...it was cruel, and ultimately Jack's fault for delegating such an important task. He'd discovered only this morning what had happened, and the irony of his situation was hard to miss. He'd taken the assignment because he'd feared Hannah didn't love him, yet how he left her gave Hannah ample reason to hate him now that he was back.

Vivian O'Grady covered her mouth, hiding a nervous, sympathetic smile. Pepperidge had provided a briefing packet on the team, and Vivian's file described a talented tech who had a bit of the savant about her; the team's designated caregiver. The thirtysomething looked like a small-town librarian. Jack could easily suppose she had a house full of cats, maybe porcelain figurines in a china cabinet, so his gut said Vivian wasn't the type to join Hannah's mutiny.

Detective Ferguson snickered, catching Jack's attention. He was a big guy. The Boston Police Department's point man on the task force. His grin told Jack he was enjoying Hannah's push back. Ferguson would gladly join Hannah's mutiny.

"Special Agent Benton, I'm not going anywhere," Hannah said. "I've been leading this case for a month. Leaving would hamper the investigation when I need it running smoothly. It's my life on the line."

Like he didn't know that. *Why the hell did she think he was here?* And what the hell was with the 'Special Agent Benton' routine? He'd fucked up last year. That didn't mean they were strangers. He could describe down to the most intimate detail what she'd looked like when she'd climaxed in his arms. Strangers couldn't do that. "You'll follow orders."

Hannah's eyes narrowed. "Taking me off the case is a bad idea."

Stubborn. That's what she was. "Put your ambition on a back burner."

He detected a flicker of hurt in her gaze, the first real emotion she'd shown since he'd arrived. Even when she'd attempted to knee him in the groin, her face had been an unemotional mask, her thoughts hidden. She'd reminded Jack of his father, a cold man. Detached, too, especially when the bastard had doled out pain. His father never loved Jack, either.

"Well." Pepperidge clasped his hands loudly. "Now that we have that settled, everyone back to work."

"You hear that, Special Agent Benton? It's settled," Hannah repeated. "I'm working the case."

Pepperidge glanced between Jack and Hannah. "I have a meeting with the captain. Have this ironed out before I come back." Then he left the room, disappearing into the hall.

Hannah seemed primed for battle, but Jack didn't want the team witnessing her losing this fight, so he waved everyone toward the door. "Give us the room, but don't go far," he said.

Vivian and Ferguson hustled into the hall, helping themselves to doughnuts as they left. Ferguson walked most of the way backward, smiling ear to ear, looking between Hannah and Jack. It was enough to make Jack want to test Ferguson's Ranger skills against his Quantico training. Almost, but then the door closed behind the two, focusing Jack on the battle ahead with Hannah. It was coming, was long overdue, and she had every right to be pissed.

Hannah surprised him by grabbing his hand and dragging him into the lieutenant's office.

When she slammed the door behind them, he frowned at her, not knowing what she had in mind. Then she grabbed his lapels and pulled him in for a kiss.

There was no hesitation. No moment of shock. Her lips were on his, and his tongue slipped inside her mouth, as if that's where it belonged. He pulled her close, clutching her to his chest as he reacquainted himself with her taste, the smell of her, and how she felt in his arms. Thinner than he remembered, but good. So good. She felt right.

Hannah broke the kiss. "They told me you were dead." She was gasping, suppressing sobs as she pulled his jacket off, peeling it down his arms until it fell to the floor. "I saw the body, Jack."

He shook his head, while dropping kisses on her face. "I'm sorry."

"Do you have a condom?"

"Huh?" He blinked at her. "Yes." He pulled out his wallet, she grabbed it and rifled through until she found the condom, which was old enough to give him pause.

"Thank heaven." Then she kissed him, her hands fluttering on his chest as if she couldn't believe he was real. When she loosened his tie, a jolt of arousal had him sucking in a breath, and reminded him what he'd given up when he'd left. This...hunger. And he was hungry for her. Raw need blocked out common sense, and he felt no shame, no worry as he helped her unbutton his shirt. All he wanted was Hannah touching him. To touch her skin, to taste her, to bury himself deep and forget this last year ever happened.

Then his hands were on her, unzipping her pants with shaking hands. He was desperate for her as she kicked off her shoes and pants, her gaze never leaving his body. Jack slapped at the doorknob, locking the door as she unsnapped her bra. Then Hannah launched herself at him, jumping on him. He caught her and buried his face in the hollow of her neck, inhaling her glorious scent, tasting the tender skin beneath her earlobe. She locked her ankles behind his hips as Jack lifted her higher, cupping her ass, holding her weight as he relished the feel of her warm, wet core brushing against his belly.

"Damn, Hannah. *Damn*, I've missed this." He'd missed *her*.

He made it to the nearest wall without tripping over their clothes and pressed against her, his weight holding her in place as he freed a hand to cup her breast. She trembled, tasting him, running her tongue up his neck, nipping at his earlobe. When his thumb brushed her nipple, it pebbled, she gasped, reminding him how responsive a lover she was, and how that had always turned him on. As it was turning him on now.

Jack handed her the condom. She reached between their bodies, rolled it on, and then it was his turn to touch her...wet, hot, and ready for him. He buried himself with one thrust as he slid his tongue into her mouth, sealing their lips with a kiss.

She moaned deep in her throat, something he'd never thought to hear again, and it was heavenly. She gripped his shoulders, restless, moving her hips. Impatient. So like Hannah. His smile broke their kiss but allowed him to watch her reaction to his deep thrusts. Her obvious surrender sent a jolt of pleasure through him, but he forced himself to *savor* the moment, her gasps of desire. Like a starving man eating his last meal, Jack's possessiveness was back, but he knew she wasn't his to keep. Not anymore. Not for a long time. *What the hell was he doing?*

Hannah pulled his head toward her and kissed him, their tongues meeting. Jack's control buckled, and he took her hard, fast, and then it was Hannah breaking their kiss. She threw her head back, crying out in climax, destroying Jack's last thread of control. All thoughts became about Hannah's release, how her body melded with his, how amazing it felt to be inside her again as she clenched around him—consuming and being consumed. She sighed and gasped each time he buried himself inside her, and when he found his release, she was on her second one.

They were left gasping, their chests heaving as he continued to pin her to the wall with his body. When he could think again, he rested his forehead on hers, not wanting this moment to end, knowing it might be his last shot to have her like this. It had always been this way with Hannah. She always made him feel as if she were a breath away from being gone. A comment away from leaving him. Last year, he'd left so he wouldn't have to live through her leaving him.

Now, he felt like a fool.

Drawing his lips along her jawline, he moved up her neck until he could brush his nose against the skin behind her ear. She smelled of fruity shampoo, and her hair had escaped the clip, tickling his face. Jack couldn't get enough of kissing her, tasting her lips, capturing her tongue, and sealing her mouth with his…breathing the same air.

Neither attempted to speak as they reacquainted themselves with each other's body and scent. Her fingertips caressed his shoulders, drew down his arms as he cupped her ass with both hands, keeping her firmly in place, them connected.

It was a homecoming.

Hannah. The only woman he'd ever loved.

Just as these thoughts filled his head, Hannah broke their kiss, unhooked her ankles, and slid her feet to the ground. It forced him to pull out of her, but her legs were wobbly, so Jack used that as an excuse to continue holding her close, keeping her cheek pressed to his chest. She clung to him as Jack tried to understand what had just happened. Honestly, he wasn't sure, but knew it wasn't just sex. He knew how that felt; impersonal, fleeting pleasure. This was different. It always had been with Hannah.

She took a deep breath, then pushed away from him, turning her back as she gathered her clothes. Hannah was never one to argue from a weak position, so she predictably dressed as quickly as they'd disrobed, acting as if she were alone in the room. Jack followed suit, not wanting to be the only naked person when the inevitable discussion began. He counted himself lucky she'd waited until he was dressed before unlocking the lieutenant's office door and storming from the room, but her behavior confused him. Surely, she had questions.

He followed her out, and when she sat at her desk as if she intended to ignore what they'd just done—to ignore *him*—it took Jack a moment to gather his thoughts and come up with a strategy to respond. He stepped to the refreshment table and poured himself a coffee, but didn't drink it, not wanting to lose the taste of her on his lips.

Glancing over his shoulder, he saw she was reading a report that she'd picked up off her desk. If she was absorbing any information, he'd be a monkey's uncle, because he'd be hard-pressed to spell his last name right now. Hannah had to be putting on a show, otherwise, he had no idea who this woman was. He stepped to her side. She ignored him still, even when he sat on the chair next to her desk.

On assignment, he'd told himself he felt fine living without her. Less stressed, despite working the Coppola syndicate case, surrounded by a bunch of sociopaths. It was a relief to clock his time on the job and not worry about a personal life. He'd missed her, but assumed he'd have missed anyone he'd recently broken up with. He'd missed the sex, that's for sure. No one rocked Jack's boat like Hannah, and he wasn't interested in anything less, so it had been a dry year. A lonely year. He'd missed her companionship, too. Working side by side with Hannah had been bliss, and then coming home to her, making love until they had nothing left... That had been an amazing life they'd shared.

Looking at her now—stone-cold expression, sitting at her desk, ignoring him—he was reminded of their past challenges, too. Her silences. And how things got real bad, until he'd cried uncle and left, falling back on what he knew. The job. Something he was good at.

"I'm sorry." He wouldn't blame her if she never spoke to him again. "You deserved to be told I was on assignment. I was assured you would be, but, well, you know what happened. I'm sorry things went down the way they did."

"Apology accepted." Her eyes remained on the reports, her gaze scanning left to right. She *was* reading, and it flabbergasted him. Who was this woman? Didn't she just strip him to the skin and fuck his brains out mere minutes ago? He had to assume she wanted more of an apology, so he dug deep and tried to come up with something that revealed exactly how horrible he felt about the whole mix-up.

"A job presented itself," he said, "and it required me to go deep undercover. It's a long story."

"I'm sure it is." Her eyes flashed with anger, but it came and went so quickly, he could almost convince himself it didn't happen as she continued to read whatever the hell was in that fascinating manila folder. He wanted to throw it across the room.

"I'm sorry I didn't call." Was she furious or bored? Or annoyed he was still talking?

She barked out a laugh, still avoiding his gaze, but Jack noticed she wasn't reading anymore. She simply stared at the paper, her lips pressed together so tightly they'd lost all color. Progress, he supposed, but… okay. She was angry. She had that right, but other than apologizing, he didn't know what else to do. Hannah wasn't like him. She got angry for reasons that wouldn't even occur to him. It left him feeling like a kite in the wind, its string clipped, its demise assured when it collided with the ground. *And so it begins again,* he thought. This is where he and Hannah left off a year ago.

"Once I realized you hadn't been informed, I thought it best to tell you in person," he said.

She took a swift breath through her nose, then released it slowly. "And you did. Thank you for that courtesy." *Cold.* Cold enough to freeze him solid. And she *still* wouldn't look at him.

"Listen. I don't know what you want me to say. Goodwin was supposed to tell you. He dropped the ball, and believe me, when I found out this morning, I called and gave him hell." Jack adjusted his position on the chair. "I'm saying I'm sorry, Hannah. Stop busting my balls."

"I accepted your apology," she said. "Stop busting *my*…chops." His Hannah, bristling with anger, face flushed, was shaking with barely controlled emotion, and she was the most beautiful thing he'd ever seen. He found himself sighing, and that reminded him that he hadn't slept in who knows how long, and yeah, he was tired. Best to get this over with.

"The assignment required me to die on paper, so I could have a life after the op." Hannah's cheeks drained of color, panicking him, so he pushed his coffee toward her, thinking the caffeine might help.

"You had a life *before* the operation. With me." There was hurt in her gaze again, and it confused him. When he'd left on assignment, they'd been fighting more than not. He was almost positive she hadn't even *liked* him by then.

"I'm sorry."

She grabbed a random paper clip off her desk and kept her eyes on it, using her fingers to twist it into pop art. "I moved to Boston because I thought my life was on the line. I was told you were murdered because of the Murtagh case, the case we were working, and Murtagh is still in the wind, Jack. Your car was rigged with explosives. Every time I stepped into a car I wondered if it would be my turn next." She met his gaze squarely now. "I had to leave D.C. How could you do that to me?"

Now *that* made sense. She'd thought she was in danger, and her reaction was to take steps to protect herself, upending her life. Realizing they'd been unnecessary would piss Jack off, too.

Her breathing hitched, then her chin quivered, and her breathing became labored. Jack saw panic color her expression, and it freaked him out. "What the hell?" he said.

"Shut—" She sucked in air. "—*up!*" Hannah squeezed her eyes shut, and focused on inhaling and exhaling. He didn't know what was happening.

"Go home, Hannah. Let me take it from here." It was the least he could do.

She shook her head, her expression a cross between amazed and confused now. "And what? Catch up on my to-be-read pile? Is that how you envision my life until the killer is caught?" She covered her face, still breathing heavily.

"I don't care what you do as long as you're at a safe house under round-the-clock protection. Do your nails. Catch up on sleep. It's with pay, so order out, have a party." Jack had noticed the dark circles under her eyes, and that she was thinner than before, but it only now occurred to him that it was indicative of something bigger. He didn't recognize this side of Hannah. Delicate. Vulnerable. He didn't like it *at all*.

She dropped her hands and glared at him, still puffing away. It made Jack replay his last words, wondering how they could possibly have warranted this reaction.

"You're going to keep me on the case," she said between gasping breaths.

"No. I can't." He couldn't do his job efficiently while babysitting Hannah, and he would have to babysit. It wasn't as if he could trust her safety to someone else if she went all free-range on him. "You need to be gone. At least until we have some idea of what's going on." Her cheeks had flushed beet red by now, and she was seriously worrying him.

"I know what's going on," she said. "That's why I need to stay on the team." She narrowed her eyes. "I understand how I can't lead the team.

I'm the target. But it's my life, Jack, and if this perp kills me, I don't get to come back a year later for a do-over." He flinched. "It will take you a week *at least* to be up to speed on this case, and I don't have a week." She closed her eyes again, this time holding her breath. When she opened them again, she released her breath slowly, sounding like she'd managed to control herself. "Our perp's pattern is three days max after the emailed message, sometimes less, but never more, and I don't have time to cater to Lieutenant Pepperidge's fears for my safety."

"That's unfair," he said. "Pepperidge is thinking of you. And yes. The case. No one has the time to cater to your ego." She squeaked with outrage, sitting up ramrod straight. "Admit it," he said. "If the target was Vivian or Ferguson, you'd have their ass in protective custody so fast their head would spin."

"It's not the same and you—"

"Stop!" The job was the only thing he was good at. "Hannah, let me do this!" He didn't trust anyone else to keep her alive. Any chance they had of being together died a slow death even before he was offered the Coppola syndicate case last fall, but that didn't mean he wouldn't give his life for hers.

Hannah lowered her chin, and though her breathing was under control, her hand shook as she lifted the coffee. "If you don't agree to my continued involvement in this case," she said, "I'll still refuse protective custody, and then take what vacation days I have left to run an investigation on my own."

Her threat chapped his ass. "Typical."

She sipped, and then set the coffee aside. "How would you know? In case it's not abundantly clear"—Jack was horrified to see her chin quiver again—"I am not the person you left. I'm...stronger. I have more to lose." She looked everywhere but at him.

More to lose, huh? What the hell did that mean?

Ferguson glared at them through the incident door's glass panel. He looked possessive. And in love. Jack glanced between Ferguson and Hannah, wondering if this is what she'd meant by "more to lose." Was she in a relationship with the detective? Jack couldn't believe it. Not after what just happened in the lieutenant's office, but...maybe.

I am not the person you left, she'd said. Well, he believed her. He'd done a considerable amount of growing up, too. Enough to realize he was a fool when it came to Hannah.

"I won't agree," he said. "You're a target now. The killer is coming for you. We need to be ready for him, and you running around the city only makes it harder to protect you. You'll make it more likely he'll find an opportunity to kill you."

She shook her head, dismissing his concern. "Let me worry about that."

"I'm heading this task force. Not you. It's my call."

Her eyes narrowed. "You're a bastard. Do you know that?" she said.

Yeah, and so did she. He could see the moment Hannah realized what she'd said, and its connotations. He wondered if she would apologize, and waited for it. He felt no pain from the accusation, felt no ownership of the moniker, but he was curious to see where her brain was at. Did she care enough not to hurt his feelings? The old Hannah would be horrified at pushing his buttons.

Ferguson's patience seemed to be at its end. The detective pushed through the door and walked to Hannah's side. Vivian trailed after him. "You okay?" Ferguson exchanged glances with Hannah, while Jack stewed over Hannah's silence.

She had no problem calling him a bastard. Duly noted.

Ferguson was glaring at him, and some small part of Jack's mind wondered if the detective would clock him. He was a bit surprised at himself for wishing he would. After Hannah's mind-fuck, he was in the mood for a good brawl.

Hannah stood and indicated Vivian should move closer and join them at her desk. "This is how it's going to go. Special Agent Benton will lead the task force and I will consult. The perp's pattern is to strike three days after the emailed warning, but because it was sent so late last night, it messes with our timeline. It could be three days from when I would most likely be expected to receive the email, or three days from late last night. Either way," she grimaced, "I'm dead soon, so let's get to work."

Jack stepped in front of Hannah, glaring, his hands on his hips. Yeah, that pushed aside his black suit jacket, exposing his holstered 9mm Glock. Yeah, he looked ramped up and aggressive, but she was purposefully being insubordinate, contradicting what he'd declared had to happen. He could throw her over his shoulder and toss her ass in the hall. That would send the team a strong message. Or he could simply say no and have uniformed officers do his dirty work.

Every eye was on him. They wanted what Hannah said to be true, but she'd clearly transferred her authority to him, so they waited for his agreement or denial. He could tell from their tense expressions that everyone hoped he'd give the green light to Hannah staying on the team, and Jack wasn't stupid. Life within this team would be easier if he gave them what they wanted. Hannah had earned their loyalty, and that was no small thing.

"On one condition," Jack said. "Nonnegotiable." He saw her skepticism, and maybe a little unease. "You never leave my side. Ever." Was her expression one of surprise, and maybe curiosity? The possible benefits of being effectively shackled for the duration of this case occurring to her? Jack licked his lips, and found he could still taste her. Hannah, he saw, was watching his tongue at work, so maybe her thoughts weren't far from where his had gone.

Hannah shook her head. "Sergeant O'Neil said he'd allocate patrolmen to keep an eye on me. There's two beefy, highly trained Boston's finest guarding my apartment. *I don't need you*, especially since you'll be busy finding the perp."

First Ferguson, and now...what did she say? Beefy? It was just raining men for Hannah in Boston. "Nonnegotiable." He prepared himself for a sharp *go to hell*.

"Deal," she said. The glint in her eye told him he'd been played. She'd hung the arrangement around his neck, and got what she'd wanted. Equal access to the case.

With one word she'd flipped the bird to a serial murderer and him at the same time. Now, *that* was the Hannah he remembered.

Chapter 3

Hannah told herself to be grateful Jack didn't stick to his guns and send her packing, but instead of gratitude, she felt numb, exhausted from fending off her latest anxiety attack. She had to consciously move her facial muscles to project whatever the correct expression was for whatever was being discussed, all the while feeling as if everyone was staring. *Breathe in, Hannah, breathe out.*

"Jack, what did the lieutenant tell you about the case?" Hannah approached the murder board, turning her back to it, feeling like a schoolteacher rather than a trained FBI special agent. One look at Jack's face and she could see he was angry about their deal, so why did he agree? He was all about control. How did giving in to Hannah's demands buy him control?

"Our perp started killing four months ago, and—" Jack grimaced. "He likes poetry."

"If he is a *he*." The incident room's door swung closed behind a gorgeous blue-eyed blonde whose red Kate Spade bag hung from the crook of her elbow. She approached the team, tall in her heels, dressed in a black haute couture pantsuit.

Hannah adjusted her plain, black, off-the-rack suit jacket, and told herself not to care that her hair was escaping the clip at the nape of her neck.

"This is Special Agent Cynthia Deming," Jack said. "I stole her from Quantico's Behavioral Sciences Unit." Hannah couldn't help but notice that Deming was the type of woman Jack usually dated. Or had before he and Hannah had become an item. "Deming," Jack said, "this is Detective Ferguson, our point man in homicide." Deming shook Ferguson's hand. "And this is BPD's tech, Vivian O'Grady." Deming shook hands with the tech. "Where's Special Agent Gilroy?" he said.

Deming tilted her head, giving a little shrug. "Since you gave Special Agent Modena the week off, Gilroy's finishing the paperwork on the Coppola syndicate case." Deming's gaze settled on Hannah, who Jack had yet to introduce. "He should be here soon." Deming stepped in front of Hannah, smiling. "Hello."

Hannah nodded. "I'm Special Agent Hannah Cambridge."

"Of course you are." Deming smiled. There was a twinkle in her eye.

"Most serial killers are men." Ferguson's scowl was aimed at Deming. "Why would we assume otherwise in this case?"

"Deming is our profiler," Jack said, "who specializes in serial killers. She didn't get much sleep last night after poring over the files, so don't give her a hard time."

Deming's cheek kicked up. She seemed, if anything, amused at Ferguson's behavior, and gave no indication the detective had gotten under her skin. Hannah suspected Special Agent Cynthia Deming was a badass.

Deming indicated the room's desks with a flick of her manicured nails. "Where do you want me?" Hannah could give a damn where Deming sat, so glanced at Vivian, who stepped forward.

"My desk is over there." Vivian pointed to the back wall of the room, toward a desk decorated with African violets and candy dishes. It was neat, stacks of manila folders and thousands of dollars of tech hardware all in their places. "You could take the one next to mine." Vivian smiled sweetly.

Deming followed the tech to the proffered desk, dropped her bag on it, and then made a beeline to the coffee machine off to Hannah's right. "Dunkin's!" She opened the pink and orange pastry box, and then glanced at Hannah. "May I?"

"Of course. The lieutenant's wife brought them. Help yourself." Hannah could see Jack champing at the bit, impatient to continue the meeting. He looked rumpled, and it reminded her that she'd ripped his clothes off in the lieutenant's office mere minutes ago.

When Deming had her coffee in hand and was nibbling on a doughnut, Jack arched a brow. "Are you ready, Deming? Or do you want to braid hair next?"

Deming bit her lip to suppress a smile. "You can't wave a Dunkin' Donuts box at me and expect me to pass it up, Benton. Give me a break."

Jack grit his teeth. "Is there anything you'd like to share *about the case?*"

Deming gave no indication of being intimidated, solidifying Hannah's suspicion that something romantic was happening between the two of them. And why wouldn't there be? Well acquainted, worked hand in hand, both extremely good-looking...

Deming sipped her coffee. "Ferguson is right."

"Of course Ferguson is right," Ferguson growled, storming back to his desk.

Deming ignored him. "Our perp is probably a male, but lightning strikes once in a while, so we can't rule out the perp being a woman." She leaned back in her chair, getting comfortable. "He's educated, smart enough not to get caught yet, lives in the Boston area or has lived here most of his life. Maybe a commuter. His choice of crime scenes—North End, adjoining wharfs—they're easily accessible via the JFK Expressway and Causeway. Economic status still unclear, but from the files I was given to look over, I'm leaning toward middle class, upper middle class." Deming glanced at Ferguson, and then smiled brightly. If the profiler did that to irritate Ferguson, mission accomplished. "Mostly because there are more working-class killers in the world than rich killers. And rich killers have more to lose, tend to be more educated, so rarely are caught."

"You sound like a bookie," Ferguson said. "Playing the odds."

Deming turned her attention back to Jack, who sat on the chair next to Hannah's desk. "This guy wants us to catch him," she said. "They all do. He's obsessive, compulsive, asexual as far as the evidence shows, which makes this case unusual. Or, more likely, we just haven't found the pertinent evidence yet."

Jack arched a brow. "Clarify."

Deming sipped her coffee. "If our guy is getting his jollies, it's not with the victims." She frowned, revealing her first sign of unease.

"That it?" Jack said.

"He likes poetry, or at least William Blake's 'Broken Love.'" Deming took a bite of glazed doughnut. "It is interesting that every kill is preceded by an email sent to the victim. He's not as cryptic as…say, the Zodiac Killer, but he certainly wants to play."

Hannah studied the back-and-forth between Deming and Jack, looking for more definitive clues to see if they were an item. As much as Hannah hated to admit it, it was a joy to watch him in action. Just listening to his voice calmed her. And it was reassuring to see Jack's and Deming's frustration, because it meant she and her team hadn't missed anything.

"Someone tell me about this poem." Jack adjusted his weight in the seat and leaned his elbow on the desk. "It might surprise you all, but my training at Quantico didn't extend to poetry analysis."

Vivian raised her hand, smiling. "It's about death, longing, and regret. It's *gorgeous*."

That's my cue. Hannah ignored the butterflies in her belly, opened the appropriate manila folder on her desk and found her list of pertinent information. "We contacted a professor at UMass Boston and he gave us notes. The most relevant being, 'The narrator [of the poem] is a mysterious figure dealing with regret, talks of withholding love for fear of rejection, then losing that love to death, losing the opportunity to win the object of his affection and is tortured by it, forced to live with just the memory of her, and his broken heart. Struggling to move on. Her power over his heart stretching from the grave.'" Hannah felt her face flush as the words finally sunk in, though this had to be the hundredth time she'd read them this month. They perfectly described the fallout of her relationship with Jack; how it ended, Jack dead, Hannah struggling to move on. This couldn't be a coincidence... But it had to be.

"Huh?" Jack's face scrunched up. "What does all that mean?"

Glancing at the team, she wondered if any of them made the connection, then realized her fears were silly. Only Jack could know how it pertained to them, and he looked clueless.

"I find the poem haunting and romantic," Vivian said. "Sad, too."

"The killer is using the poem as a weapon," Deming said. "Jacques Derrida penned, 'The poet...is the man of metaphor...[who] plays on the multiplicity of signifieds.'"

"Cool." Vivian's smile couldn't have been wider.

"Who the hell is Derrida?" Ferguson leaned against the edge of his desk, arms folded across his chest. "And what the hell is he talking about?"

"I'm sorry, Ferguson." Deming contemplated her manicure. "I shouldn't have expected a hammer to understand a nail."

"Excuse me?" Ferguson narrowed his eyes.

Hannah stepped in, hoping to smooth the detective's feathers. "He's a dead French philosopher."

Deming nodded, eyes now on Jack. "In other words, the killer has no qualms about twisting reality and defining it to his specifications."

"Maybe he's a profiler," Ferguson mumbled.

Vivian snorted, and then covered her mouth. "Sorry, Special Agent Deming. Sorry."

Deming ignored them both. "The perp is lashing out. Someone he loved died, maybe, and he's doing what he wants, when he wants, to ease the pain."

Jack waited, and when no one added anything more, he lifted his hands expectantly. "The kills started four months ago, people. That's May. What triggered him?"

Hannah studied Jack's face, reacquainting herself with it, and saw the same frown Ellen sported when things weren't going her way. *Jack.* She still couldn't believe he was alive. How would he react when he discovered he was a father? Hannah caught Deming studying her, so wiped her expression clean. *Stay numb, Hannah. Survive the moment, and schedule your meltdown for when no one is looking.*

"There are no previous cases in the FBI databases that we can link to this MO," Deming said. "Gilroy and I scoured them with a fine-tooth comb."

"We knew that already," Ferguson said. "All you had to do was ask. With all due respect, Special Agent Benton, you and Special Agent Deming are acting as if we've been sitting on our asses doing nothing, when in fact, I've been here from the beginning."

Hannah nodded. "Detective Ferguson is the one who discovered we have a serial killer on our hands."

"This meeting is to put everyone on the same page. Can we continue?" Jack said. Ferguson pressed his lips together, as if forcing himself to stay silent.

"Four months ago," Deming said, "our perp set in motion his plan to kill using the poem 'Broken Love.' Did he have a psychotic break, act out when he lost a loved one? Maybe. Or maybe it just took this long for him to act on his urges. His use of the poem tells me this guy is a planner." She lifted her brows, absently nudging her coffee cup on the desk. "Could have been planning this for a long while, but I believe we can rule out we've missed prior kills. We have stanza one's victim clearly marked by the killer. It could be a diversion, yes, but until we discover otherwise, I believe it's safe to say the killings did start this May."

"With James Twoomey," Vivian said.

"Could. Thinking. *Maybe.* We have nothing." Jack scowled. He was acting as if Hannah's team had failed him. Failed *him.* How had this case become about Jack? Anger bubbled up, but Hannah pushed it down with the rest of her inconvenient emotions.

"We have plenty of evidence," Hannah countered in a quiet voice. "It just doesn't point to any suspects yet." She left her desk to hand Jack a folder containing the email copies, and a breakdown of what the individual stanzas meant in the literary world. "Our perp informs his victims they're targets by emailing them the words 'Weep No More for Broken Love' in the body of the email, leaving the subject line blank."

"Pretty ballsy, giving them a heads-up." Jack flipped through the printouts as Hannah took a few steps back, needing to distance herself from him. "And that's all he writes? Nothing else?"

"We hope one day he'll sign with his real name," Ferguson said, "but so far, no dice."

Jack gave him a *fuck you* look, but Ferguson didn't seem impressed. Hannah blamed herself. Ferguson wasn't stupid. He'd seen her try to knee Jack in the groin, and because he was on Team Hannah, and protective as hell, he'd be at loggerheads with Jack forever unless she did something about it. It wasn't as if Jack would be able to de-escalate tensions. Jack's idea of smoothing out problems was to destroy his opponent—a reflection of his personality, no doubt. She'd take Ferguson aside and have a talk with him about his attitude. *After* she stopped smelling like Jack's cologne. She discretely sniffed, knowing it wouldn't be anytime soon.

"We discovered most of the emails in the victims' Delete Items or Spam folders," Hannah said. "All opened, and discarded. The victims had no way of knowing they'd been targeted, or that they needed to seek protection. We've come to suspect the perp wasn't warning them so much as consoling them. To let them know their pain was about to end."

"Deming? Your thoughts?" Jack said.

"On the plane last night, Gilroy and I talked about this at length," the profiler said. "We agree with Special Agent Cambridge's assessment. The guy isn't warning anyone. He wants these kills."

"Where did you say Special Agent Gilroy was?" Jack pulled out his phone, glaring and swiping at the screen.

Deming flipped a length of her silky blond hair over her shoulder. "I left him on the first floor, looking for a secure server to submit the Coppola syndicate report. I said I'd do it—"

"Heaven forbid," Jack muttered, never taking his eyes off his phone's screen.

"Unfair. It's not my fault." Deming glanced at Ferguson and then narrowed her eyes at Jack, as if he were spilling the beans on something Deming didn't want spilled. It made Hannah extremely curious to know what they were talking about. "Like I said, Gilroy will be here. We all know how important this case is." When Jack continued scrolling on his phone, Deming rolled her eyes. *"He'll be here."*

"So..." Jack adjusted his weight on his seat, and then put his phone back in his suit jacket pockets. "William Blake." He glanced at Hannah, his eyes more guarded than usual. It made her wonder what he'd been looking at on his phone. "This poetry angle should help whittle down our suspects," he said.

"To English majors?" Hannah folded her arms, hating the derision in her tone. It was important to her that Jack believe she didn't care enough to be upset with him. More than important. It felt imperative, if only to retain a shred of her tattered dignity. "This is a college town, Jack."

"Nineteenth-century poets, then," Jack said. "How many people even know Blake exists?"

"I'm surprised you do." As soon as she said the snippy words, Hannah realized she'd lost all control of herself.

Jack arched a brow. "I know 'the Google.'"

Vivian raised her hand, waving it back and forth. Jack pointed to the tech as if her behavior were normal, which was a good sign that Jack was attempting to go with the flow. Vivian could be odd, but she was a damn good IT tech. It was a positive that Jack seemed willing to humor her.

"I followed the email IP addresses that the perp used to send his messages." Vivian futzed with the silk bow at her blouse's neckline. "The North End branch of Boston Public Library on Parameter Road, and two different internet cafés, both in the North End."

Hearing the North End mentioned triggered Hannah's to-do list. "Deming, we were promised a geographical profile. Did you have a chance to pull one together?"

"Almost done." Deming licked her fingers and eyed the doughnut box across the room. "Long story short, the North End is his killing grounds."

"Our taxpayer money at work," Ferguson said. "We already knew that."

After a pointed glare at the detective, Deming smiled at Hannah. "I'll have specifics soon. Promise."

"Special Agent Cambridge," Jack said. "Please give us the rundown on the victims." He had yet to call her 'Hannah' in front of the team, suggesting she was just another member, which she should have been grateful for... but wasn't. Gratitude was far down on the list of emotions she was feeling. "I said *please*." His barely audible remark made her aware that she was glaring at him, yet he was making an effort to get along. She looked bad.

Hannah blindly faced the murder board, wanting to walk from the room and go home to Ellen. Instead, she poked the first photo with her index finger and kept it there as she spoke, projecting a calm she didn't feel. The photo was of a smiling older man in a blue suit and red tie; balding, thin, strong jaw.

"James Twoomey," she said. "Retired salesman." *Nothing like her. Why did the killer target her?*

Vivian read from an index card she held. "My Spectre around me night and day, Like a wild beast guards my way; My Emanation far within, Weeps incessantly for my sin." The IT tech caught Jack's attention by waving the card. "The first stanza of Blake's poem."

Hannah couldn't separate her past and the poem anymore, not since Jack had come back from the dead. It seemed so obvious, so how had she missed the similarities? Poetry was like that, she supposed. It reflected what you threw at it; an inkblot test, personalized to the reader. Did that mean there was no way the team could find the killer by dissecting the poem? If so, all this seemed hopeless. Hannah *felt* hopeless.

"'Broken Love's' first stanza was printed on regular copy paper and then pinned to Twoomey's chest with a safety pin post mortem," Hannah said. "No witnesses. No finger prints. No identifying markers on paper or safety pin."

Deming grimaced, staring at Twoomey's after picture. "It tells us the killer has a strong stomach."

"'My sin,'" Vivian said. "The stanza has to be about sin." She stood, leaning against her desk as she studied Twoomey's picture from across the room.

"We've interviewed the guy's family," Hannah said, focusing on the picture, too. "From all accounts, he was a saint. Lonely, but a saint. If he had a sin, we couldn't find it." Hannah stepped back to compare the picture of Twoomey in better days, side by side with what witnesses found that morning. The after picture *was* grisly.

"Everyone sins," Vivian murmured, barely loud enough to hear. "It's the nature of the beast."

Hannah glanced over her shoulder at Jack. "He was ravaged by a pack of unregistered large dogs. Mastiffs."

"So I see." Jack didn't take his eyes off the picture. "Forensics found...what?"

"They matched fur found on the body with the dogs," Hannah said. "Saliva, too. The pound caught and euthanized the animals. Casts of their teeth were conclusive. They killed him. Ferguson, please give Special Agent Benton the vic's file." It felt weird to be so formal, reminding her of the months she and Jack had pretended they were nothing more than partners back in D.C. They'd pretended so well, their past relationship continued to be a secret.

Hannah knew that couldn't last. Jack was a father now. She had to tell him.

"No DNA on the perp?" Jack glanced between Ferguson and Hannah. "The killer touched the body after Twoomey was mauled. Forensics found nothing?"

"Nothing. Except this." Ferguson stepped forward and dropped a fat file on the desk next to Jack's elbow, and then returned to his desk, never once looking at him. "If there was DNA, they'd have found it."

Jack bristled. Yup. She had to speak to Ferguson, because *this* behavior was not productive. Everyone's focus had to be on finding the killer, not on a pissing contest between Hannah's dead lover, who wasn't dead, and— Who exactly was Ferguson to her? A coworker. Nothing more. None of this mattered, she reminded herself. She had a job to do, a killer to catch. She needed to be tougher, more focused. *She could do this.*

Jack flipped through copies of photos, and forensic pathology reports. "Death by mauling. Poor bastard." He flipped the file closed. "It's too early in the day for photos like this." He indicated Hannah should continue with a wave of his hand.

Hannah poked her finger at the picture of a young, blonde woman with elfin features. "Carey Stone, administrative assistant at Kelly Services, a staffing agency downtown."

"Nothing like Twoomey," Jack said.

Or me, Hannah silently added.

Vivian raised her hand again. Hannah could see Jack hesitate, as if playing with the idea of asking the tech to stop with the hand-raising, but he nodded instead, indicating she should speak.

"Carey Stone's stanza." Vivian glanced at the Stone crime scene photos. The before picture was a high school graduation photo, primped and posed, and the after picture was when she'd been dragged from Boston Harbor; bloated and fed on by fish. Vivian composed herself. "A fathomless and boundless deep, There we wander, there we weep; On the hungry craving wind, My Spectre follows thee behind." Sympathy tightened the tech's expression.

"Stone was found attached to a cinder block in the Boston Harbor at Constitution Marina," Hannah said. "A nonfatal contusion on her forehead suggested to the forensic pathologist that she was rendered unconscious before being submerged and then drowned. That could suggest some sort of conscience on the perp's part. Maybe squeamishness."

"More likely a struggle," Deming said.

Vivian hurried to Jack's side, providing him with a file.

"Thank you," Jack said.

"I don't know if you've been told what I do." Vivian avoided his gaze. "I oversee the data, categorizing and logging evidence. I'm also responsible for disseminating pertinent information to patrolmen upon request. Your request, now that you lead the team." She nodded twice, glancing at Hannah.

"Thank you." Jack arched a brow, glancing at the profiler. "If Deming asks to touch any of your equipment, tell her no. She's notorious for crashing hard drives." Vivian startled, and gave Deming a look that should be reserved for monsters that kicked puppies. "I'm not sure how she does it, but she does," Jack said.

Deming grimaced as she flipped through a manila file, but didn't deign to lift her gaze from the page. "Ignore Special Agent Benton, Vivian. I promise to go nowhere near your tech. As much as tech hates me, I hate it."

Vivian glanced between Deming and Jack, and then pointed to the file she'd delivered. "A summary of all the searches I've completed over the course of the investigation, and a log of the evidence we filed with the various departments, all cross-referenced with the DA's office and the bureau."

Jack opened the file, as Vivian's rose perfume wafted toward Hannah. The scent turned her stomach, reminding her of Jack's memorial service. The bureau had filled the room with roses. Now she couldn't abide the smell.

"Thank you, Vivian." Hannah forced a smile. "Twoomey got the first stanza, Stone the second." She pointed to the third photo, and then approached the murder board. "Harold Zelezny, retired plumber. He received the third stanza."

Vivian recited the stanza from memory. "He scents thy footsteps in the snow, Wheresoever thou dost go, Thro' the wintry hail and rain. When wilt thou return again?"

"Did you memorize them all?" Jack said.

"Most. There are seventeen, so I'm still working on some of them." Vivian blushed.

"Impressive." Jack's expression darkened. "Seventeen, huh? The perp is in it for the long haul."

"I'm number four," Hannah said.

Jack seemed as if he wanted to chastise her, but instead shook off her words. "'When wilt thou return again?' Does this guy think they'll come back from the dead?" Jack flipped through the files as Hannah forced herself not to remind Jack that he'd done just that! "He fucking locked this guy in a freezer," he said.

"St. Stephen's church's basement freezer," Ferguson said. "He was found when they were stocking it for a reception. If he wasn't killed in such a public place, no one would have known he'd been murdered."

Hannah contemplated the murder board, all the vics, their information, and it shouted one thing. These people were all alone. But Hannah *wasn't* alone. She had Ellen. She had Mrs. Branaghan. And Natalie was coming to help her on the weight of one phone call. That was friendship. Just because Hannah didn't have any living family, a husband, or a boyfriend who was astute enough to realize his girlfriend was unexpectedly pregnant and not up for the baby daddy to be fake murdered...that didn't mean she was *alone*. She did not fit the criteria of these kills. Yet the perp had targeted her.

Hannah scanned the faces in the room. Did they all think Hannah was alone? The perp did. Maybe even Jack did. *Damn.* Everyone must think she was pathetic.

"Hannah's stanza." Vivian cleared her throat before starting her recitation. "'Dost thou not in pride and scorn, Fill with tempests all my morn, And with jealousies and fears, Fill my pleasant nights with tears?'"

Hannah turned her back to the room, ostensibly concentrating on the murder board. It was becoming harder and harder to keep her composure. Her hands were shaking even more than before, and the damn poetry reading was getting on her nerves.

"How's the perp going to kill Special Agent Cambridge?" Jack said.

"Nice," she said, narrowing her eyes at him.

He shrugged. "The only thing that sounds ominous in that stanza," Jack continued, "is the word *tempests,* and unless we're in a Shakespearean play, even that's not scary."

Deming, ankles crossed and propped on her desk's edge, contemplated the murder board with her head tilted to the side. "The stanza is about torment," she said, "being tormented by...thoughts."

"Pride, scorn, jealousy, fear, tears," Hannah said. "Death by pity party." It was true. Bereft of the ability to beat the crap out of Jack, incapable of keeping a lid on her rage, she was left with directing it inward. *Jack left her.* He didn't die. He left her. What was wrong with *her*? Even enraged as she'd been upon realizing he was alive, her first instinct had been to make love to the lout.

"Not funny." Vivian leveled a delicate frown at Hannah.

"He's a prick," Ferguson said. For a moment, just a *tiny* moment, Hannah thought the detective was referring to Jack. "The perp thinks he's being cute with this poem stuff."

Deming shook her head. "No. I don't think he's being cute. I believe this poem means something to him. Something important. Everything he does is done for a reason. Remember? He's a planner. This is Hannah's stanza because he wants it to be hers."

"But why this stanza for Hannah?" Jack said.

So she was *Hannah* now. Was it her status as potential victim that made him loosen his protocol standards? Or maybe it was because he realized he now owned her. One wrong move and she was off the task force. Special Agent Cambridge, leader of the FBI task force designed to track down Boston's latest serial killer, was now Hannah, the woman here at *Jack's* largesse.

"Come on, people. Why?" Jack said, his impatience near the boiling-over mark. No one answered Jack, prompting him to throw his hands up in frustration. "Fine. Let's leave that question for now. What do we know about the victims' personal lives?"

Hannah stepped back from the murder board to give the room a better view of the pictures and information, and then pointed to Twoomey's picture. "Widowed. Like I said, he was a salesman. Retired. From all accounts, a regular guy. No children." Hands shaking, Hannah tucked them into her suit jacket pocket.

"Any clubs? Gyms? Restaurants he frequented regularly?" Jack said.

"Nope," Ferguson said. "Didn't even get the newspaper delivered. If he had a hobby, we couldn't find one."

"Tell me about the Stone woman." Jack walked to the coffeemaker against the wall and grabbed a cup, studying the murder board as he poured and then sipped.

Ferguson waved a notepad in the air. "I asked around. Midtwenties, pretty. Unattached. Quiet, by all accounts, lived alone, not even a goldfish. The only person I know that doesn't have a Facebook account. In fact, no social media. Not even Pinterest. Carey Stone wasn't openly dating, so if there's a crazy boyfriend in the picture, we couldn't find him. And we looked. No red flags. Nothing suspicious."

Jack pressed. "Clubs? Gyms—"

"YMCA," Ferguson flipped the pages on his pad, reading the information. "And only the last few months. I asked if anyone remembered her there, but got nowhere. The manager said she swam in their pool, but he never spoke to her."

"And our plumber? What about him?" Jack said.

"Zelezny was eighty years old," Hannah said. "Alone. No children. Wife dead. Plenty of acquaintances, but they hadn't spoken to him in weeks, didn't know where he lived, or anything about him."

"Is Stone the only vic with a Y membership?" Jack said. Ferguson nodded, prompting Jack's scowl to deepen. "Lot of dead ends."

"Too many," Deming said. "It's almost a thing. There is no connection between the vics whatsoever. What is the statistical probability that our victims had nothing in common, yet lived their lives in the same tiny section of Boston?"

"One hundred percent," Vivian said.

Jack shook his head. "Hannah, you moved here when? A few months ago?"

Wrong. Jack didn't know so much about her after all. She'd been in Boston since last November, but on this case since mid-July.

"Why a hundred percent probability, Vivian?" Deming said.

Vivian smiled. "Because it happened." Deming chuckled.

"The poem is connection enough," Hannah said. "And that the victims had no personal attachments, no significant others. All of them. Twoomey, Stone, and Zelezny all were—" She had to say it, even knowing they'd try to make her profile fit the killer's MO. "Alone. That's a big similarity."

And there it was, Hannah thought. The looks. The whole team *looked* at her like she was a thing to pity. It was too much to handle. A small voice inside her blamed Jack. If he'd stuck around, her life would have been different. Less hard. Less filled with grief. She felt her body tremble as she struggled to suppress her emotions. *Shut it down, Cambridge. Stop thinking.* Hannah crossed her arms and turned her back to the room again, pretending to stare at the murder board.

"The world is filled with loners. Why these loners?" Jack said. "We'll never find the guy if we can't answer that question." He tossed the files on Hannah's desktop, and the noise made her jump.

Ferguson stepped to the coffee machine, refreshed his coffee. "Hannah was leading the task force yesterday. This guy is just spitting in our faces with this email, messing with us. She's not alone." He glanced at Hannah, but then quickly averted his gaze. "She has us," he said.

"Interesting theory." Deming shrugged. "But as far as we know, the press isn't even aware an investigation exists. How could the perp know? Pillow-talk?" She winked at Vivian, who blushed and quickly concentrated on organizing files on her desk. "Despite Ferguson's razor-sharp analysis—" Ferguson glared at her. Deming ignored him. "—serial killers have patterns for a reason. They're fulfilling fantasies and required rituals. We need to concentrate on why the killer believes Hannah fits into his pattern, instead of hoping she doesn't. To do otherwise—" Deming pursed her lips.

"Could get her killed," Jack said.

"I was going to say that it wastes valuable time," Deming said. "But yeah. It could get her killed."

Hannah didn't agree; not because Deming's conclusion wasn't based on sound science, but because the profiler didn't have all the facts. Deming didn't know about Ellen. She didn't know anything about Hannah.

"It has to be my role as task force leader, otherwise I don't fit," Hannah said. "Like Jack said, I'm new to the area. I don't live in the North End, and…and I'm not alone." She stared everyone down, not willing to concede that *extremely* salient point, and not willing to argue. It would be pathetic. How could it not be?

"You're guessing, Hannah. We *know* a few things," Jack said. "This perp plans out his kills. You got the email. We can expect a move on you defined by your assigned stanza in three days or less."

Ferguson scowled at Deming. "You're the profiler. Give us something we can use. Mauling by dogs is nothing like freezing to death, or drowning. As far as I can see, there are no patterns except for the locale. North End and the Waterfront."

"That's not true. The emails," Vivian said. "And the poem."

Deming nodded. "And the victims are all," she glanced at Hannah, "segregated from social contact." Hannah cringed. Deming didn't pat her on the head, but she might as well have. "And they have nothing in common."

Ferguson narrowed his eyes. "Stop trying to make a *lack* of clues a clue. That's not how we catch killers. It's how we explain why we *don't* catch them."

Jack nodded. "We need clues not handed to us by the killer, which means we need to be more proactive. I'm not willing to wait for him to make a mistake, or heaven forbid, kill again. We need to get out in front of this. Why haven't we enlisted the help of the media? Let the public know what to do if they get a weird email with the words 'Weep No More for Broken Love'?"

Hannah caught Jack's attention. "No media was the district attorney's call and I agree with him." She nudged a few files away from the edge of her desk. "The lieutenant and the DA are adamant. We announce, even vaguely, that the killer is sending emails, and we'll be inundated with false alarms or copycats, making it harder to see the real leads. As it stands, we're lucky the next threat was toward me."

Jack's jaw dropped. "Lucky?"

Hannah nodded. "I know I'm a target, so nothing's going to happen to me." She waved Ferguson over. "Show them the map."

Ferguson gripped the edge of a spring-loaded laminated map affixed above the murder board, and pulled it down until the map unfolded, covering the victims' pictures and notes. The map had three *X*s drawn in red, marking the crime scene locations.

"Here, here, and here," Ferguson pointed. "A straight line right through the North End of Boston. First." He pointed to Paul Revere's house. "Twoomey. Murder by dogs on the street. Second," he pointed to the coastline. "Directly east is Constitution Marina. Stone was drowned." He pointed to the final crime scene. "Directly west of Twoomey's kill—

see the straight line it's making on the map?—is St. Stephen Catholic Church. Death by freezing, or heart attack, depending on which came first. Charlie Foulkes—"

"Charlie Foulkes?" Deming seemed almost to panic.

"Yeah. He's the head of our forensics team. The forensic pathologist," Ferguson said. "You know him?" Deming nodded, but said no more. "Well, he found cause of death was most likely heart attack brought on by freezing, so let's go with what the perp had in mind. Death by freezing." He traced the map with his finger, linking the crime scenes with a smeared red line. "All in the North End of Boston."

Hannah walked to her desk and sat. "If this geographic alignment of the crime scenes holds, it might allow us to anticipate the next crime scene, especially if we find ourselves deep into the stanzas."

"Which won't happen," Jack said. "We're catching this fucker before he kills again. Got it?" He leveled a frown at Hannah, and for a moment there, she believed him, until she remembered that Carey Stone died even though the team had known pretty much all the information they had now. This killer wasn't making mistakes.

"Like I said, I'm writing up a formal geographic profile." Deming approached the map and, in red marker, drew wide circles around the crime scenes and then connected them with lines. "But this should give you a general idea of where the perp lives or works."

Jack didn't hide his skepticism. "People would recognize him if he lives there. These neighborhoods are dense, people walk the streets. They'd see the perp in places they know he's not supposed to be."

"Agreed, which is why I'm leaning toward commuter status, but we can't rule anything out." She pointed to the JFK Expressway and Causeway Street. "Heavy traffic thruways lead straight to these tourist spots." She used the red marker to stab at the maps' crime scene marks, making her shiny blond hair sway with her movements. "And there's the line Ferguson was referring to connecting Constitution Marina, St. Stephen Church, and Paul Revere's house." She seemed surprised. "Hmm. Ferguson's right. I'll have to incorporate that in my profile."

"Are you admitting I knew something you didn't?" Ferguson pretended to be shocked.

"The crime scenes are not random sites." Deming appeared to ignore his snark, though her cheek briefly kicked up with a smile.

"*Damn right*, Ferguson's right," he mumbled under his breath.

"This perp knows the area," Deming said, "so with what little evidence we've gathered, and a dash of statistics, our best bet is he's a local who commutes, but not very far."

"Our own personal Ted Bundy." Vivian wrinkled her nose, showing a hefty level of disgust marred by unmistakable excitement.

"No," Deming kept her attention on the map. "Bundy was a disorganized serial killer. Impulsive. Though charismatic, he had few social skills. His murders were opportunistic and haphazard. He'd break into random houses and bludgeon people to death. Pick up hitchhikers."

Ferguson grimaced. "Have sex with victims *after* he'd murdered them. A real go-getter."

Vivian neatened up her desk, looking uncomfortable. "I just meant, you know, a serial killer. It's my first."

Deming continued to focus on the map, seeming to work a problem in her head. Hannah stepped closer to the map, studying it, trying to see what Deming saw.

"People like Bundy," Deming said, "lack knowledge of normal sexual behavior, and make it up as they go along." She erased half a circle's circumference and redrew the edge, expanding the circle.

"Like Ferguson?" Vivian said.

Ferguson's jaw dropped. He turned to the IT specialist, and seemed to struggle to find words. Deming barked out a laugh, her eyes twinkling with amusement. "Vivian made a funny!"

Jack had a coughing fit, his eyes revealing his amusement. Hannah frowned at him, needing him to play nice if only for a little while longer.

"Funny, O'Grady." Ferguson's usual scowl melted and in its place grew a smile. Then he laughed. "Didn't know you had it in you."

"Deming's point, I believe," Hannah said, "is the perp isn't a guy who uses opportunity to dictate his kills. He scopes out the crime scenes and somehow lures his victims into a predetermined place so he can play out his fantasy dictated by the vic's assigned stanza. All very controlled. Orchestrated." Hannah turned to Jack, wondering what he was thinking. Of all the people in the world who could help her find this killer, Jack was the one she was most confident could get the job done. He'd had more experience with serial murderers than she did, and he could write a book on control issues.

"That's right. As I said, the kills were planned." Deming nodded. "Our guy's a hunter."

"Maybe. Too many *ifs* to be sure." Ferguson contemplated Deming's handiwork on the laminate map. "Big deal if the guy knows Boston. Tons of people do, too. If they're not random—"

"They're not. The emails rule that out." Jack stepped forward, studying the map. "Deming's right. Each murder is meticulously planned."

"*Damn right* Deming's right," Deming said, smirking at Ferguson. "And I don't think the perp is using highways to get to the North End. I don't think he's traveling even half an hour to reach the crime scenes. Everything seems personal. Like he knows these people." She startled, turning to Hannah. "He knows them. If that's true..."

It would suck, but it certainly would cut down on the suspects. Hannah barely knew anyone in Boston. Most of her time here had been working from home, or being stuck in a hospital bed. She felt all eyes on her, and Jack's gaze was the heaviest, squeezing the air from the room.

"Gut feeling, Deming?" Jack's tone carried no teasing, no humor. Hannah didn't need interpretation. Jack's gut solved many a case. He knew its value.

Deming dragged her fingers through her long hair, clearly frustrated. "His kills are staged in a big way and by design. Tourist traps. If he knows the vics, he really doesn't like them."

"He's a psychopath," Ferguson said. "Liking, hating—hell, emotion probably doesn't even factor into it." Deming nodded.

"We need to beef up police presence at tourist destinations dictated by the perps geographical profile. He's sending a message." Jack caught Hannah's gaze, as if silently asking something, but Hannah had no idea what the question was. She looked back, and all she could think was *Jack is alive. So, why does the ache in my heart remain?* Shouldn't her grief have dissipated a bit? He was alive, dammit, why didn't she get to be happy about that?

Ferguson stepped next to Hannah, arms crossed over his massive chest. Gently, but purposefully, he nudged her shoulder, surprising her with the physical contact. Hannah sought the detective's gaze, only to discover he was waging a staring contest with Jack.

"Staking his claim," Jack said, gaze now locked with Ferguson's.

"He's sent a message, all right." Vivian leaned her hip against her desk. "'Broken Love' is rife with messages."

Hannah purposefully stepped away from Ferguson, needing to distance herself from whatever silent battle the men were waging. Approaching the board, she retracted the map and exposed the murder board beneath. She wrote her kill date under her picture. "The kills are one month apart. The first was May 15. Three days from now will be August 15. We were due for the forth stanza. If all goes as scheduled..."

The room fell silent. Jack approached her from behind and touched her arm. She saw his concern. His worry. Everyone else was looking at her as if they didn't know what to say, but she suspected they were all thinking the same thing.

Hannah was as good as dead.

Chapter 4

"Stop it." Jack knew how Hannah was finishing that sentence in her head, and he was having none of it. No one was getting to her, not while he had breath left in his body. And Ferguson? He needed to back off. What the hell was all his touchy, touchy, feely, feely with Hannah? That was not happening on his watch either.

"We'll get the perp, Hannah," Ferguson said. "In three days this case will be in your rearview and you'll have a big win on your resume. We'll celebrate."

Ferguson's smoldering look left nothing to the imagination. Jack wanted to sock him in the nose. He blamed fatigue, the long flight, and he was hungry. He didn't blame the sex in the lieutenant's office. No one could interpret that as anything but letting off steam. He and Hannah were something from the past...by design. A year ago, they'd read the tea leaves, and nothing had changed—except, thanks to their old boss, she hated him even more now. Jack grabbed a blueberry muffin from the Dunkin's box and counted himself lucky she was still talking to him.

"What are you going to call him?" Ferguson stepped to Hannah's side again, hunched his shoulders, bringing his face closer to hers...cutting her from the herd. "I'm sure Special Agent Benton wouldn't begrudge you the honor. You got us to this point, and I sure as shit am not going to allow you to die, so—"

"We're not calling him anything." The hand Hannah used to nudge her bangs from her eyes shook. Jack wondered if it stemmed from a natural fear of a serial killer targeting her—that would give anyone the shakes—or maybe Ferguson's flirting was flustering her. That possibility bothered him almost as much.

Deming's expression lightened with approval. "Good for you, Hannah. To name it gives it power."

"Good for you," Vivian echoed.

Hannah glanced at Ferguson, still standing close, and flushed. Damn. Now she was blushing. Jack hated Ferguson. "I'm not that erudite," she said. "We won't name him until we know what makes him tick, but mostly because you can't keep things like that a secret."

Hannah, being Hannah, didn't recognize the team was trying to compliment her. She was oblivious, as usual. Jack had always found her impossible to compliment, and she'd never reacted as expected. If she didn't roll her eyes, or give a dismissive shake of her head, she would act distrustful of the praise. After a while, Jack just stopped trying. If he had it to do again, he'd compliment her until she collapsed under the weight of his admiration.

"Vivian, we need that poetry expert back to pick his brains," Hannah said. "The perp gave us the poem. It's the key to unlocking his identity. It has to be."

Ferguson snorted. "Poetry means whatever the reader thinks it means, so it might as well mean nothing."

"You don't know what you're talking about." Vivian seemed truly upset by Ferguson's words. "Poetry is life and death and everything in between."

"Isn't that what I just said?" Ferguson scanned the room, gauging everyone's reaction.

"Enough." Jack didn't have patience for this. "Ferguson, if you're done raining on Ms. O'Grady's parade, maybe you could interview our poetry expert from UMass? Pick his brain. Deming, go with him and keep him out of trouble."

Deming's smile was naughty. "Oh, I'd love that," she said, "but don't you think Vivian should come with me? Ferguson might scare the guy."

Jack wanted Ferguson busy and away from Hannah, but couldn't say that, so when Deming glanced at Jack, he widened his eyes and managed to convey the importance of his profiler doing what she was told. She glanced at Hannah and then laughed. *Damn.* Deming was doing her voodoo on him and Jack's motives weren't as hidden as he'd hoped.

Hannah stood in front of the murder board, studying her photo, a reprint of her FBI ID headshot. In it, she was smiling, her hair pulled back as it was now, and she seemed happy. It had been taken before Jack had met her. Guilt forced him to acknowledge that he hadn't been able to make Hannah happy when they were together. Now, she appeared fragile and flustered, lost in thought. He told himself that optics were deceiving. Hannah was one of the strongest people Jack knew. And smart. He knew it had to be the stress of the case that was getting to her.

"Hannah. Can I have a word with you?" Jack stepped to the incident room's door, holding it open for her. "Okay, everybody," he scanned his team's curious faces. "You know what you have to do. We'll get this guy. We just have to work the case."

"So I can sleep at night." Hannah mumbled the words as she walked past him into the hall, Jack close on her heels. He closed the door behind them.

"You'll sleep," he said, doing his best to sound confident. "You'll be safe. Nothing will happen to you, Hannah, because I'll be with you." Gun drawn, sleeping with his eyes open if need be.

She scanned the hall, saw it was empty. Then she stepped so close to Jack her breath warmed his face. "Excuse me?"

It occurred to him that maybe he'd insulted her by suggesting she couldn't keep herself safe, but for the life of him, he couldn't care. He needed her to acknowledge that he'd be there for her. That *he'd* make sure she was okay. "I know you're a capable agent. Don't take this the wrong—"

"*You* happened to me, Jack. Who's going to protect me from *you*?"

"What?" He thought back to the meeting, searching for something he'd said that might have ticked her off.

"You died." Hannah's chin quivered as she stared back at him.

Now didn't seem a good time to hash that out, but Hannah wasn't asking. She was demanding answers. "Look. We both know things were bad when I left."

"They were worse when *you died.*"

"You know you could barely stay in the same room with me without yelling. I assumed you'd be happy to see the back of me."

"*You were murdered.*" Hannah was shutting down. He recognized the signs. Whenever they had a disagreement, she shut him out, making him think she was measuring the drapes for some other apartment. An apartment away from him.

"Goodwin should have—"

"*You should have*, Jack. Said goodbye. Given me that, at least." Taking a big breath, she released it in a burst and turned away from him. "I refuse to do this now."

She had him off balance. "I'm sorry I didn't say goodbye." He scanned the hall. People could walk by, and explanations would then have to be made. "I'm sorry, Hannah."

She shook her head, covering her face with her hands. "You died—"

"I don't know what else to say."

"—and now you're just dead to me." She dropped her hands and met his gaze, and it was the look on her face that convinced him she meant every word she'd said. He was dead to her.

He took the hit with as much aplomb as he was capable of, and kept his peace as she hurried down the hall. Away from him. Always running away from him.

Chapter 5

As soon as the words left her mouth, Hannah regretted them. They were the truth, but Jack didn't deserve the truth. He didn't deserve to understand how much his abandonment had damaged her. Tears spilled over her lashes as she hurried down the hall, desperate to escape emotions that shadowed her. She didn't get far before Jack grabbed her elbow and hustled her into Interrogation Room 1. He flipped the "Occupied" switch that lit a red light outside the door and locked them in.

"Get it all out, Hannah," Jack said. "Say everything you need to say now, and then I'll have my say, and then we need to focus on working together to catch this killer. Deal?"

She couldn't look at him. Didn't want to. Not until she could control her expression. The sound of a metal chair scraping against tile grabbed her attention. There he sat, watching her, the image of a concerned boss, or an inquisitor seeking a confession.

So this is happening. Whatever. Might as well get it over with.

Hannah dragged a chair to the other side of the interrogation table and sat, facing him as an adversary. "How fitting." She lifted her hands, indicating his choice of venues. He was expecting an interrogation, but their relationship was dead. This was an autopsy.

"We won't be interrupted." By locking the door, he had made sure of that. "I have questions, Hannah."

Jack's resemblance to Ellen jumped out at her, reminding her he didn't know he was a father, and that he didn't know the joy of holding their baby in his arms, the sweet smell of her fuzz-covered head. He'd never heard Ellen's gurgle of happiness, felt the fear of losing her. In this room, there'd be no way Hannah could tell him without, by default, appearing to use

Ellen's existence as a weapon. That Hannah wouldn't do. Ellen was a gift, and deserved to be presented as such. Until Hannah's temper cooled, or at least became manageable, the only gift she was willing to give Jack was a black eye and a bloody nose, but she had questions, too.

"Do you want to draw straws to see who asks first?" she said, hastily wiping telltale tears. When she'd become pregnant, her emotions were always a hair's breadth from teetering out of control, and now that she wasn't, her hormones were all over the place trying to level out. She'd become a crier. Something else to blame Jack for. He was staring as if he expected her to blow up. She couldn't blame him. Since he'd arrived in the incident room, her behavior has been erratic at best, questionable at worst. Sex in the lieutenant's office? What was wrong with her? She was happy Jack was alive. She was. But also devastated. It was confusing as hell, and she wasn't handling it well.

Sure, he didn't *knowingly* allow her to believe he was dead, but it'd happened. It could have been averted with one phone call. He could have just been honest with her. Instead, he left with no explanation, relying on an unreliable source to cut his ties. He bore responsibility for that, and the repercussions of his decision. Yet Hannah was the one suffering from aftershock. It wasn't fair. She wished he was the man she'd thought he'd been. That man, she'd have thrown her arms around and cried for joy when she discovered he was alive.

This man, she feared. As Ellen's father, he had endless opportunities to hurt her, and always would. How could she defend herself against that kind of power?

Sprawled on his chair, leaning back, he was the picture of relaxation. She might have bought what he was selling if his expression wasn't guarded. Too serene. Too in control. He'd have to be a robot to not feel the tension in the air.

"What do you want to know?" he said.

Ever the G-man, trying to suss her out, looking for hints of what he had to admit, and what he could hold back. She took the same interview classes in Quantico. She had to choose her questions carefully, or risk exposing herself more than she already had. That meant she couldn't ask, *how could you leave without talking to me first*? It would tell him she needed closure. She couldn't ask, *what case could be more important than me, your lover, hell, your partner*? She and Jack had never exchanged words of love. She'd held back because she refused to be the first to say it, and he never seemed inclined.

The last time Hannah saw Jack, she was hoping to reveal the big, scary news. She was three months pregnant and couldn't put it off any longer. She'd begun to show. Jack was in a mood and looking for a fight. He got one, and then stormed out of their apartment. Four hours later she got the call from a coworker that he was dead. Car explosion. Planted bomb. Murder. Body burned beyond recognition.

Hannah threw the first volley. "Whose body did I say goodbye to in the morgue?"

"I don't know." He looked uncomfortable. "I don't want to know."

The experience had been grisly, and the memory had staying power. She'd traced her PTSD to that night, that visual of the burnt corpse of her lover on a metal slab. "What we had was secret. No one knew I was more than your partner. Did that change at any point? Did you tell anyone?" She couldn't even name what they had been together. For two years, they'd had sex, then secretly roomed together, worked together. They'd been partners in a professional capacity, but to officially claim anything beyond that was stretching it. He never told her he loved her.

"We weren't secret. We were discreet," he said. "I didn't want our personal life to be part of the gossip mill."

Bullshit, she thought, and regret scourged her heart raw. She should be feeling relief that she hadn't exposed herself to ridicule by declaring herself to him, but all she felt was self-doubt. Would he have left if she'd told him she was pregnant? Looking at him now, all defensive and closed off, she supposed he might have stayed, but she'd never have known if it was for her or because he was an honorable man ready to do the right thing. What was obvious to Hannah was Jack didn't love her. But she'd loved him. How else to explain the grief she'd suffered over this last year? *She'd had to have loved him.*

But not now. He'd killed it, and what was left was suppressed rage. And grief, dammit, never-ending grief, because the man she thought he'd been *had* died that night. This man, sitting across from her, was Jack's pale shadow.

Her inclination was to shut him out and move on, but there was Ellen to consider. Always Ellen, pulling her out of the doldrums, reminding her life continued no matter the losses, no matter how weighed down with grief and rage she was. Hannah would have to tell Jack about his daughter, and it would be easier without a river of acrimony spewing between them. To do that, she'd be a grown-up and learn to forgive, or at least not care.

"Why did you have me as your emergency contact?" she said.

Jack didn't like the question, and shrugged it off. "You were my partner."

He was studying her reaction, calculating, she supposed, what she was feeling. It took all her energy to give him nothing for his efforts, but his words hurt. His memory of her was of a partner, not a lover. She swallowed hard, trying not to allow more tears to well in her eyes.

"When did they give you the assignment?" In other words, *how long did you know you would leave me and not give me the heads-up*?

"That morning. It was important no one knew."

"Not even your *partner*." She arched a brow.

Jack's eyes flickered with some unknown emotion. Hannah was too busy wrestling with her own to recognize what it was. "I was assured Goodwin would take you aside and clue you in. I'm sorry. I shouldn't have left it to someone else. I should have said good-bye."

Not, *I should have discussed taking the job*. Not, *I shouldn't have left*. Just, *I should have said good-bye*. His leaving was always in the cards. Hannah felt her body break into a sweat. It beaded on her upper lip, and suddenly she couldn't tolerate the stuffiness of the room. Stripping off her suit jacket, she hung it over the back of her chair. "For a dead man you certainly have pull in the bureau. More than a few strings were pulled to get you here, taking over this case. *My* case."

"Yes. I admit I called in favors." He shifted in his seat, betraying his discomfort with her line of inquiry.

"Why?" This was the first thing he'd said that didn't make sense. Why did he pivot so quickly to come to her rescue? He didn't love her. That was abundantly clear.

Jack leaned forward, folding his hands on the table. "You know why, Hannah."

This serial murder case would put whoever solved it in the FBI history books. It was a coup for her to land, and now Jack was swooping in to take over. She smirked. "Yeah. I get it."

He interpreted her response correctly and took umbrage. "No, I don't think you do."

She had to get out of there before she lost it. Hurrying to the door, Jack at her heels, she reached for the doorknob. He leaned on the door, stopping her from opening it. "Move out of my way," she said.

"We're not done talking."

"We are."

"If you want to continue working on this case, you'll listen." She could see him digging his heels in, and when Jack got that way, there was no budging him. Well, fine.

"OK. Your turn." She stepped away from him and leaned against the wall, arms folded over her chest.

"I take your safety very seriously." Jack looked her over, as if contemplating the best way to attain that objective. She wouldn't be surprised if her duct-taped to a wall became his solution. She'd be out of the way and completely controlled. Just the way Jack liked things. On his terms. "I wasn't kidding when I said we'll be attached at the hip. That's nonnegotiable. Whoever this killer is, he's gotten away with it so far, and I'm not willing to take any chances with you. Tell me you understand that."

"I'm not going to a safe house." Just the thought of her and Ellen trapped in a stuffy apartment under lock and key was enough to make her squirm. She'd make other plans if she had to. Her words got the expected results. Jack rolled his eyes.

"Fine," he snapped.

"Fine," she snapped back.

"Look." Jack sounded exhausted. "I'm working on no sleep, I smell of airplane, and all I have with me are the clothes on my back. If you don't mind, we'll stay at your apartment." Hannah didn't try to hide her displeasure. She *knew* there had to be a catch, and here it was. "Please?"

"Do I have a choice?" Jack being at her apartment meant he'd meet his daughter tonight. It was too soon.

"It's that or you're in a safe house."

The pressure of the case, the fear for herself and her daughter, all combined to make having Jack around a little easier to stomach. He would be another layer of protection for her helpless baby. Their baby. That's *all* she was thinking about. Jack was nothing to her now. Like she'd said, he might as well have died last September. "Whatever," she said. He'd have to be told tonight, and then he'd have to agree to keep Ellen's existence a secret or she'd quit. No job was worth her daughter's safety. "Anything else?"

"Did you happen to save any of my stuff? Like I said, I have no clothes with me, and I've been wearing this suit for two days." The suit she'd helped him shuck an hour ago. It wasn't a leap to assume his mind had jumped there, too. She saw it in his eyes. But instead of being embarrassed, she bowed to the inevitable. She'd enjoyed the sex. It was amazing. It always had been with Jack. That didn't make it healthy for her to be with him. Hannah needed a man she could rely on. Surely there was a guy out there who made her feel like Jack made her feel, but didn't have such an antipathy for commitment. She wanted that man. "Hannah? Did you save any of my stuff?"

"Clothes. Right," she said. There were two boxes of his stuff hidden in the back of her bedroom closet. Out of sight, out of mind. She'd been unable to give it away, blaming her weakness on nostalgia, that Ellen might want to see something of Jack's when she grew up. But it was a lie. She'd had little enough of him as it was when he'd died. She'd found herself unable to give any of his stuff away. "I might have something hidden away somewhere."

His sigh of relief annoyed her. "That makes things easier."

"So happy to accommodate." She stepped toward the door, hoping he'd move aside so she could escape. Instead, Jack met her halfway and pulled her into his arms. His lips connected with hers in a kiss that shocked. Her body instantly reacted, and before she made a conscious decision to respond, she was kissing him back. Her hands clutched him close. Her breasts mashed against his chest. Like a switch flipped, he turned her on.

Jack walked her back against the wall, never breaking their kiss, and his hands were everywhere, caressing her, exploring, doing things that made her knees weak. Yes, he'd put her through hell, and yes, she'd never forgive him, but damn, he was alive and she knew, even if logic resisted, she *knew* him being alive was the key to digging out from the grief and sadness that had dogged her since he'd gone. *This*. One more chance to hold him. *This*. One more kiss from Jack Benton. Hannah trembled under the onslaught of his passionate kiss, overwhelmed by desire, humbled by gratitude.

It was Jack who pulled back, wearing an expression of guilt and concern. Cupping her cheeks, he licked his lips, and she knew he was tasting the saltiness of her tears; a staple of her diet since he'd been gone.

"Hannah, I'm sorry. I was wrong to go the way I did, and now I'm wrong again. Your life has gone to shit. You don't need me complicating it, but I can't seem to stop myself from—Hannah, I can't stop touching you." He pressed his forehead to hers, closing his eyes. "I'm a selfish ass."

Not a confession of love. It wasn't his style, or it was beyond his emotional capacity. She tried to tell herself she didn't care, that she wouldn't believe him if he said the words, but her heart sank anyway as the insanity of the moment faded, bereft of the fuel of his kiss. He was acting as if he loved her and she suspected that was all it was. Acting. He needed her compliance to make his role in this case work. Interrogation Skills 101, Quantico. Use the tools available. She'd always wanted him and sex together had always been phenomenal. It was just another way for Jack to control her. He hadn't changed one bit.

"How do you not get it, Jack?" Her words were shaky, her body trembling. The helplessness she saw on Jack's face made the decision for her. It was past time to tell him the truth, and maybe if she allowed him in this one last time, he'd understand why she couldn't trust him again.

"Hannah—"

"I loved you, Jack." There. She thought once she said the words, she'd feel relief that the truth was out there. She didn't feel relief. Hannah felt incredibly sad. Heartbreakingly so. "I know I never said it, but I did. I loved you. When you died, it broke me. I'm broken." He had to understand now. Yet he looked as if her words didn't compute. Impatient with his stubbornness, she pushed out of his arms and reached for her jacket on the chair, forcing herself to project a nonchalance she wasn't feeling as she slipped her arms into the sleeves, wiping evidence of tears from her cheeks. "I'm a faucet. Sorry. Now you know why I stopped wearing makeup." She chuckled, and hated that it sounded forced.

"Hannah." Jack stepped toward her.

She held up her hand, stopping him. "Just so we're clear, I'm done with you. I can keep myself safe. And FYI, you'll never find this killer without me. I think you're beginning to see that already. You might get the credit for this win, Jack, but even you have to admit you're poaching my case."

Jack reacted as if she'd smacked him. "That's not why I'm here."

Shaken, barely able to keep her façade in place, all Hannah wanted to do was run and hide her vulnerability. "I like to think I'm teachable." She wiped her cheek. "I was so gullible…crying over *a stranger's grave.* Well, excuse me for not falling for more of your lies."

Someone banged on the door three times. Jack ignored it. Hannah stared him down. The door was hit again, more insistently. Spitting out expletives, Jack whipped it open, unveiling a stranger. A bald, large, handsome man, in a black suit and tie. FBI, if she were to guess.

"Gilroy. Not a good time." Jack moved to close the door again, but Gilroy held out his hand and easily stopped the door's movement.

The man glanced at the ceiling, indicating the room's camera. The red light was on. "When you hit the 'Occupied' switch," Gilroy said, "it turned on the incident room's video monitor. When I arrived, I found the team watching. All that was missing was the popcorn."

Hannah recoiled, replaying everything she'd said and done. Then she couldn't move fast enough, hurrying past the men, down the hall.

"Hannah!" She didn't look back, but it sounded as if Jack was following her.

"Uh, Benton, maybe you should let her go," Gilroy said.

"Step aside, Gilroy." Jack sounded furious.

Hannah wanted to die, but didn't want witnesses. Pushing through the stairwell door, she closed it behind her and leaned back to stop anyone from following. She covered her face, humiliated. *Breathe. Breathe.* Her heartbeat raced and her throat kept closing, strangling her as she swallowed back tears. Sick to her stomach, she wrangled with the knowledge that her team knew everything now. Well, almost. They still didn't know about Ellen.

Hannah forced herself to look on the bright side. Sure, she was a mess. Swollen eyes, red nose, twitchy as hell. Sure, her life had been threatened, her job was in limbo, her secrets were aired in front of her peers and subordinates, but damn, the love of her life miraculously was alive.

Hannah slid down the door into a crouch, resting her head on her folded arms. She had to think. First, Ellen's safety. Second, catch the killer. Her pride had to be a distant third.

Ellen was under police protection, so she could focus on the case. Somehow Hannah got on the perp's radar. Her being targeted was not a coincidence. If it was, they might as well admit defeat now, because there'd be no rhyme nor reason to the killer's motives then.

She had to believe she was chosen for a discoverable reason. The perp's ritual, or rules, had to be met before he chose a victim, and Hannah fit some predetermined criteria. Even with the full roster of information they had, she couldn't see the connection. Deming might, given enough time, but that was slim consolation when time was something they didn't have. Three days, if she was lucky.

Something bought her a ticket into the killer's pool of targets. What the hell was it?

The door shoved her forward, tipping her, forcing Hannah to catch herself against the floor. Vivian O'Grady's head popped into view. "Oh, sorry, Hannah."

As Hannah moved to accommodate the tech, dusting off her pants, Vivian squeezed through into the stairwell landing.

"No worries," Hannah said, sniffing. "Just trying to get my head on straight."

"Yeah," Vivian said. "We heard." The IT tech flushed, biting her bottom lip.

Hannah cringed. "How much and who was there?"

"The whole team." She clasped her hands. "Don't get mad. Ferguson was mad. Deming? Shocked. Yeah, Deming was shocked."

"Did you all hear everything?"

"Saw everything, too. Sorry. We're a curious bunch. So...you know him, I gather. Well, that's the way it looked."

There was no denying it now. They'd seen the lip-lock. "We worked together in D.C. As partners."

Vivian waited, and when Hannah didn't offer more, she prodded. "That doesn't explain why you tried to unman him earlier."

Vivian had seen that, too, huh? Well, Hannah wasn't about to explain. Whatever the team imagined couldn't be any worse than the reality. "Long story."

"I would be surprised otherwise." She smiled, but with kindness.

Considering Vivian was in her early thirties and still single, Hannah supposed she had her fair share of *long stories* involving men. Vivian probably understood more than most. Still. This wasn't only her story to tell—it was Jack's, too—and Hannah's habit of reticence was ingrained. There would be no further declarations of her sordid past, and if she had her way, the past would stay in the past.

"Special Agent Benton is leading our team," Vivian said. "None of us could resist a little snooping, especially when the monitor started making noises and the interrogation got juicy. I'm not excusing our behavior, just trying to explain a little."

"Ferguson was mad, huh?"

"Was he *ever*. I think he has a crush on you. He nearly turned over a desk in his rush to put a stop to your clinch, but Special Agent Gilroy arrived and once he figured out what was going on, he told him to stay put. Ferguson saw the sense in it, I guess, because you're FBI, and so is Gilroy, so I think Ferguson figured he had the right to intervene more than him." She put a hand on Hannah's shoulder. "If you ever want to talk, know you can talk to me."

"Thanks, Vivian." Hannah did appreciate the offer, but knew that just wasn't going to happen. She had Ellen, and any sort of heart-to-heart would involve revealing her existence. Hannah just wasn't ready for that.

Vivian nudged her. "Choose Ferguson. He's half in love with you."

Hannah took a cleansing breath and tried to release it slowly. Instead, it came out as a sob. "Love is totally overrated."

Vivian nodded. "Unfortunately, that kind of wisdom never comes until it's too late." She gave Hannah a sympathetic smile. "When we met, I suspected we had a lot in common."

Hannah couldn't imagine what. The tech seemed apples to Hannah's oranges. Their temperaments, even taste in clothing were widely divergent, but if Vivian wanted to see them as alike, who was Hannah to cry foul?

Hannah readjusted the clip in her hair, and pushed her bangs out of her eyes. "Do I look okay?"

Vivian's sigh was wistful. "Hannah, if you looked any more okay, I'd hate you. It must be nice to be so pretty. Do angels sing when you wake in the morning?"

Vivian's wistfulness was delivered with enough tongue-in-cheek to prompt Hannah's dimples to make an appearance. Smiling felt like a breath of fresh air after so much heavy emotion. "Sure. And bluebirds help me dress." She nodded to the manila folder the tech was holding. "Is that why you tracked me down?"

Vivian handed it over. "And to see if you're all right. Everyone feels bad."

"Well, tell them to stop." She flipped open the folder. "What do you have?"

"Deming finished the geographical profiling. Boston and its suburbs, like she said, but I think you need to hear what else she's come up with." It was hard for Hannah to disguise her hesitancy at the thought of seeing the team so soon after being humiliated. Vivian's smile was meant to encourage her, but it didn't. Hannah wanted to hide. "You have to see everyone sooner or later. Better to get it over with."

Hannah nodded, reminding herself that no one died from embarrassment. "Then let's get this over with."

Chapter 6

Jack's stomach clenched as he watched Vivian open the door to the incident room and then held it open for Hannah to enter. When she stepped inside, everyone was professional to a fault.

"What are you two doing here?" Hannah said, upon seeing Deming and Ferguson. All poised and professional, Hannah acted as if she and Jack hadn't just been caught kissing. He envied her the ability to go with the flow. Jack wanted to find a bottle of whiskey and get shit-faced. "I thought you two were chasing down our poetry expert," Hannah said.

Ferguson wouldn't meet Hannah's gaze, and Deming shrugged. "The professor had class, but I scheduled an appointment. We'll get it done. I had a thought." Deming wasted no time approaching the murder board, pulling down the laminated map again. After a perfunctory glance Hannah's way, Jack forced himself to keep his attention on Deming and her carefully drawn boundary lines around the map of Boston. He and Hannah had more to say to each other, but it would have to wait.

Deming stood back from the map and eyeballed her handiwork. "This is where our perp most likely lives, works, or has a reason for visiting frequently. As you can see, it's a much wider net than the actual crime scenes indicate. Twoomey and Zelezny's bodies were found on the Freedom Trail, but Stone was found at Constitution Marina, *not* on the Freedom Trail."

Vivian walked to the map, her arms folded across her chest. "Still a historic site."

"But *not* on the Freedom Trail," Deming said.

"You're suggesting the Freedom Trail isn't part of his ritual? That something else about these sites attracts him?" Ferguson said.

"I'm not ready to rule out the Freedom Trail as being significant," the profiler said, focusing on Jack. "But I believe the wharf is an outlier, maybe our perp made a mistake."

"Your gut again?" Ferguson said. Deming grimaced, but kept her focus on Jack, who sympathized. Ferguson irritated the hell out of Jack, too.

"It bears extra scrutiny," Deming said. "Someone needs to check out Constitution Marina again."

"*Again*," Ferguson said, looking ready to blow a gasket. Jack figured the detective's attitude was probably more about what happened in the interrogation room than trolling the marina, though Jack felt his pain. He wanted to put his fist through a wall, too.

"We need to go back if only to rule out missing something," Deming said. "So yeah. We need to interview the witnesses one more time, and recanvas that crime scene. If the marina *is* an outlier, maybe the perp made a mistake. It could be the lead we've been hoping for."

Jack didn't have anything to lose. They were getting nowhere staring at the murder board. "You and Ferguson go to the marina. See what you can see." It would give him and the detective some much needed space.

Deming shook her head. "If you don't mind, I'd like to check out Lewis Wharf and Copp's Hill Burying Ground."

Vivian frowned, taking a step toward the map. "Neither place is on your geographic profile."

Deming pointed at the two sites she mentioned on the map. "The killer likes the North End. He's already gone to the border on both ends of the line he's created. He's run out of real estate if he wants to use Freedom Trail tourist sites. Copp's Burying Ground is on the Freedom Trail. Lewis Wharf is as far as you can go in the opposite direction before you hit ocean. It's not on the Freedom Trail, but the Freedom Trail *might* be incidental to these kills. We need to hedge our bets, and not assume anything."

"You're saying we don't know anything," Ferguson said, looking furious.

"So the Freedom Trail might have nothing to do with these kills. Gotcha," Vivian said, looking uneasy.

Deming shrugged. "It's a theory. Worth a try."

"Fine," Jack said. "Then Hannah and I will canvas the crime scene at Constitution Marina." It would give him time to calm her down, maybe set right some of the damage he'd created when he skipped out on her last year. Maybe make her not hate him so much. Well, maybe hate was too strong of a word. They did have sex. It was confusing. *She made him nuts.* He glanced at Hannah. "Let's go," he said, and immediately regretted his harsh tone.

Hannah grabbed her gun and badge from her locked desk drawer, and then led the way into the hall. He told himself to ignore her swaying hips, the wisps of curling blond hair that had escaped her hair clip at the base of her long neck. He needed to model his behavior on hers; professional, distant, cold.

He'd find the perp. Make Hannah safe again. Then he'd fade quietly into her past and leave her for good this time. That should make her happy, and Jack wanted Hannah happy, because at some point—and he wasn't sure exactly when it happened—Hannah's happiness became more important to Jack than his own.

Chapter 7

Hannah stepped into the hall as Jack followed, pointing toward the elevator, not slowing his gait. "I can't wait to get out of here. Talk about putting on a show," he said.

She felt a pang of embarrassment, and then it morphed to anger as she tried to keep pace with his long strides. "Whose fault is that?"

Jack, being Jack, shrugged off her chastisement. "Deming's profile of the perp says he's a hunter who lures his victims to predetermined crime scenes. So, you and me, we're stuck like glue. Let's make sure you don't get lured." When they reached the elevator, he hit the button, and they waited.

"Don't get lured," she said. "Why didn't I think of that?"

Jack frowned at her, and Hannah had to suppose he was taking umbrage because of her sardonic tone. When he opened his mouth, looking on the cusp of arguing, the elevator door opened. Hannah stepped on, leaving Jack to gape after her. For a moment there, she wasn't sure if he would step onto the elevator with her, but then the door pinged, and Jack was standing next to her when the doors closed them in. He pressed the ground floor button with such force, Hannah had to suppress a flinch. Then elevator music filled the void of conversation, giving her time to compose herself.

Jack hadn't asked her about why she'd lured *him* into the lieutenant's room. On some level, she knew she should be insulted. They'd had *sex*, for heaven's sake. She was still tender from his hard thrusts. How could he not want to talk about that?

Jack kept his eyes front, though he stood so close she could feel the heat of him, even though he wasn't touching her. "Have you noticed," Jack said, "the perp doesn't leave forensic evidence he doesn't want us to find? He knows something about how we work. Maybe he's a cop."

"Or DVRs *Criminal Minds*," she said.

Jack wasn't like regular people. Nothing about him was regular, but she'd known that when she got involved with him way back when, when things were...simpler. Hannah knew she had only herself to blame for how their relationship went up in flames. But still. *They'd just had sex.* And it was so damn good. How could he act as if they'd simply shared tea and cookies? It was insulting.

Hannah felt a growing pressure in her chest, and then suddenly it was hard to breathe. Just like that. Like a switch was flipped. She knew it was stress. Knew it, but it didn't help to dispel the horrible tightness. She and Jack were alone again, and the last time they were alone, well, *they'd had sex.* She was furious with him, but she couldn't stop thinking about the damn sex.

It had been heartbreakingly wonderful. No lie. She'd enjoyed every bit of his kisses and his hands on her body. If she could be assured of not being caught, she'd beg him to take her again, here, now. The elevator was large enough to accommodate, but it wouldn't be emotionally healthy for Hannah to give in to that desire. Jack was like a drug. She craved him, forgot all her worries and responsibilities when she was in his arms, but ultimately, he always seemed to be in the center of her heartache.

Jack was heartache in a rumpled suit.

"There are never any signs of struggle from the victims," he said. She refused to meet his gaze until she could stop thinking about their kisses, and his mouth on her breast. "What did Deming say about that?" *Still,* she could not look at him, especially now when her blush kept growing. She kept remembering. How it was a full-body experience to have him sheath himself inside her, his tongue thrusting into her mouth. It was... wonderful. "Hannah? Just so we're clear, I'm not here to make your life difficult." The elevator music was interrupted by a *bing,* indicating the doors were opening.

Hannah glared at him, too angry for the conversation they were having, but just angry enough for the conversation they were avoiding. Exiting the elevator, she attempted to outpace him as she hurried down the hall. She wanted to outrun her thoughts and the temptation to act upon them—to find some empty room and strip his clothes off again, to touch the body she'd mourned this last year, that had visited her only in her dreams.

"Why are you here, Jack?"

"To catch a killer."

"Then we're clear." They were not going to attempt to repair the past. They'd have a new beginning as peers in the bureau, and co-parents with

Ellen...if he wanted to be in their daughter's life. *Damn*. Nothing was ever easy with Jack.

"As mud," he muttered under his breath. Approaching the glass exit doors, Jack tugged on her sleeve, stopping her from leaving the building just yet. "There's a target on your back. Every moment, Hannah." He glanced around the area, making sure he couldn't be overheard. Then he lowered his voice. "A serial—"

"Stop. I know. Okay?" She swallowed the lump in her throat, and attempted to breathe through her escalating stress symptoms.

"You will stay close. The deal is—"

"Attached to your hip. Or do you want the glue analogy? I get it. Let's go. Shall we?" She stepped away from him, fighting light-headedness, and hurried outside. On the sidewalk, she used her hand to indicate the bureau's parking lot. "My car is in there." She attempted to discreetly hold her breath, because she feared she was hyperventilating. She had all the symptoms.

Jack shook his head, and led her down New Sudbury Street as he surveilled their surroundings. "No."

No? What the hell did that mean? No. He was so high-handed, it made her want to scream, but Hannah kept pace with him despite her urge to bitch-slap him. *Calm down, Hannah.*

"You should let me drive," she said. "You don't know the area." Whereas, Hannah did. She'd been on her own, fending for herself and then Ellen for nearly a year now, and she'd lived to tell the tale. But now that Jack was here, she was supposed to turn every life decision, personal and professional, over to him? Even whether she drove her car or not? *Hell, no!* She stopped walking and glared.

Jack stopped, too, his eyes still on their surroundings, and the roofline of buildings on the street. She resisted the urge to remind him that their killer used poetry and mind games to make his kills—*finesse*. Execution by scoped rifle was too ham-fisted for their perp—but with Jack, it was best to pick her battles.

"Let me drive," she demanded.

"I'm driving," Jack said. "You'll navigate." His tone said he wouldn't argue, which made Hannah want to argue even more, but then he tilted his head to the side, indicating a tomato-red 2SS Camaro Coupe. It looked new.

She snorted out a laugh, and then continued to laugh. It released some tension, and felt so good she was forced to acknowledge she hadn't done much laughing lately. More than lately. Since Jack died.

"You and your flashy cars," she said. "You're a glutton for punishment." Admiration fought with her practical streak as she studied the sleek lines of the gorgeous automobile. "Every ding, every scratch, every college student who uses your car for target practice will break your heart a piece at a time. If this work of art isn't stolen within the week, I'll be surprised, and I'm rarely surprised."

"Which is ironic, considering you never fail to surprise me." His eyes were on his car, though, and he was smiling, as if the car's very existence made him happy. Hannah wondered what it would feel like to be on the receiving end of that smile again. "Don't jinx me." He unlocked the door, and slid behind the wheel.

Hannah slid into shotgun, and couldn't resist caressing the glove leather seat. "Kiss that stereo goodbye. Statistically, it's the first to go."

Jack smiled, and Hannah's heart hurt. She hadn't seen that rendition of his smile in a long time. It was uncensored, boylike, and her favorite. "Me and this car is long overdue. I saved up and now it's mine." He turned the key and listened to the engine's purr.

Hannah buckled in, telling herself to be cool. "Nothing wrong with a good rental." She should know. She was leasing a white Camry, a good family car with all the safety features a new mother could possibly want. Ellen wasn't getting anywhere near this sports car. She suspected it was not child-friendly, and she'd tell Jack that very thing...as soon as she told him about Ellen's existence.

Jack shrugged. "Nothing wrong with fast food, but sometimes a man wants a real meal." He patted the dashboard and winked at Hannah.

The wink had her shaking her head. They were friends again, huh? Fine. She'd ignore the sex, the drama in the interrogation room. She'd even ignore that he took her job, and count herself lucky. For Ellen's sake. Didn't mean she had to like it.

Hannah pointed down the street, giving directions as if nothing out of the ordinary was occurring, as if every day her dead lover appeared out of the blue and took over her world.

"The Constitution Marina is a little over a mile away," she said. "Follow New Sudbury to Cross Street, take a right and then go north on Atlantic Avenue. It's south of the Coast Guard base in Boston Harbor." Jack merged into traffic, and with Hannah giving directions, arrived at the marina in under fifteen minutes. For Boston? They made good time.

"We could have walked faster," he said. Jack pulled into the lot and searched for a parking space. "Refresh my memory on the Stone murder."

"Pull up to the dockmaster's office and park in front." She pointed toward the water's edge where yachts, sail boats and shuttle crafts bobbed in the water, next to the small building with a blue placard declaring it

Kris Rafferty

Constitution Marina. It was a sunny day, so people were milling on the docks, coming and going. Jack parked by the office door.

"Stone, Hannah. Tell me about Stone."

"A witness saw something in the water," she said. "Reached down to see what it was, and found a human hand. Homicide discovered her attached to a cinder block. The killer wanted the body found. The depth of the water at that dock is shallower than the rest of the marina, so the length of rope used made the body's discovery inevitable. We found the stanza in a closed Ziploc bag duct-taped to the rope. Mariner's rope. No fingerprints. No forensic evidence that could narrow down to something even resembling a lead."

Hannah stepped out of the car, slammed the door behind her and caught Jack's wince as he closed his door with more care. "Take it easy, will you?" he said.

"It's a car, Jack. Closing the door won't break it." He glared. She held his stare, not willing to give an inch. "Are we doing this, or are we going to argue about the car?"

It was rare Jack admitted to caring about anything. That he admitted to loving his car was a big deal, and showed emotional progress. Hannah knew she should encourage it. The greater capacity he had for love, the more he had to give to his daughter, but she resented he'd evolved for a car, and not for her.

He grimaced, and scanned the parking lot, then waved Hannah into the office first. When she stepped inside, mild salty breezes gave way to crisp air conditioning and the smell of aromatic coffee. A doorbell overhead pealed, announcing their arrival as her shoes sank into a lush, white carpet. Silver walls and whitewashed wainscoting shouted *tasteful*, and white satin-clad chairs with carved wood bases screamed *money*. The office was like stepping into a showroom…with snacks. Against the right wall, a white lacquered table supported silver platters of artfully arranged pastries on individual paper doilies, and a glass coffee carafe, with accompanying white porcelain cups. On the left was a brochure rack touting tourist sites, membership packages, and boating and slip sales paraphernalia. Ahead was an unmanned counter with an open guest book next to a cash register. A man appeared from a door behind the counter as Jack took pictures of the signatures in the book.

"Can I help you?" A tall, lean man stepped from the back room, running his fingers through his hair as if conscious that it was ruffled and needed repair. Hannah's lack of reciprocating smile didn't dampen his smile's enthusiasm, highlighting his white teeth which contrasted sharply with his dark tan. Though graying at the temples, he still looked no more than late thirties. His fitted IZOD polo shirt stretched tightly over his muscular chest, and his khaki slacks were expensive, if untidy, as if hastily donned.

She flashed her credentials. "We have a few questions."

The dockmaster absently ran his fingers through his hair again, glancing over his shoulder. "I'm in a meeting—"

"It won't take long." Jack indicated the nameplate, also showing his credentials. "You're Peter Bolger? The dockmaster, right?"

"Yes." Impatient resolve replaced his earlier curiosity. "What can I do for the FBI? *Again.*"

Hannah indicated the room behind him. "Is there someone back there?"

"Janice," he called over his shoulder, keeping his gaze on Hannah. "Come out. The jig is up." Bolger's cheek kicked up.

A barefoot blonde, early twenties, holding a pair of sandals, stepped into the reception area in the process of buttoning her shirt. Her curls bounced and her white blouse and brief khaki tennis skirt appeared expensive. "Hello." Though markedly embarrassed, Janice's smile was nonetheless bright. "Peter, I'll come back later."

"I'm counting on that." His gaze still on Hannah, Bolger winked.

Jack slid a picture of Stone onto the counter. "Do you recognize this woman?" The bell above the entry door pealed as Janice departed.

Bolger nodded. "Her picture made the papers, and this isn't the first time I've been questioned about her. Some cop. Big dude." Bolger spread his arms, and frowned fiercely, doing a pretty good impression of Ferguson.

"What do you know about the woman?" Jack tapped the photo with his index finger.

Hannah didn't like Bolger. He was too measured in his responses by far, too cavalier given that they were talking about a murder that took place in his marina. She reminded herself that he was a salesman, and only worked here. It was his job to be smooth, especially when situations got tense. But still…she didn't like him.

"I know what everyone else knows," Bolger said. "Some chick tied her ankle to a cinder block and went for a swim off the one dock we have shallow enough for her to be found." He shook his head, as if more annoyed the body was found than that the woman was dead. "People are still talking about it."

Jack exchanged a measured glance with Hannah. No one who knew *anything* about the Stone case thought it was a suicide, and this guy's job was to know everything that went on in the marina. It made a person wonder where this theory originated.

Bolger dropped his gaze to Hannah's chest. He smiled a small smile, and it was so obnoxious, she had to assume he'd done it to distract her, so Hannah made a point of not being distracted.

"Why do you assume the death was a suicide?" she asked. His eyes remained on her chest.

Jack slapped his hand on the counter. The dockmaster startled, as if only then remembering Hannah wasn't alone. When his gaze collided with Jack's, the man frowned with annoyance.

"The papers say it's murder," Jack said. "What do you know that they don't?"

"Nothing," Bolger said with growing impatience. "You're the FBI. *You* should know." He glanced between the two of them. "Which begs the question, why is the FBI asking? This is a local matter, right? Why aren't the *police* talking to me?"

Hannah's fingers tapped on the counter, one after another, creating a rhythmic beat of fingernails on wood. So far, Peter Bolger hadn't answered one question, and she'd lost her patience. "*You don't know. You don't know.* I'm thinking we should bring him downtown, Special Agent Benton. What do you think? Maybe his memory will strengthen if his ass hits one of the cozy chairs in the interrogation room."

Bolger threw his hands in the air. "Listen! I'm doing my best. I know nothing, okay? Just gossip. Some people think it's murder, some think it's suicide. She wasn't tied up, or drugged, so maybe suicide." The dockmaster leaned on the counter, staring at her chest again, as if that were normal behavior. "Nobody around here knows her, so maybe murder. If we knew her, even I'd think it was suicide."

Jack stepped into Bolger's line of sight, which meant he had to nudge Hannah aside. At first, she didn't know what Jack was doing, so she stepped back and waited to be read into his reasoning. But Jack acted as if nothing out of the ordinary had just happened, leaving her marginalized.

"*Even you?*" Jack said. "What does that mean? Who *does* think it's suicide?"

Hannah stared at his back, attempting to cool her anger. Jack had his reasons for crowding her out of this interview. She was almost positive. He'd tell her when he was ready. Yet her stomach tightened, and her face flushed as she struggled to control her feelings.

"The marina's board of directors think it's suicide," Bolger said. "They've been selling suicide since we found the body. They don't want rumors that people are being murdered at Constitution Marina. Can't blame them, can you? Not good for business." Bolger didn't look all broken up by the possibility, but then again, Hannah wasn't sure what would break through Bolger's demeanor of affable, carefree bon vivant.

Hannah peeked around Jack's broad shoulders to catch Bolger's attention. "Have there been any other unusual happenings around here?" she asked. "Strangers milling about? Residents acting out of character? Disturbances?"

Bolger craned his neck to see behind Jack, and his disappointment was palpable when he couldn't lower his gaze to her chest. "The most action we have around here is revolving bedmates, and nobody seems all that disturbed by it." Bolger's saucy smile returned, until Jack slapped his hand on the counter again. It had the benefit of stopping Bolger's creepy leer, so she began to appreciate Jack's caveman behavior. "A few foreclosures, maybe. Nothing worthy of note."

"We want to take another look around the marina," she said.

"I'd give you the tour, but, well—" Bolger lifted his hands, indicating there was nothing he could do. "I've got a lot of work to do."

The tour. Hannah shuddered at the thought, thinking nothing could be less appealing then having Bolger leer at her for the length of time it would take for a tour. "Thank you for your time," she said, heading for the door.

"Stick around long enough," Bolger said, "you'll witness *my* murder. I'm supposed to report to the board that another millionaire isn't paying their bills." Then Bolger disappeared into the back room, mumbling, "Who names a two-million-dollar yacht *Teapot*?"

Jack bumped into Hannah's back as she stopped short in the doorway. Looking back, past Jack who stood between her and the now unmanned counter, Hannah gave herself a moment to process Bolger's words.

"What? Why'd you stop?" Jack said.

Hannah turned and stepped around him, back into the office. "Teapot?"

"What of it?" Jack was so close his breath warmed Hannah's face. It reminded her she wasn't wearing makeup, and made her self-conscious. It also had the unfortunate result of making her forget why she'd stopped short in the first place.

Bolger turned back to his spot behind the counter. "I'm sorry, did you need something else?"

Jack was impatient to leave, and was pressing on her lower back, but Hannah muscled past him, and walked back to the counter. She had to wave her hand in front of the guy's face to make him look at her face. "How long has the *Teapot* been docked?"

"Three months. They been ducking my calls for two months now. Why?"

Jack's disgruntled expression gave way to curiosity. "What are you thinking, Hannah?"

Kris Rafferty

"Hannah?" Bolger's smile brightened. "That's a beautiful name."

She ignored the dockmaster, and held Jack's gaze, feeling foolish. "Tempest in a teapot."

"Shakespeare," Bolger said, nodding.

"No." Jack said. "William Blake?" He lifted his brows and Hannah nodded. He saw where she was going with this.

"No." Bolger shook his head. "That is definitely a Shakespeare reference."

She could see Jack's instant skepticism, but dismissed it. "Listen," she whispered, attempting to exclude Bolger from their conversation. "The victims are lured to the crime scenes, right?" She pressed her palm to her chest. "I'm here. I was led here by the killer's geographical profile." Bolger peered at them, attempting to overhear. "Death by *tempest*, Jack. Remember?"

"It's a coincidence." Jack shook his head.

"It's a lead." And if Jack wasn't so stubborn, he'd admit it. "You," she pointed to Bolger. "Get me everything you have on that vessel. Owners' contact information, specs, contracts, dock logs, everything. Do you understand? I want the owners here, if possible, if not, on the phone. Tell them it's a federal investigation, so if they refuse, there will be obstruction of justice charges. No joke."

"You're making my life difficult," Bolger said. His grimace was full throttled, but it didn't look as if he would push back. "These people are rich. When they find out the feds are looking for them, why wouldn't they head the other way? I need them to pay their bills."

"Do I need to explain 'obstruction of justice,' Mr. Bolger? Get it done!" Jack didn't wait for his answer, but turned his back on the dockmaster and pulled out his phone. The line must have connected quickly, because he was talking into it soon thereafter. "Ferguson, we might have something. Tell Pepperidge we need a warrant ASAP for the *Teapot*, a yacht docked at Constitution Marina. We're trying to locate the owners, but they've been missing for two months." He waved a hand to garner Bolger's attention. "What kind of vessel exactly?"

"A 2001 Sanlorenzo yacht. A small one," the dockmaster said. "No one's been on her for months. Like I said, the owners haven't answered calls, texts, or certified letters so I don't know what you expect me to do."

"It's a yacht," Jack said to Ferguson. "We're thinking a *tempest in a teapot*. Get Charlie Foulkes and his forensic team down here." He hung up.

"Where's the yacht?" Hannah opened the door, impatient to start. "What direction? How far down the dock, Mr. Bolger?"

Jack leaned toward her, keeping his tone quiet. "Ferguson thinks this is a dead end."

"And what do you think?"

"I think if you're right, you're in danger."

"Right now, it's just a lead," she said.

Bolger pointed. "Take a right, and it's the third dock down. The corner dock."

She took off, leaving Jack behind. He caught up with her, grabbed her arm, preventing her from sprinting ahead. "What did we agree on, Hannah?" he said. "Attached to my hip. That means you're not barreling into a situation without backup."

"Don't pretend you think we'll find something." She pulled her arm from his grip, and he didn't make it easy. "You think I'm crazy."

He put his hands up, as if trying to gentle a colt. "I trust your instincts, just...let's act accordingly."

"Of course." It galled Hannah that yesterday she answered to the lieutenant, and today, when she needed all obstacles leveled, her decisions had to be vetted by Jack. She forced herself to take his advice without snapping, when what she wanted was to sprint to this *Teapot* yacht and end this threat to her and Ellen. Their daughter. Her frustration was making it hard to think.

"We wait for the warrant," he said, as if expecting an argument.

"Of course." She reined in her impatience.

The sky was deep blue, not a cloud in sight, and the breeze smelled salty, like seaweed. Tourists were meandering, enjoying the temperate day. It was the least conducive setting to violence she could imagine, yet as moments stretched to minutes, there was a tingling between her shoulder blades, as if she were someone's target. "Tempest in a teapot. If it's not a coincidence, the killer could be here, right now, watching us," she said.

"Maybe we should wait inside." Jack surveilled the parking lot. She could tell he was fighting the urge to drag her away. "We can wait for the warrant in the office." Fearing his suggestion would morph to an order, she threw caution to the wind and headed down the walkway toward the third dock on the corner. He caught up with her just as the *Teapot* appeared ahead; white, sleek, as big as a house. "Hannah, you said you'd wait for the warrant!" His eyes locked on the *Teapot*. "*This* is a small yacht?"

"A lesson in perspective." Hannah indicated the larger yachts in the distance, moored in open sea, requiring their occupants to use a dingy to travel from dock to ship. The *Teapot*, however, was easily accessible. She stepped onto its gangway.

"Hey!" Jack said. "We agreed. We're waiting, Hannah."

"I hear something. Maybe a call of distress." She pulled her gun, bending her knees, trying to see into the portholes from that angle.

"Bullshit. Come back." He folded his arms across his chest and grimaced at her, as if there was no doubt in his mind she'd follow orders.

The more Jack resisted, the more she became convinced there was something to be seen on this yacht. "Maybe there's a crime in progress. Don't know. Sure would like to." She jogged across the gangway, making a considerable amount of noise.

"Without a warrant, nothing will be admissible." He threw his hands in the air, his frustration on full display.

"So you *do* think this might be a solid lead." Ha! She could see the truth on his face. Hannah took the final step onto the yacht's deck and heard his truncated curse.

"Come back!" Jack hurried after her, making a racket. "This is not our deal, Hannah."

True. And she couldn't help but silently list the protocols she was breaking. She knew them all, because Hannah was a by-the-books kind of gal, but she recognized this case wasn't a by-the-books kind of case. Her reality had changed dramatically the moment she got Ferguson's call this morning. It made her less worried about an eventual court case and more worried about surviving.

The stairs leading into the belly of the yacht were halfway to the stern side, and if there was anything to be found, it would be down there. She quickly descended, afraid Jack would physically attempt to stop her. When she reached the stair's bottom, she halted just inside the door. It was almost as if an unseen hand had barred her way.

Ahead was a wall of photographs. Of her. Of Twoomey, Zelezny, and Stone.

"Shit." Jack jostled her aside as he stepped inside, his gun at the ready.

Yup. *Shit.* They'd found their killer's lair.

Hannah approached the wall, in a daze. One picture jumped out at her. She pointed, making her index finger hover over the photo, but careful not to touch it. "This was taken last month, first day on the case. That afternoon I'd spilled coffee on my shirt. See that?" She pointed to the stain. "I've yet to bring it to the cleaners and it's still on the bottom of my laundry basket."

"The date, Hannah. What was the date it was taken?"

"July 15. Maybe around 5:00 p.m. Stone's body had just been discovered."

It was creepy to realize that someone had taken Hannah's picture without her consent. It was *horrifying* to realize they took the picture with the purpose of hunting her.

Jack pulled out his phone and dialed.

She pressed her hand to his arm. "The killer has inside information, Jack. My first day on the job? I was targeted long before I received that email." Her pulse raced as she processed this new development. Did the killer know about Ellen? "We have to think about who might be leaking information, or maybe—" She didn't want to say it, but felt it had to be said. "Maybe the killer *is* law enforcement."

Phone to his ear, Jack nodded. "Let's worry about that later. I need to get you to a safe place." He peered out the door, looking up the stairs, his back to her. "Lieutenant? Yeah, it's Benton. We have a shitload of evidence on a yacht in Constitution Marina and we need help expediting a warrant. Yeah. It's the marina where the Stone woman was killed." Using her phone, Hannah snapped one photo after another of the board. "Get uniformed officers here ASAP. I don't want Hannah anywhere near this place, and need to hand it off to forensics. Ferguson should be with Deming. We need everyone on the team here. I'll call Gilroy when I hang up."

Hannah was having a hard time believing what she was seeing, but so far, there were no pictures of Ellen, so that was good. Seeing these photos made her precarious situation seem more real...real in a way that an innocuous email hadn't driven home.

"He's not coming back here." She shook her head. "Odds that he'd keep his home base next to a crime scene are statistically nil. It makes no sense."

"Yet here it is." He glanced at her, waiting, still on the phone.

"He's not coming back, Jack."

"You don't know that." He turned away from her, focusing on his phone conversation. "What's the soonest you can get a cruiser here?"

Hannah snatched the phone from Jack's hand. "Lieutenant, Deming was right. The Stone girl must be an outlier. She must have stumbled upon this site, got caught, and the killer took her out."

Jack snatched the phone back, glaring at her. Hannah faced the photos, forcing herself to see them as an investigator rather than a potential victim. She took wide shots of the wall in case the photos were arranged in a pattern that could be a clue. Then she approached the wall and studied a photo of her leaving her brownstone. She'd still been carrying baby weight around the middle, so had worn her jacket buttoned to disguise the bump. It was only a month ago, yet seemed like forever.

Jack's fingers were white-knuckled as he clenched the phone, holding it to his ear. "Okay. Yeah. I will." Then he disconnected the line.

Hannah didn't reholster her gun, but kept it at the ready. "I'd give my left arm to know if Stone was on this yacht."

"She was knocked unconscious, then dumped in the harbor. Seems risky to kill her here and then dump the body so close to all this evidence."

"Maybe hauling her body to a second site was riskier."

"Like the Freedom Trail?" Jack scanned the room, fairly twitching with pent-up energy.

"Exactly." A shudder ran the length of her body. "This photo board is freaking me the hell out."

Jack scowled. "Don't tell me that, because if you tell me that, I have to assume you can't handle this—"

"I'm handling it. This is me handling this. Let's not fight. Not now, when"—she pointed her gun's muzzle at the photos—"that's staring at me."

He sighed. "You know the files better than I do. Maybe Stone was at a bar and someone brought her here. That would indicate the perp is young enough to gain a twentysomething's attention. Did Stone say she was going to a bar? Maybe a party."

"She had no one to tell, Jack. Stone was a loner. They're all loners. No close family, and Stone's coworkers said she kept to herself."

Jack glanced at his watch, and then at the stairs leading out of the yacht. Even if a cruiser was in the area, it would still take them time to find the yacht. Jack's impatience spoke volumes about his unease, and it mirrored her own.

"Pray we get the warrant quickly, and this place gives us DNA to work with." Jack's lips pressed together, and his expression clouded with anger. "You might have just broken this case wide open."

"But? For the life of me, I know you didn't say *but*, although it sure sounds as if *but* was implied."

"*But* you put yourself at risk by coming onboard, and by definition, you put my life at risk, too. You've broken protocol and our deal, so you're going into protective custody. No more arguments. Got it?"

"Bullshit." Hannah shook her head. He couldn't make her, and knew it. "I want to interview the owners of the yacht."

It was his turn to shake his head. "You heard Bolger. They're long gone. And I don't see them good for the murders, anyway." He indicated the wall of photos. "They'd be fools to leave this here, then not pay their bills. It's just inviting attention."

True, but... "Every serial killer wants to get caught."

He looked over his shoulder toward the door, fairly bouncing on the balls of his feet. "Yeah, but they want to get caught when they're good and ready. This is here for a reason, and so are we."

She agreed. "He wanted me to see this." She peered closer at the photos. "Jack, how could he have known I'd find it? That I'd make the connection between the stanza and the yacht, or even that Bolger would mention its name?"

"Bolger didn't need to mention it. Sooner or later you'd look at the marina's list of yachts moored here. You'd have found it." They exchanged glances, and Hannah recognized his worry. "We need a good long talk with Mr. Peter Bolger, dockmaster extraordinaire."

"No." She shook her head, not believing his implication. "I just can't—" Then she thought on it a moment more. "Yeah?" *The dockmaster?* A serial killer? Was it horrible that she hoped it was true? Hannah scanned the rest of the yacht's interior.

Pollen had gotten inside and covered everything with a fine yellow powder. Paintings were missing off the walls and large squares of dust marked where they'd hung. All personal items were gone: lamps, doodads, all missing. The only evidence beyond the photos were various disturbed layers of dust and pollen, confirmation that activity in the yacht happened at different times over the last months.

"The place is stripped clean," she said.

"An abandoned million-plus yacht. And this." He pointed to the wall of pictures. Evidence. "We can't stay any longer," Jack said. "The police will be here any moment, hopefully with a warrant."

Then a cell phone rang, and they looked at each other, but it wasn't Hannah's, and Jack pulled his from his pocket and found his wasn't ringing, either.

Hannah followed the sound to a door in the corner that she'd presumed was a utility closet. Thinking there might be someone hiding in there, or worse yet, a body with a phone, she gripped her gun with both hands and raced to the door. She waited at one side of the door for Jack to approach and back her up. Jack gripped the doorknob, paused, then pulled the door wide, revealing two propane tanks duct-taped together with a small block of C4 and a cell phone attached to a detonator. There were seconds left on the countdown to zero.

Hannah's body flooded with adrenaline. Jack grabbed her arm and pivoted toward the stairs, and up, until they were in the salty air, under the pristine blue sky. She heard her breathing, a stream of expletives spilling from Jack's mouth, and the sound of the ringing cell phone. When her foot hit teak decking, Jack hauled her to his side, lifting her off her feet as he continued to run, his long legs eating the distance to the gangway.

Kris Rafferty

The bomb went off with a concussive *boom* that forced the air from her lungs. Her eyes closed. She was separated from Jack in that instant, and sailed through the air.

Next thing she knew, she was plunging into the cold, dark harbor water, alone, and her descent seemed never-ending. It continued past the assumption that she could ever hold her breath long enough to break the water's surface again. Her world became shock, a muffled ringing in her ears, and the disorienting blackness that made it impossible to know what was up or down. She froze, steadily moving in the water, not knowing if she was still sinking, or if she was floating back up.

Then she panicked as pain racked her body. She couldn't breathe, and her lungs burned. Kicking, clawing the water, she saw a flicker of light, and swam toward it, though its distance seemed unreachable. But she did it for Ellen…for Jack. They urged her on, gave her a reason to push past her fear and suffering, to fight the promise of oblivion.

When her head broke the water's surface, she was more surprised than relieved, because she was in so much pain. But she was alive. Gasping, coughing, orienting herself in a world of floating, burning debris. The yacht was on fire, crackling, and people were gathering along the dock, shouting and pointing.

She was alive. Sobs made breathing harder as she slapped the water's surface, barely afloat. "Jack!" She turned this way and that, struggling to tread water to find him. "Jack!" Did he even know how to swim? The topic had never come up. Had the explosion's concussion rendered him unconscious? Was Jack drowning? He couldn't die. Not again.

Hannah dove under the inky water, blindly searching with her hands, desperate to find him. When her lungs gave out, she kicked to the surface long enough to regain her breath and then dive again. It seemed to go on forever. Reaching, swimming in circles, feeling for his body. Hannah popped up for air again, shaking and crying.

"Jack!" She'd been helpless when he'd died before, and was helpless now. She couldn't live though it again. "Jack!" People along the shore were pointing at her, shouting to the gathering first response teams on shore. She wanted to scream at them, tell them Jack needed their help, but couldn't find the breath to make a sound.

"Hannah!" Jack's shout echoed over the water. She saw him! His powerful strokes quickly had him by her side.

Sobbing, never so happy to see another human being in her life, Hannah treaded water, breathing deeply. He was alive. *Thank you, thank you, thank you, Lord.* It had been her idea to board the yacht. It would have been her fault if he'd died without knowing he had a daughter. She felt her body sinking, her arms no longer strong enough to keep her above the surface.

Jack grabbed her from behind, keeping them both afloat as he swam them to shore. "Are you okay?"

"Where were you?" She leaned her head back, staring at the blue sky, tears blurring her vision. "I looked for you, was calling you."

Jack dropped a quick kiss on her head, his strong kicks and arm strokes keeping them moving. It was hard to breathe through her sobs, and now that she knew he was safe, she was humiliated by her weakness, but she couldn't stop crying. "I'm here," he said. "We're safe, but we have to get out of the water." Jack was looking around, on guard. "We don't know who's watching."

That reminder gave her a jolt of energy. "I can swim." Pushing out of his arms, she fought her exhaustion and swam. "What the hell happened?" Stroke after stroke, Hannah slowly made progress to shore with Jack easily keeping pace next to her, still scanning the shore.

"A bomb," he said. "The fucking boat blew up."

"No. I mean, where were you?" Anger was replacing sorrow at a fast pace.

"We were thrown on different sides of the gangway. I heard you calling, but you didn't hear me respond."

Because she'd been swimming underwater looking for him! She felt even more a fool, and weak. Every arm stroke was a little less effective in getting her to the damaged gangway. "You're bleeding."

He shook water from his eyes. "My forehead burns."

They were finally at the gangway and the crowd had grown. Witnesses. Maybe the perp. She didn't see the dockmaster. "Bolger? You see Bolger?" Her kingdom for a camera. She studied faces as she patted her pocket, searching for her phone. It was still there in its protective case, containing the only record of what they'd seen on the yacht…the wall of pictures.

"No." Jack swam behind her and used the leverage of the gangway to hoist Hannah out of the water. Charlie Foulkes, rushed forward, pushing through the crowd.

"Are you two all right?" He set his case down and reached for her. Hannah grabbed his forearm to steady herself as she climbed the last bit onto the mangled gangway. His blue Forensic BPD windbreaker was slick against her palm, but Charlie held tight. He was strong, pulling her the rest of the way out, one-handed. A handsome and muscular redhead, Charlie had a bit of the geek about him. Just a bit. She wondered how Deming knew him, and told herself to ask at some point. Later. When she didn't feel like she was dying.

Jack pressed up onto the gangway, dripping harbor water. He slipped his hand into his pocket and pulled out his phone, testing that his waterproof case had done its job. She wiped the water from her eyes, blinking, and peered at her own phone. It turned on…a relief. They weren't leaving empty-handed.

Hannah's wobbly smile fizzled under the weight of Jack's angry stare. He obviously blamed her for their current predicament. He had to. Pepperidge was going to bench her for sure.

"What happened?" Charlie was scanning the radius of the blast.

"It went boom." Hannah was suddenly freezing, though it was mid-August and the sun shone brightly. The sea breeze made it worse.

Jack gave his head a shake and sprayed them with water. "Could this water smell any worse?"

Charlie frowned. "The bomb. What did it look like?"

"An IED; two propane tanks, small block of C4, detonated by a ringing cell phone." Jack pressed his palm to his bleeding brow.

Charlie extended his hand. "Charlie Foulkes, by the way. We've talked on the phone, but haven't met face-to-face." They shook. Charlie indicated Jack's head wound. "EMTs pulled up behind my truck. I'd patch you up, but my skills lean toward the dead."

Jack gave his head another shake. "Other than a ringing in my ears, I'm fine."

Charlie nodded, but his interest lay elsewhere: the burning yacht. "I'm going to need you to describe in detail what you saw. It will increase our chances of finding any surviving pieces of the bomb."

Hannah's shaking had grown worse. Shock and exhaustion had drained the last of her reserves, and she knew if she didn't sit soon, she'd collapse. Jack didn't look any worse for wear. His clothes were plastered to his body, showcasing his amazing physique. Minus the smell, he could have been a model that had been wet down for a photo shoot. It wasn't fair. Hannah knew she had to look like a drowned rat. An exhausted, pale, drowned rat. Pregnancy and then extended bed rest did nothing for the cardiovascular system. She'd been working out a bit, but still wasn't up to her fighting shape, so reality was, she'd welcome a gurney with a heated blanket right about now.

"We could have been watched," Jack said. "The phone rang while we were in there." He flagged down a uniformed officer racing toward them, and flashed his credentials. She recognized Sergeant O'Neil immediately. "My name is Special Agent Jack Benton. I'm liaising with the New Sudbury precinct," he nodded to Charlie, who nodded in agreement. "I want the marina's dockmaster tracked down," he said, pointing toward the office.

"Have your men bring him to the precinct and have him wait there for me. In fact, ask Detective Ferguson to sit with him, see what shakes loose."

"I know who you are." The sergeant turned to Hannah, concern written all over him. "Special Agent Cambridge. You good?"

She nodded. "Thank you, Sergeant."

Jack's impatience with the man sharpened his tone. "The dockmaster, Sergeant." O'Neil nodded to Hannah, obviously conflicted, but he left on task, though the look he gave Jack said he wasn't happy.

"How to make friends and influence people," she said. "He's been kind to me, Jack. Try to play nice with others for a change."

"The dockmaster a suspect?" Charlie said.

"Maybe." He indicated the burning yacht. "How long will the search take?"

"It's still afloat. There's a chance we'll find something that might lead to the bomb maker. Maybe shrapnel with a finger print, if we're lucky, but don't count on it happening any time soon. No way to give you a realistic timeline. Best guess is damned if I know." Charlie indicated their dripping clothes with a glance. "How are you two alive?"

"We flew." She hid her trembling hands behind her back and could have kicked herself when her own words brought the scary incident back, as if it were happening in real time. Which triggered a panic attack. "Nice seeing you again, Charlie. Jack? We've got to go." Her words echoed in her ears as her vision narrowed. She started walking, hoping to hide before she unraveled with an audience.

"Go?" Jack took her arm and forced her to stop walking. "We're not going anywhere. This is our perp's last crime scene."

Charlie picked up a shard of decking. "It could take us days to pick through this flotsam. And if the yacht sinks, we'll need divers, which will lengthen the process." Hannah swayed on her feet. "My people are taking photos of the crowd, Special Agent Benton," Charlie said. "You might as well get cleaned up."

"Sure." Jack released her arm, allowing Hannah to walk again.

"I'm not feeling well," she whispered, trying to walk past him, but Jack wouldn't back off. He kept pace with her. "Please. Let me meet you back at the precinct."

"The ambulance first. We need to have you checked out," Jack said. "That was a hard blast."

She shook her head. There's be no hiding her panic attack from medical professionals. She'd be pulled from the case. That was not acceptable. "I need dry clothes. Maybe grab lunch. I'll be fine." She headed back to Jack's car.

"Special Agent Benton," Charlie shouted after them. "You really should get that cut looked at. There are bacteria in the harbor you don't want infecting that cut." Whatever Jack replied was lost to Hannah as she was left to focus on her breathing, the weird buzzing in her ears, and the growing blurriness to her vision. She could make out the EMT truck parked near the office, but if Jack hadn't grabbed her elbow and escorted her past it, she wouldn't have known where she was going.

"Please tell me you still have your car keys," she said, hoping Jack would ascribe her shaking to the cold.

"I do, but we're not getting anywhere near my leather seats with Boston Harbor stink on us. One of the patrolmen can drive us back. This way." He led her toward the cruisers in the parking lot.

Great, she thought. And her heart sank. This day was killing her. "I need to upload the photos to the precinct's secure site," she said. "Vivian can access it, so she can download the pictures and print them out by the time we return." Her teeth were chattering.

"We're going to your apartment to change." His words seemed innocuous. They made sense. She needed dry clothes.

"Wait, what?" she said. He couldn't go to her apartment just yet. Her heart skipped a beat. It was too soon for him to meet Ellen! "Later. I want the team to see these photos first." She'd suffer the physical discomfort, and suck it up. She had to.

"They'll keep. You need dry clothes. So do I."

"No." Her denial came out sharp to her sensitive ears, and when she searched for an excuse to back it up, for staying in stinking, harbor-wet clothes, she didn't have to stretch the truth. It was obvious, low-hanging fruit. "Pepperidge might demand you take me off the case. Bring me to the incident room, Jack, so I can consult with the team while I still have access to them. I need their take on the photos and the yacht." She swayed on her feet, feeling dizzy.

"Fine. But I should bench you. You know that, right?" He didn't look happy, but since when did she require him to be happy? All she'd ever asked was that he be there, with her, and even that had been too much for him to commit to.

She wanted to thank him, but couldn't force the words past her lips. She was falling into a stress-induced fugue, her emotions shutting down, and even her voice sounded distant and hollow to her. Jack opened the cruiser's back door for her, and she slipped inside just in time to stop herself from falling to the pavement.

As she sat there, shivering, Jack called Vivian, told her about the upload to the precinct's secure site. With shaking hands, Hannah managed to do that simple task without help. Then she used the rest of the ride to process what had happened and calm her body's reaction. Soon, she settled into a familiar exhaustion, and thankfully, the pain in her chest subsided. Everything was going to be okay, she told herself. She would be okay.

In the twenty minutes it took to arrive back at the BPD New Sudbury precinct, Hannah managed to shed most of her symptoms. She was getting better at it, and that made her think maybe she was getting better. The panic attacks had begun when Jack died. Maybe she was right to think Jack's resurrection would make them go away.

Once inside the building, past security and up the elevator, they hurried to homicide's incident room. They were both impatient to discuss what they had found. Ferguson met them outside the door, holding it open as they rushed inside. "The dockmaster, Bolger, is a piece of work. Even Vivian doesn't like him." And Vivian liked everyone.

"Where is he?" Jack said.

"Interrogation Room 1." Ferguson scowled at Jack when he said it, making Hannah think he was remembering this morning, and the fight he'd witnessed between her and Jack. And the kiss. A blush heated her cheeks, mostly because she knew that kiss had been the least of her inappropriate behavior today. Sex in the lieutenant's office, and then boarding the boat without a warrant. "Vivian is printing the pictures now," Ferguson said. "Lot of photos. Hannah, you had no business going on that yacht. Were those pictures worth your life? Sergeant O'Neil called me and said you nearly died twice."

"It's over." Hannah knew he was right. She'd almost killed her and Jack, and it was making her see this whole case from a different perspective. Jack was right. She hadn't considered the target on her back affecting anyone but her and Ellen. It put a target on Jack's back as well. "Is there any coffee left?" She was so cold.

Ferguson rolled his eyes. "It's not over, Hannah. *You're alive.* Our guy doesn't leave his targets alive."

"Detective Ferguson, stop," Vivian said. "Can't you see she's exhausted?" Vivian was wringing her hands, noticeably upset.

"Yes, she is." Jack plopped his wet suit jacket into the trash bin next to his desk. "Everyone give her some space."

Gilroy adjusted his tie as he walked up to the gathering crowd, scanning their faces. "Death by *tempest*. Got to hand it to the perp. That's unique." He pulled out his phone and Googled the word. "Tempest is…the definition says tumult. Now I have to look up tumult. What the hell is a tumult? Here it is. 'A violent commotion.' I guess blowing up a boat constitutes a tempest." He swore under his breath. "Just my luck I catch a case where you need to be a nineteenth-century poet to understand the perp."

"It was a yacht." Jack scanned the room. "Where's Deming?"

"She said I was cramping her style," Ferguson said, "so we separated. She went to Copp's Hill Burying Ground and I went to Lewis Wharf. Nothing there labeled *here's where the perp will hit next.* Complete waste of time. I've been calling her, trying to tell her just that all morning. She's not responding. I don't think she likes me." He smiled, not at all unhappy at the thought.

Hannah poured herself a cup of decaf, gripping the pot so tightly her knuckles paled. She sipped the bitter brew, studying the murder board. The new photos still weren't taped up. Impatience with herself and the situation sharpened her tone. "Vivian, where are my uploads?" Hannah stepped to the IT tech's desk and saw them displayed on her monitor. Pointing at one, Hannah overshot the distance and slammed her finger onto the delicate screen. It startled Vivian and embarrassed Hannah. "Print that photo first," she said. Jack grabbed tissues from Vivian's desk and pressed them to his brow. "Is it still bleeding?"

He glanced at the tissue. "No. It's nothing." Hannah could see it no longer bled, but it didn't look like nothing. It looked bruised and angry; like it hurt. Turning his attention toward Vivian, Jack said, "What are you printing?"

"It's a copy of Hannah's stanza," Vivian said. "The perp thought the yacht was where she'd die. He's good. Who could hear the word tempest and not associate it with a teapot?"

Hannah narrowed her eyes at Jack and then Ferguson, refusing to say *I told you so.* But she wanted to. Badly.

Ferguson was ignoring her, dialing. "Deming," he said into his phone. "Where the hell are you? Hannah almost died." Then he hung up.

It didn't go unnoticed that he failed to mention Jack's brush with death. If she hadn't been under such a strain, she might have smiled at Jack's reaction. He did not like Ferguson.

Vivian handed Jack her pump bottle of hand sanitizer, though never once did she take her eyes off the screen. "Dost thou not in pride and scorn, Fill with tempests all my morn, And with jealousies and fears, Fill my pleasant nights with tears?" She nodded. "Yup. That's her stanza."

"Vivian, why am I holding your hand sanitizer?" Jack had blood-smeared tissues in one hand and the bottle in the other, and he didn't look happy.

Gilroy took it from his hand and squirted some on a tissue. "For your cut. I hope your tetanus shot is up to date." Then he pressed it to Jack's cut.

"*Shit.*" Jack recoiled from the pain, squeezing his eyes shut and grimacing. "That burns."

"Nowhere does that stanza refer to an IED." Gilroy released the tissue when Jack took over. Then he took more tissues and wiped his hands.

Hannah sipped her hot coffee. Its heat soothed. Then she walked to her desk and returned to Vivian's with her first aid kit. She handed it to Jack. "We didn't know I'd be on that yacht until moments before I stepped on it." She was glad they'd thought to put a protective duty on her apartment, because she knew Ellen was safe, but she was impatient for Natalie's arrival. Things were escalating fast, and Hannah wanted her friend in charge of her daughter when Hannah couldn't be. "Is the killer following me? Because there is no way it could have been planned this way. Right?"

Jack shrugged, rummaging through the first aid kit. "That bomb was for you. The stanza on the wall tells us that." He opened a few antiseptic wipes and attempted to do a more thorough job on his cut, failing miserably. Hannah took the wipes from his hand and peered at the cut, dabbing.

"Let's walk through how you got there," Ferguson said. "Maybe it will give us an idea of how the killer lured you there."

Hannah nodded. "The geographical profile." She took out a butterfly bandage and indicated Jack should lean down so she could put it on his cut.

"Our killer knows police procedure." Gilroy folded his arms over his chest. "So…what? A cop who knows William Blake? He should stand out like a sore thumb."

Jack's breath caressed Hannah's cheek as she pressed the two sides of his cut together and applied the bandage. She hadn't expected the moment to be so intimate, and it unnerved her, made her feel as if she was under scrutiny as her heart was revealed to all and sundry. Everyone knew she loved Jack. They'd heard the "interrogation" this morning, so everything she did with him would be colored by her confession. Even something as mundane as putting a bandage on a cut. When she was done, Jack didn't pull away, but instead watched her closely. Strangely enough, it was only then, when she was done, that it occurred to her that Jack would be the one who interpreted her behavior as a reflection of her feelings for him.

"Thanks." He winked at her, then straightened up.

It broke the spell he'd cast, and allowed her to move. A quick glance told her no one was paying attention, thankfully. They were looking at Vivian's monitor.

"He's using our protocol against us." Vivian leaned her elbows on the desk, staring at the photos. "But even so, he couldn't have known Hannah would be the one to check out the marina this time."

Jack met Hannah's gaze again. "Another indication he is watching you. The photos show he's been watching since you were assigned to this case."

Ferguson scowled, and folded his arms over his chest. It was an intimidating sight. "So how could he know someone else wouldn't find the yacht first?"

"Maybe someone did," Gilroy said.

Jack nodded. "Maybe *Stone* did. We don't know. Yet." Jack released a heavy sigh. "The stanza is our perp's rulebook. The stanza is assigned to a victim. I don't think he'd have blown the yacht up for anyone but Hannah."

Ferguson used his thumb to indicate the incident room's doorway, and the hall beyond. "Bolger is still waiting in Interrogation Room 1."

"He had access to the yacht," Vivian said. "Could have made the call to the cell phone. He knew you were going there."

Jack caught Ferguson's attention. "I have to get Hannah home to change. Put some pressure on Bolger, get info on his girlfriend. What's her name?" He turned to Hannah.

"Janice," she said.

"And if he drops something interesting, call me." Jack motioned to Gilroy. "I'll want verified alibis on him for the time of every murder before you release him."

"Consider it done," Gilroy said.

Ferguson gathered his badge and gun from his drawer and then hurried out of the room with Gilroy trailing behind him.

"You were lured to your death." Vivian's words startled Hannah.

One glance made it clear the tech's words were meant for her, and they were not what Hannah needed right now. She wanted to go home, hug Ellen and pretend none of this was happening.

"No." Jack's tone was harsh, and final. "Hannah's alive and she's going to stay that way."

Vivian nodded. "Charlie will find the bomb fragments and put it together like a puzzle. Then we'll know if the perp was trailing Hannah and made the call, or if it was a trap that you two happened to spring. It might help explain the other kills, too."

Jack seemed to bristle with nervous energy and anger. "We have more evidence than we had this morning, and no one had to die to get it. I count that a good day." He caught Hannah's attention. "This means the patrolmen and detectives on the Stone crime scene definitely need to be interviewed again. Deming was right. Something was missed." He turned to Vivian. "Find out what vessels were searched the day of the Stone killing. We need to know if the *Teapot* was searched, and if not, why not." She nodded. "Today Hannah and I never had the chance to do more than interview the dockmaster. *Everyone* involved gets interviewed again. This is big, the biggest lead so far. But first," he held his arms wide, staring down at his dripping self. "I need a shower. Damn, I smell."

Hannah studied Jack with as much objectiveness as she could muster. She envied his anger. It was healthier than this emptiness she was feeling. The last year had taken its toll on her physically and emotionally, and though she admired Jack's strength, she resented it, too. He wasn't the one who'd mourned a lover while creating a life, and struggled to stay gainfully employed while she overcame those challenges.

Her life was out of control because of Jack's decisions. Why couldn't she hate him?

Vivian finished scrolling through a file on her computer. "Records show they didn't search the *Teapot*. It wasn't even on the list of vessels that were near the crime scene."

Jack swore. "It's a well-maintained marina with a rich clientele. They must have a sophisticated surveillance system. See if you can gain access to it, Vivian. We'll subpoena it if we have to. And find out where the *Teapot* was during the time frame of Stone's murder to when she was found. I want pictures, video, dock records, whatever we can get our hands on. See the lieutenant if you need warrants before I get back, but get them ASAP. If the perp's been active at the marina for months, there's a picture of him."

Hannah was dripping on the floor, too, feeling more and more miserable. Jack finally noticed. "You're dead on your feet, Hannah." He pressed his palm to her lower back and led her toward the door. It was meant to be comforting, but it forced her clammy shirt and suit jacket against her skin. She shivered. "Vivian," Jack said. "*Find Deming.* Tell her I want a report of her findings when we get back. Have her study these photos, and see if she can find something new. She thinks Stone's murder is an outlier, and now Hannah and I agree." When they reached the door, he stopped, and looked over his shoulder, sweeping the murder board with a last scan. "We'll get this bastard. We'll get him." Then he led Hannah into the hall toward the elevator.

"Hannah!" Mrs. Pepperidge hurried toward her. "What in the world happened to you?" Wearing a black pantsuit with a fuchsia blouse and gleaming white pearls, her hair and makeup impeccable, the lieutenant's wife contrasted sharply with Hannah's bedraggled, smelly state.

"The Boston Harbor happened," Hannah said.

Mrs. Pepperidge hugged Hannah to her chest with surprising strength. "Poor girl." Hannah tried to ignore the sympathy she heard in Mrs. Pepperidge's voice, because in her state, sympathy was sure to turn her into a weepy puddle. "You look like you've been put through the ringer."

"I'm okay." Hannah's voice cracked, contradicting her assertion.

"Don't kid a kidder." Mrs. Pepperidge studied her face, tilting her chin up with her fingers. "You should go home. Do you have someone to take care of you?"

Hannah's lower lip quivered, so she bit it, but the lieutenant's wife saw it. Mrs. Pepperidge's face fell and her eyes welled with tears. "Oh, Hannah. What can I do? You know I'll do anything." Hannah forced a smile. Just standing next to Mrs. Pepperidge was calming.

"I'm fine." Not now, maybe, but she would be. Hannah would function because she had to. She was a mother now and Ellen needed her to be strong.

"Hannah." Jack stood at the elevator, twitching with impatience. He'd never been good with the whole "feelings" thing.

Mrs. Pepperidge finally noticed they weren't alone. "Oh, I see. Good. As long as someone is here to take care of you." Her words immediately reminded Hannah why she liked the Pepperidges so much. When you don't have family, and life is a series of bureau posts across the country, it was nice to find people you could count on.

Mrs. Pepperidge waved to Jack, gave Hannah another hug and disappeared into the incident room to find her husband. The woman had style. Not once did she acknowledge that hugging Hannah had ruined her gorgeous suit and blouse.

When they were alone in the hall again, Hannah glanced at Jack's face. It wasn't hard to see that he wanted to bench her. She could see it in his eyes and didn't blame him, nor did she have the energy left to fight him.

Taking a deep, calming breath, Hannah straightened her back and walked toward Jack; her past, her present. She couldn't wait until Jack was in her past again, but she had other, more pressing issues now.

He was about to meet Ellen.

Chapter 8

"You can let us out at the corner, please." Hannah's voice sounded weak as she gave directions to the uniformed officer driving the patrol car. A quick glance told Jack that the explosion at the harbor had done Hannah in, and hoped to convince her to stay home and recover, at least for the rest of the day. The police presence guarding her apartment would keep her safe. "I don't want to be seen stepping out of the police cruiser," she said.

The officer drove past kids playing on the sidewalks, old people lingering on stoops, then pulled up to the curb, a few houses short of her brownstone address.

Jack thought to lighten the mood. "Afraid of what the neighbors will say?" Hannah's sidelong glance told Jack he'd inadvertently hit the nail on its head. She didn't want to be seen leaving this car *with him*. It hurt his feelings and confused him.

When they'd been in the water, struggling to survive, Jack had never seen her so afraid. Devastated, really. At the time, he'd felt like railing at her, because the debacle at the marina was her doing, and just her *latest* really bad idea. First, she'd left D.C., separating herself from people who knew her best, who had her back, and then after putting herself in the crosshairs of a killer, she'd refused protective custody. It was reckless, and so unlike her. The Hannah he'd known was a methodical thinker. She'd never take unnecessary risks. But this Hannah...

She'd said that she was broken.

Well, her behavior seemed cracked, that's for sure. And she blamed Jack. He shook his head as the patrol car stopped and he could finally escape the oppressive silence in the car. Had news of his "death" truly broke Hannah as she'd said? He couldn't believe it. Hannah just wasn't thinking straight.

It was the stress of being the target of a serial killer. Yeah, that was it, and she was projecting her angst on Jack.

He rushed around the car to open the door for Hannah. His onetime woman warrior was looking delicate again. Luckily, she didn't fight the curtesy. Old Hannah would have flipped him the bird.

He caught the officer's attention. "Be back in an hour. I need to pick my car up at the marina."

"Sir." He waited for Jack to close the door, and then merged the cruiser into traffic.

Hannah hadn't waited for him. With a few long strides, he caught up with her. "Since when did you care what the neighbors say?"

She grimaced, and then shook her head. "Don't poke me, Jack."

Fair enough. Hannah took the five stairs up to the brownstone door, pulled her keys from her jacket pocket and got them into the foyer. He closed the door behind them. "Do the neighbors know about me?"

"Why would they?" She glanced at him over her shoulder as she stepped into the hall. "As of this morning, I thought you were dead."

Once again…fair enough. A door down the hall opened and an older woman appeared. Her white hair was pulled back into a bun and she wore a housedress. One look at Jack and she scowled. The vehemence of her expression took Jack by surprise, because, mostly, women tended to like him. Especially older women. This one acted as if he'd just kicked her dog.

"Hannah," the woman said. "What a surprise. Back from work so soon?" A baby cooed from inside the apartment.

"Hello, Mrs. Branaghan." Hannah's smile was tired, but seemed genuine, as if she liked the woman. Hannah lifted her arms, and then looked down at herself. "Had an accident, but I'm fine. Just need to change into dry clothes."

A stylish woman stepped into the doorway next to the old woman. She held an adorable infant girl. Presumably, she was the infant's mother, yet she acted as if she didn't know the kid, and held it at arm's length. Jack supposed the kid must have a messy diaper or something.

"Here," the woman said, aiming the baby at Hannah, but Mrs. Branaghan tsked and took the cooing child.

"Hannah's filthy and wet." She tilted her head toward the woman, catching Hannah's eye. "Natalie arrived an hour ago." Mrs. Branaghan narrowed her eyes at Jack. "Who might this be?"

Jack waited for introductions, hoping this didn't take long. He wanted out of these wet clothes. But Hannah was too busy smiling at Natalie, and then the baby. He could tell she wanted to hold it, and didn't blame her.

She looked brand-new, and sported a tiny pink bow that was dangling off a wisp of hair. Without thinking, Jack fixed it.

All three women stared at him, as if he'd done something wrong.

"What?" When they did no more than blink, he became self-conscious and looked away.

"I need to change," Hannah said. She blew an air kiss to the baby and led Jack upstairs.

He was curious to see what her apartment looked like. When they'd been living together in D.C., she'd catered to his taste. Sleek, urban minimalism. Jack missed that apartment. He missed their life together. The stability, maybe? Now, watching her slip her key into the door's lock, he guessed her new place would more reflect Hannah's preference. Girly, he supposed. Maybe flowery upholstered couches and pillows everywhere... Pinks. He could see it all. Lace maybe. Lots of antiques.

He reminded himself to ask her about his stuff. There were a few things, like pictures of his mom, a few items of memorabilia he didn't want to lose, but had abandoned when he'd 'died.' Now, however, didn't seem the time to talk about stuff like that.

"I don't think that old lady liked me," he said.

She swung the door open and stepped through. "You're easier to like when you're dead."

Burn. She must be feeling better, he thought. As he closed the door behind him and Hannah stripped off her sodden jacket, he looked around the room. He'd been wrong. No antiques. No lace. It seemed less a home than a storage unit.

"I guess I deserved that," he said. "All I can do is continue to apologize."

Hannah's wet white shirt was see-through, and her bra was negligible, hiding nothing. She couldn't have known, otherwise she wouldn't be facing him like she was, hands on her hips, treasures on display. He averted his gaze with great difficulty as he focused on controlling his body's response.

"You *guess*?" She hurried around the dining room area, picking up a few items, hiding them under pillows. Then she closed a door to a room. "You *know* you should have told me you were leaving, and you shouldn't have left it up to Goodwin, so why didn't you tell me?" She folded her arms under her chest, glaring, all very impressive...if her shirt hadn't been nearly transparent, and her arms didn't push her breasts higher, making them look even more lush. He swallowed the lump in his throat and averted his gaze again.

"You're right," he said. "I'm an ass." To go into more detail would bare his soul and strip him of what little pride he had left. He hoped she'd drop the subject.

No such luck. "What would you have done if your father had still been alive?" she said. "Would you have asked Goodwin to tell him, too?" He suspected her question was rhetorical, but it was a question he could answer truthfully, so he took the bait.

"Of course I wouldn't have asked Goodwin." When his father was alive, Jack could have cared less what he'd thought. In fact, if Jack had died first, he suspected his father wouldn't have noticed.

Hannah startled, taking a step back, prompting him to replay their conversation. His answer had him wincing. *Of course I wouldn't have asked Goodwin*, he'd said. He'd insinuated he'd tell his abusive father he was alive, yet had left without telling Hannah. Jack lowered his head, resting his hands on his hips.

"I didn't mean it the way it sounded." His ability to plumb the depths of asshood never failed to surprise him. Now, he was left to flounder, searching for words that would make her hurt go away. He settled for the truth. "Honestly, Hannah. We were fighting so much I didn't think you'd care." She swayed, reaching out to support herself against the wall. Jack panicked, rushing toward her.

She held up a hand. "Don't touch me." It stopped him cold, a few feet in front of her. She shook with...what was it? Anger? Hurt?

Her reaction forced him to admit he'd been *afraid* she wouldn't care. He'd bailed without a word, allowing Goodwin to do Jack's dirty work, so he wouldn't have to find out one way or the other if she cared that he was leaving. What did that say about him? Nothing good, and he already looked bad in her eyes, so he didn't want to share that humbling piece of honesty.

Hannah turned her back on him and disappeared into what he presumed was her bedroom. He followed, though he was positive his presence was not welcome. When he saw her rummaging through drawers, pulling out underwear, opening her closet and grabbing a replica of the suit and blouse she was wearing, he was reminded of a time when this had been a commonplace occurrence. Hannah, donning her "uniform." Did she wear the same clothes because it was easier, or because she knew she looked so damn hot in them?

"Your stuff is in boxes at the back of the closet. It's not much." She wouldn't look at him. Her eyes brimmed with tears, and her expression revealed he'd hurt her again. She stepped into the bathroom, closing the door in his face.

Jack stripped, grateful to peel the sodden, smelly clothes off until he was bare. His clothes were ruined, and would need to be tossed, so he kicked them into a pile on the hardwood. Opening the closet, he rummaged behind her hanging clothes for those promised boxes, and thought to notice there were no signs of another man's suit next to hers. His relief humbled him, because even he, dumb as a stump when it came to women, knew he had no right to have an opinion about her personal life. He'd forfeited that right when he'd left...when he hurt her.

Two boxes, side by side, were pressed against the closet's back wall. As he grabbed for them, her silk blouses caressed his face and arms. He found himself inhaling, eyes closed, reacquainting himself with her delicate scent. Memories surfaced of the first time he'd met her.

It was in the D.C. office. He'd just completed a long embed with a motorcycle gang suspected of gunrunning. Six months later, he was closing the case, having gathered enough evidence to jail the lot of them. He remembered smiling at her, checking her out, noticing how she liked it, and he smiled when he recalled how she'd responded by giving him the finger. Her. Little Hannah. So prim and proper, flipping a motorcycle gang member the finger. She hadn't known he was fresh off an undercover mission.

His hair had been long then, he hadn't shaved in weeks, and he'd been running on zero sleep for days. So, yeah, Jack had been disreputable looking and ripe. In fact, he remembered barely being able to stand his own smell that day. Combined with his motorcycle gear, gang signs, the leather, and shit-eating grin, it was no surprise Hannah had dismissed him out of hand. If he hadn't caught her checking out his ass, he might have chalked the experience up to lack of interest, but he did catch her, and later that week, after days of consistent sleep, thorough grooming and a debrief, he approached her again. By then his reputation had preceded him, and she'd said yes. On the QT, but they were exclusive for two years. It was the longest relationship he'd ever had, and every day of it, he'd wondered if that was going to be the day he screwed it up. Wanting her that much had scared the hell out of him, but fearing he'd lose her made him lose his mind. How else to explain his behavior?

Jack brought one of her blouse sleeves to his face and inhaled again. He missed her scent. Hell, he missed her. Regret clawed at his insides. Give him death-defying odds, danger around every corner, and Jack was in his element. Ask him to trust his heart to a woman and he ran like a dog whose tail was on fire.

He grabbed the boxes and pulled them out from behind her hanging clothes in the closet. They were taped shut, and weren't easy to open, so before he knew it, the cardboard was in shreds at his feet. Suits, shirts, ties, all his clothes were there, neatly folded with tissue paper to prevent creasing. It made him pause for a moment to wonder why she'd bothered to save his stuff, and to take such care of them.

"Damn, Jack."

He turned, and saw Hannah standing in the bathroom doorway. She was in a white terry cloth robe, a yellow towel wrapped around her hair, and was staring at him.

"What?" He knew *what*, of course, and it made him smile. He was naked as a jaybird.

Hannah scowled, took the towel off her hair and threw it at him with enough force to land at his feet. Not a small feat, considering he was at least ten feet away. He suspected her angst was more about being caught checking him out, than that he was naked.

"You never did have a modest bone in your body," she said, clearly struggling to keep her gaze above his waist.

Jack was growing hard. "You never complained before." He walked toward her, enjoying her blush as she stepped to the side, allowing him to pass. Their fingers brushed, surprising him enough to pause. Hannah kept her gaze averted, but didn't protest or move away when he took her hand.

Earlier, in the lieutenant's office, and then in the interrogation room, he'd touched her because he couldn't help himself. And he suspected neither could she. *He'd* been fantasizing about making love to Hannah since he'd left her, so it was a no brainer for him to long for her kisses, but until now, it didn't occur to him to wonder why Hannah had kissed him back. *She* was the one who'd instigated the sex in the lieutenant's office. Why? Hannah had never been casual about anything, least of all sex. He found it hard to believe she was now.

Her behavior confused him, especially since she was clearly pissed. Because he'd died on her, or because he'd lived?

Hannah was statue-still, breathing shallowly, as if she couldn't catch her breath, and he was fully aroused. She had to know that, and had to know that with one glance, one arch of her brow, he'd bury himself deep inside her and not come out until they were both blind with ecstasy.

She had to know that, yet...said nothing. No glance. No arch of her brow.

So why wasn't she walking away? Should he touch her, nudge her over the edge of reason and into his arms? Maybe if he loosened her robe's belt, she might allow him to touch her, make love to her. Would she kiss him back, or slap him down, scornfully dismissing his need for her? He wasn't sure. He never was with Hannah.

"Jack." She blinked a few times, and then met his gaze. He saw confusion there that matched his own. Then her hands went to the lapels of her robe, clutching it closed.

Her body language was at odds with what he saw in her eyes. She wanted him back, and his body was taut with need, demanding he grab her and convince her that she wanted him just as much. His lips parted as he thought of how she'd taste, how he'd feel when she touched him back. She licked her lips. He leaned toward her, intent on tasting them.

"You smell." She swallowed hard.

He blinked. "Yeah." She was right. He smelled of the harbor. Stepping into the bathroom, he shut the door, shutting her out. He told himself it was for the best, that he'd dodged this latest chance to screw things up with Hannah, but he knew he was lying. His body was aroused to a painful degree, and he was in hell. A Hannah-smelling hell.

It took a few moments for his vision to focus on his surroundings. The room was devoid of anything male. Flowery, feminine bath products were propped against the tile rimming the tub, supporting his hunch that Hannah hadn't devoted a drawer to another guy. Not yet, anyway. There was no Axe bodywash or second toothbrush in the holder, and that made him happy.

He stepped into the tub, tugged the floral shower curtain closed, and picked up the least girly shampoo, envisioning the fair amount of shit he'd shoulder when he arrived at the precinct smelling like Johnson's Baby shampoo. He lifted the bottle to his nose and inhaled, shrugging. It smelled good, so the hell with it. He turned the shower on and set the temperature to ice cold, needing to multitask. A hard-on with Hannah pissed was just looking for trouble.

It took him ten minutes to achieve that cold, calm state of mind necessary to defend himself from all that was Hannah. Waterlogged, he found her in the eat-in kitchen drinking coffee with a half-eaten ham and cheese in front of her. She'd put on a pot, so he poured himself a cup and sat. She pushed a plated tuna fish sandwich in front of him. His favorite.

"We need to talk." She popped a chip in her mouth.

Understatement of the year. He took a bite of sandwich. "I'm starving. Thanks."

"I was upset earlier, acted unprofessional."

"Which time?" He glanced at his watch. He'd resurfaced in her life only this morning, yet it felt like forever ago.

"I shouldn't have attempted to knee you in the groin," she said.

"Oh. That." She hadn't tried very hard.

"There are extenuating circumstances," she said, "but that's no excuse. My behavior was unprofessional and I appreciate you being a sport about it." She held up her hand to stop his attempt to interrupt. "I have a lot going on."

"I'd say that's an understatement." He could list on both hands the amount of shit she'd had to deal with just today alone. Add whatever had been going on this last year with her change of jobs, and the move, and he was positive it was a *gross* understatement. "Maybe you should take the rest of the day off. Hang around here for a while."

She studied him, not giving him a hint of her thoughts. "When you showed up, Jack, I was doing fine."

"No. You weren't. I'm here because you're being threatened. In no way does that mesh with fine."

"I've spent the last seven years proving myself within the bureau. I can handle this. I don't need you to save me. I never have. And no, I'm not taking the rest of the day off."

Hannah didn't want his advice, and she wanted him gone. Big surprise. Well, she broke their deal, so it was time to play hardball. "I gave you a choice. Protective custody or—"

"You gave me an ultimatum. A babysitter, or exile. Neither is necessary. You have to stop acting as if you're my hero. You're not. You're someone I used to know."

Bullshit, he thought. He'd caught her looking at his ass. They'd had sex. "It's like that, huh?"

"Yeah. It has to be. This is my career we're talking about."

He didn't know what was going on in her head right now, but he had a sneaky suspicion it wasn't what they were talking about. "We're talking about your life. A bit more important than a job."

"My career. I need to think beyond this case. When it's over, what will I be left with? The reputation of being a victim, of needing you to solve my problems? No, thanks. I'm a big girl. I'm an agent. I *need* to be integral in catching this killer. I can't be sidelined into protective custody."

"Like I sidelined you as you boarded the yacht *despite* my direct order?"

"You never should have given the order, Jack. This was my case—"

"If it wasn't me, it would have been someone else replacing you." She was reaching, and had to know that, so what the hell was this about? "I was right. You never should have boarded that yacht. Forensics should have gotten first crack at that room. They would have found the bomb, maybe even defused it. We almost died, and now countless man-hours will be spent gathering evidence out of the harbor."

She shrugged. "You didn't think my lead was legit at the time. Given your druthers, we never would have looked at the yacht." She leaned back in her chair, scowling. "And that's not what this is about, anyway. Last night's email is a lead. My lead. But you swoop in using the excuse that it was directed at me. Then you find a way to leak our past to my team. *Undermining my authority.* And on the yacht—"

"You're living in a fantasy world." He popped a chip in his mouth.

She threw her hands in the air. "You nearly drown, and I'm the one who's seen as the basket case?"

Jack shook his head, totally confused. "I didn't nearly drown. You just didn't see me and freaked out."

"Same thing." She was scowling so hard that her face was red with it.

"No. It isn't." He saw an opening, so he took it. "What was that about, anyway?" Did she still have feelings for him? His heart pounded and it was easier to inhale than exhale, and suddenly he didn't want to hear her answer.

Hannah dropped her gaze to the table as her expression shut down. "I thought you'd drowned, or was drowning. Was I not supposed to care? What would the team think of me if I allowed you to die on your first day?" She took a big bite of sandwich.

Jack smiled. She still had feelings for him. He could be dense, but not that dense. It made him want to put his cards on the table and ask her outright, but he wasn't the same man who'd left. Walking away had the unexpected result of humbling the hell out of him. He'd spent this last year pretending he hadn't just royally destroyed his life. Now, there was no denying it. He saw that his stubborn pride had cost him dearly, and that it was about fear, and his freaking childhood damage. How else could he explain leaving Hannah without even saying good-bye? All because of the *possibility* she was leaving him.

Hannah glared at her sandwich, not happy she still had feelings for him, he supposed, or maybe it was the grin he couldn't seem to wipe from his face. Well, join the club, he thought. They had something, and neither seemed happy about it, or capable of doing anything the easy way. They cared. Jack was now a guy who cared.

"I meant it," he said. "What I said earlier."

She sipped soda and ate her chips. "And that was?"

"I didn't think you'd care if I left." He saw her anger flare. "I know for you it was *died*, but for me it was *left*. I've enough sins to carry without putting Goodwin's on my shoulders. I was wrong to leave it to him to tell you. I'm sorry. Really, Hannah. It kills me to know what you were led to believe. It was…needlessly cruel."

She kept her eyes on her plate, being miserly about revealing her emotions. "Like I said earlier, apology accepted. Let's move on." She sipped her soda again. "I really want to move on."

"So why haven't you?" *Because she cared.* That had to be it. Right? He ate his sandwich, worrying if he was wrong, and impatient to hear if she would lie to him. It's what he'd do. He'd lie through his teeth to protect his heart. He'd done it in the past, and though it kept him from true happiness, it also kept him from having his heart ripped out.

Hannah leveled a stare at him that brought his wonderings up short. "I loved a man who died, and I'm not good with that. Not good at all." She finished eating and put the plate and her empty glass in the sink. "Do me a favor and don't treat me like a victim at work. It's my career, my livelihood, but mostly, because I'm *not* a victim. I'm a survivor." She picked up her keys, slipped her suit jacket on and headed out of the apartment. "Come on. We might as well get this over with."

Jack guzzled his soda and grabbed his sandwich, finishing it as he followed her out. "Get what over with?" She ignored him and hustled downstairs. She stopped at the old lady's door. Mrs. Branaghan?

"If you don't mind, I'll wait outside." Jack continued down the hall toward the front door.

"No. I need to properly introduce you. I should have done it before, but—" She shook her head, blushing. "When I had the chance, I buckled. That was wrong. And this is important."

The door opened and Mrs. Branaghan stood before them, seeming nervous. Jack wanted to leave, but Hannah grabbed his sleeve and tugged him into the living room. The baby was in a wicker carrier on the floor. That Natalie woman was nudging the drapes aside to peer outside. Her movements exposed her holstered Glock 22, standard bureau issue. An odd sort of stillness came over him.

"Hannah, who the hell is Natalie? Really." Natalie turned to him and arched a brow. *All attitude, this woman.*

Hannah picked up the baby and approached him. "Ellen is yours. And mine. I was three months pregnant when you...left."

Jack heard the words, but they didn't compute. Pregnant. He thought back to her mood swings, her tears. He'd thought she'd wanted out.

His eyes landed on the baby. *His baby.* She had his eyes.

Jack forgot to breathe, took a step back and sucked in as much air as his lungs could hold.

He couldn't be a father. He'd be a horrible father.

Chapter 9

Hannah watched as Jack went from scowling at Natalie to scowling at her. She reflexively pressed Ellen against her chest and kissed her soft hair. "Natalie is FBI. A friend. I asked her to watch Ellen while I worked this case. I mean, after I discovered I'd been targeted." Jack's scowl grew darker, and suddenly Hannah couldn't stop talking. "No one knows about Ellen. Between moving from D.C., working from home, and my extended hospital stay and then maternity leave, only a few people in HR and the Special Agent in Charge know about her. I thought our last case together got you killed. I was afraid for the baby. I've been trying to keep her safe, Jack. I was afraid Murtagh would come looking for us."

"Murtagh is dead," Jack said. For a long moment, his words made no sense, and then the truth sunk in.

"Well, *no one told me.* No one tells me anything, apparently."

"He didn't kill me." Jack seemed confused.

"Obviously." Natalie snickered from her position at the window.

Hannah didn't think Natalie was helping, and the tension in the room was beginning to upset the baby. "I have a serial killer on my tail, so Ellen still needs to remain a secret." She turned to Mrs. Branaghan, looking for moral support, but the woman was frozen, staring at Jack. "You have to keep her secret, otherwise I won't be able to continue working for the bureau. And I love my job. I'm good at it, dammit. Jack, for heaven's sake, say something!"

Natalie turned her back on them, surveilling the front yard. "I think he's incapable, Hannah. Maybe you should slap his face. Bring him to his senses."

"I'll do it." Mrs. Branaghan's three cats weaved their way around her calves.

"No one's slapping anyone." Jack cleared his throat, blinked a few times. "She's mine. My baby."

Hannah supposed she should be glad he wasn't arguing the point. "She's mine. You died."

"Ouch," Natalie said. The special agent had always been a phone call away from the beginning; when Hannah had discovered she was pregnant to Jack's death. Natalie had a right to her opinion, but she wasn't making this confrontation with Jack easier. Hannah was in the mood for easy.

Jack stared at Ellen. "Can I hold her? Ellen, right? Your grandmother's name."

His words triggered unwanted tears, but there was nothing she could do about it. Her arms were filled with Ellen, so they trailed down her cheeks. She held her daughter out to Jack. *Ellen's father.* Then she prayed she wouldn't collapse into a heap of ugly sobs.

This is what she'd always hoped for—Ellen knowing her father, him accepting her. Loving her. Hannah knew he was probably just curious, and that this fascination might ebb when Ellen became less cute, cried, or her diaper began to smell, so she cautioned herself not to expect much. That he knew she existed was a first step. It was important to remember that commitment wasn't Jack's forte. She'd known it going into their relationship, even before their first date, but she'd been helpless to resist him then, and feared she was still helpless.

Jack took Ellen, holding her in front of his face, staring into her eyes. The father meeting the child. They *both* seemed fascinated by the other. Hannah had to turn her back on the sight. It was just too much. Mrs. Branaghan sniffling told her she was in good company.

Wiping her cheeks, she sat on the couch and waited for the inevitable questions, but Jack said nothing. He just held Ellen, silently, exchanging curious looks. The tableau would forever be etched in her mind.

"He's smiling like an idiot," Natalie said.

"Natalie, *stop*," Hannah said. Jack looked…amazing.

"This is probably a bad time to bring this up," Mrs. Branaghan said.

"I'd say it was the perfect time," Natalie said. "Even I can't handle this awkwardness, and they need to know." She wrinkled her perfect nose in distaste. "Jack, your daughter is drooling on your suit."

Jack laughed, making no effort to rectify that problem. He dropped a gentle kiss on Ellen's forehead. *"My daughter."* He shook his head, amazement his most notable emotion. "Poor kid."

"Natalie, need to know what?" Hannah couldn't keep her eyes off Jack and Ellen. He looked like he was already in love with her, and though she fully understood Ellen's allure, she couldn't suppress a twinge of jealousy. Jack wouldn't have left her if he'd known about the pregnancy. That much had become abundantly clear. She told herself it didn't matter, that she wanted a man who wanted her for herself, rather than the child she was pregnant with, but it still hurt. She hadn't been enough to keep him.

Mrs. Branaghan answered for Natalie. "Do you remember when I told you a week ago someone was trampling the vegetable garden out back?"

Hannah vaguely did. "Did they do it again?" Ellen was cooing at her father, barely blinking as she stared at him.

"Yes, they did." Mrs. Branaghan adopted a sly expression. "And I have proof this time."

Hannah forced herself to look away from father and daughter. "No one doubted you. It's just there's not much to be done. We could ask the landlord to put up fencing, but I've had trouble getting ahold of him when the heat goes wonky. The guy's not reliable."

"I have a phone." Mrs. Branaghan held up an iPhone. "And I know how to use it."

Hannah stepped to her side. "Why, you crafty old lady. Let me see." The three cats wove their way around Hannah's legs as Mrs. Branaghan handed over the device.

At first, Hannah only saw pictures of Mrs. Branaghan's thumb, and cats, but then she saw a photo that showed a figure in the back gardens holding a camera. With a long lens. It was at night, so the only lighting was from the streetlights and whatever moonlight there had been that night, but it clearly showed a figure of medium height and build dressed in black pants, black hoodie, and gloves.

Hannah exchanged weighted glances with Natalie. Her friend knew what these pictures meant. "When did you take these? Would you allow me to email these to myself? I want to look at them closer. Have the team look." If Pepperidge hadn't already put her on administrative leave, she thought.

Mrs. Branaghan's face brightened. "I was hoping you'd say that. I want to give this guy a piece of my mind."

"Hmm." Hannah knew if this was a picture of who she thought it was, there was a killer trolling the building. "Natalie, I need you to make sure the tenants in this building understand the danger here. They need to keep their windows locked, and their doors locked, too. Best case scenario, it's a burglar casing the building. Worse case, it's the man trying to kill me."

"And I'll tell the building crime watch." The old woman clapped her hands, smiling. "This is so exciting!"

Hannah was dumbstruck. "You're not afraid?"

Mrs. Branaghan scoffed. "Natalie is armed to the teeth and is staying with me, so what's to worry? I've never felt so safe in my life."

"Staying with you?" Hannah had thought Natalie would be staying upstairs, with her and the baby. In fact, she'd kind of relied on that, hoping a third person in the apartment would serve as a buffer between her and Jack.

Natalie gave Hannah a wry look. "I said I'd bodyguard the baby. Don't try to get me involved in," she indicated Jack with a flick of her wrist, "your mess. You know I'm not good with stuff like that."

Hannah glared at her. "Stuff? Like empathy? Pity?"

Natalie smiled. "Yeah. Like that."

Hannah emailed herself the photos and then handed the phone back to Mrs. Branaghan. "Jack and I have to go." He and Ellen were in their own little world. Ellen was gumming Jack's tie, soaking a good portion of it with drool.

Hannah approached them and pulled the tie from the baby's grip, and then took her from Jack's arms. Ellen kept reaching for her father, kicking up a fuss, until Jack pressed his index finger to Ellen's tiny hand. When her daughter gripped it, Jack's smile made Hannah wonder if he noticed the moment's symbolism; Ellen forming a physical connection between the three of them. It was startling, and scared Hannah, because Jack hurt her when he left without a word. Maybe beyond repair. She wouldn't allow him to do that to Ellen.

"I think she doesn't want us to leave," Jack said. Keeping his voice low, he put his hand on Hannah's back. Without warning, she found herself blinking back tears. How many times had she dreamt of a moment like this? Them, together. *Countless.* But Jack came back from the dead with baggage. He'd betrayed her trust, *damn him.* She didn't know what to think.

Hannah lowered her face until it pressed against Ellen's cheek, allowing her to hide her emotions behind a brief kiss. She had to walk away, even though separation anxiety told her to stay. "You be good for Natalie and Mrs. Branaghan, okay?" She kissed Ellen's tiny nose and then lifted her high enough to smell her diaper. "Stinky girl."

"Is that what I was smelling?" Jack's complexion reddened and his smile took on a strained quality. "She was making a lot of noise in her diaper, but I wasn't sure." Ellen still gripped Jack's finger as Hannah handed the baby over to Mrs. Branaghan. Only when the transfer was complete did Ellen release him.

"Don't let Natalie make you change all the diapers," Hannah said. "I know, deep down, she's longing to learn."

Natalie snorted, but otherwise allowed the comment to stand as she took her place back at the window, nudging the drape aside to peer outside. "There's been no activity since I arrived. I'm bored already and rooting for a carjacking, or a pickpocket, something, anything to make it interesting."

Jack was wiggling his fingers at Ellen, looking silly and adorable. He was in love with their daughter, and all it took was an introduction. Relief flooded her. "Natalie, I wish you many more boring days as you guard my child. I'll be back tonight, and if you change your mind about staying with Mrs. Branaghan, there's plenty of room upstairs." Hannah lingered, hoping Natalie would take her up on her offer, but her friend made a big show of shuddering, dashing Hannah's last hope. "*Fine.*" She left with a parting glare.

She'd be alone. With Jack. All night.

The possibilities were endless and more dangerous to her heart than the killer was to her body, because… Hannah had no defenses against Jack.

Chapter 10

Jack didn't want to leave the apartment, or his daughter. He had a daughter! Ellen. Hannah walked past him and out into the hall, so he had no choice but to follow, leaving his *daughter* behind. It was hard to leave her. Painfully hard.

"No wonder you hate me," he said.

"Pay attention. Mrs. Branaghan found us a lead."

His first thought was, *really*? She wanted to pretend that—back in the apartment—didn't happen? He wanted to confront her, to have it out on the sidewalk, but Hannah was already flagging down the cruiser idling on the street. As they waited for it to drive to the curb, Jack forced himself not to blow up. Had she planned it this way? To drop a bomb—an amazing bomb, but a bomb nonetheless—then make it impossible for him to talk about it? It was cruel. Yet, he had to admit, he did have it coming. Knowing that didn't make it easier to take, though.

She slipped into the cruiser's passenger seat and waited until Jack got in the back. "Thanks for picking us up again."

The patrolman smiled and gave her a flirty look. "I'll pick you up anytime, anywhere, Special Agent Cambridge."

Hannah glanced at his nametag. "McCarthy? We have an O'Grady back at the office. And then, of course, there's Sergeant O'Neil."

"You like the Irish? I'm second generation. Second generation cop, too." The officer gave her a blinding smile, so blinding, Jack wanted to dim it with his fist.

"Rein it in, lover boy," he said.

Hannah said the baby was a secret and for Ellen's protection had to remain a secret, but then she flirts in front of him. *Not cool, Hannah.* Not cool. What exactly would lover boy think if he discovered they just left their baby girl at the house? His and Hannah's baby girl. Just thinking about it made Jack's heart warm. He was a father. It was amazing and terrifying. It wasn't something Hannah would ever forgive him for. His heart sank. He figured he should be satisfied she was willing to let him in on the secret.

Staring out the patrol car's window, he saw none of the Back Bay's scenery. Released from the thrall of Ellen's sweet smile, all he saw were memories of fear. His father's legacy. Damn, Jack didn't know a thing about being a good father, and knew less of little girls. Ellen would eventually want him to braid her hair. He'd fail. Sooner or later there'd be some parenting problem he couldn't Google himself out of.

Hannah was having a party up front, laughing, and winking at McCarthy. It was annoying to witness. He caught her sneaking a peek at him, and realized Hannah was as unsettled as he was, and putting on a show. For whose benefit? His or the wet-behind-the-ears officer driving this patrol car? Hannah held Jack's gaze as the officer continued to chatter away.

"Jack, Mrs. Branaghan's lurker was carrying a professional grade camera with a long-range lens. Some of those pictures on the boat were of me in my apartment, and this was not the first time she saw this guy in the backyard. I believe we now have a picture of our perp."

Which raised the concern that Ellen might not be as secret as Hannah believed. She had to understand the necessity of moving to the safe house now. Hannah scowled at him, as if reading his mind. He saw her waiting for that argument, her retorts locked and loaded. Hannah was a fighter, and this would be a knock-down, drag-out fight for the books, but not right now. No way he could argue effectively with McCarthy in the car. Not and keep their secret.

Ellen. Hannah had effectively boxed him in. Smart girl.

Other than the officer's awkward flirting and subsequent dinner invitation, and Hannah's gentle refusal, the drive to New Sudbury precinct was silent. Once they arrived, Jack took her place in shotgun, and waved her inside the building. "I'm going to get my car. I'll see you inside in twenty minutes."

He didn't allow McCarthy to drive off until she was within the safety of the precinct walls. It took him half an hour to return, but it was time away he'd needed to gather his thoughts. He parked the Coupe at the curb, his assigned space, and patted the hood as he walked past. Minutes later, he was barreling into the incident room, intent on pulling Hannah aside to ask questions about Ellen, her future, and where Jack could be involved.

The team had ordered pizza. Pepperidge called out a greeting. Ferguson nodded in his direction, and then turned back to the group hovering around Vivian's monitors. Jack met Pepperidge halfway between him and his office. Gilroy approached, too.

"I told you to keep her out of trouble," Pepperidge said. "She almost died on that boat."

"Won't happen again." Jack glanced at Gilroy, who returned his gaze with a noncommittal grimace.

Pepperidge wasn't placated. "Ferguson! Tell them about the interview with the marina guy."

"Bolger?" Jack said.

"Yeah," Gilroy said. "They came up with squat."

"We've released him," Ferguson said, walking up to the group. "His alibis hold up and he's threatening to sue."

Hannah was sitting at her desk, looking fatigued. She pushed her bangs off her forehead, and clipped the rest at the nape of her neck. "He didn't fit the build of the person in Mrs. Branaghan's photos anyway. At least we won't waste any more time on him."

"We've looked at the photos Hannah took on the yacht," Gilroy said.

Pepperidge scowled at Jack. "When you were gone, I yelled at her about that stunt, boarding the boat without a warrant. I'm sure you had a few choice words, too, but—"

"Yes, sir." Jack narrowed his eyes at Hannah, who was ignoring him.

"Good. But we can't count on her to keep herself alive anymore. It will take all of us to do it," the lieutenant said.

"I'm sitting right here." Hannah opened a file that rested on her desk, focusing on the pages inside. "Listening."

"Reining Hannah in is a full-time job, Lieutenant." Jack was beginning to think it was an impossible task.

"Screw you," Hannah mumbled, eyes still on the file.

"I'd bench her if I could," Jack said. It would keep her and Ellen safer, but he knew Hannah would find a way to be involved in the case no matter what restrictions he placed on her, and then he'd lose control of her. His briefing by Charlie Foulkes, who was still at the marina, forced him to acknowledge she'd be safer with him anyway.

Hannah slapped the file closed, and stood so abruptly, her chair skidded on the polished tile. She stepped to Vivian's desk and peered over her shoulder, noticeably annoyed. After a moment, she frowned, pointing at the tech's monitor. "Zoom in on that and print it, please."

"Of you leaving your apartment?" Vivian peered at the monitor, working her mouse.

Pepperidge was scowling, his arms folded as he watched Hannah. "Our guy is going to be pissed he didn't kill our girl."

Hannah snorted, though kept her eyes on Vivian's monitor. "Not as pissed as I am he tried. But we got him to break his pattern."

That got Ferguson's attention. "How so?"

"He didn't kill me." She smiled ear to ear.

Gilroy rolled his eyes, not amused. "She should be in protective custody. You know that, Benton, and so does everyone else in this room. You're taking a huge risk."

And didn't he know it. "From where I stand," Jack said, "he's leading us around by our noses. He somehow predicted you'd find the *Teapot*, Hannah, or he followed you to the yacht."

"We need to be smarter than him," Gilroy said, eyes on Jack. "We need to start predicting *his* behavior."

"It's puzzling, though," Hannah said.

Ferguson sat behind his desk and leaned back in his chair. "Okay, I'll bite. What's got you puzzled?"

"She's wondering why the perp didn't kill us," Jack said. "The pictures on the wall in the yacht, the posting of the fourth stanza of 'Broken Love' next to them…it was the perp's handiwork."

Gilroy nodded. "He'd staged the crime scene, just like all the other crime scenes."

"So why aren't we dead?" Hannah said.

Vivian smiled at Jack. "I heard you threw her over your shoulder like a caveman."

"Not quite, but would you be surprised?" Hannah said, her cheek kicking up. "Where is Deming? I want her thoughts on why I'm still breathing."

Pepperidge's gaze settled on Deming's desk. "I've been leaving messages for hours now. Vivian, give Deming another call. The rest of you, figure this out. I want a report on my desk by end of day detailing our next move." The lieutenant left, unhappy.

Well, Jack wasn't happy either. Five hours later, he still wasn't happy. The team had pored over transcripts of interviews, the critical analysis of the poem, photos from the yacht and Hannah's backyard, and still were no closer to any answers. It didn't help that all he could do was think about Ellen and when he would see her again.

He glanced at his watch and found it impossible to dismiss his unease any longer. It was 6:00 p.m. and Deming was still AWOL. "Vivian? She answering her phone yet?"

"No," Vivian said, clearly worried.

"I've been calling, too. Nothing." Gilroy disconnected the line. "I've pinged her, but got no signal. Her phone is probably dead; tech hates her."

"Still…" Vivian said, her brows furrowed with worry.

Gilroy smiled. "Don't worry about Deming, Vivian. She's the scariest thing out there."

Hannah leaned a hip against Ferguson's desk. Jack joined them, and when his gaze met hers, for once there was no hurt or accusation marring her expression. She was too frustrated, apparently, to allow their personal life to distract her. "We're missing something. What's different about me?" she said.

Let me count the ways. "You knew you were a target. The others didn't." Jack thought that was obvious enough. "You're a trained investigator. That matters."

Gilroy shook his head. "The perp made a mistake." He was sitting at his borrowed desk, leaning on his elbows, glaring off into the distance.

"What mistake?" Hannah said.

Gilroy shrugged. "When we find that out, we'll be close to finding this bastard."

Jack caught Ferguson sizing him up, and from the look in his eye, he instantly knew it had nothing to do with the case. Ferguson wanted to know what kind of competition Jack was for Hannah's affection. Jack wanted to tell him. To come right out, get in his face, tell the huge guy to back the fuck off, because Ferguson was officially the proverbial wall to Gabriel's celestial horn. Or rather Jack's horn. *Ferguson couldn't have her.* Hannah was his. Breaking his silence about Ellen was the fastest route, of course. Ferguson would understand that kind of claim. It would be so simple to allow Ellen's existence to slip, to bring everything out into the open, but Hannah would never forgive him and he was still on the shit list for dying last year. He'd have to be patient with the detective, and hope he didn't escalate the battle for Hannah's affections.

"It's the killer's first mistake," Hannah said. "That has to mean something." She walked to the murder board and taped up a photo of the shadowy figure Mrs. Branaghan's camera caught trolling her garden behind the brownstone. "I wish we could tell if this is a man or a woman."

"I sent Charlie and his forensics team to the brownstone," Jack said. "Maybe they'll get a footprint. Maybe the guy smokes." Jack flipped through the list of victims' characteristics. "First victim, James Twoomey," he said under his breath, as if for his own benefit. "Male, middle-aged, salesman. Died by mauling."

Hannah nodded. "Second, Carey Stone, young woman working as an administrative assistant for a staffing agency. Drowning. Third, Harold Zelezny, a retired plumber. Death by freezing. And then there's me. I was supposed to blow up on a yacht named *Teacup*. We all have something in common that is not in our files, and it can't just be our lack of social lives." Hannah seemed nonplussed. "We need to interview the victims' families again. Interview the witnesses at the marina again." Ferguson ran his fingers though his hair and sighed loudly, his frustration equal to everyone else's. "I know, I know," Hannah stared him down, "but we're missing something. The interviews must be a priority. They're our best bet to find a new lead."

"I agree," Gilroy said. "This guy is practically throwing clues at us, so why can't we identify him?"

Deming burst through the incident room's door, walking inside with hands lifted as if to stave off any complaints. "I'm sure you all left a million messages, but I got locked out of my phone—the damn thing. I keep replacing it, but it keeps— Oh, forget it. Long story *longer*, it died just as I suffered a flat tire that *I had to change myself*, so please don't give me a hard time. I'm hot, cranky, and hungry. Is that pizza? I haven't eaten since breakfast. I'm *starved*."

Ferguson smirked, turning his swivel chair toward the room's entrance, eyeballing Deming as she walked toward him and the pizza box on his desk. "Hannah and Benton were blown off a yacht by a bomb, then half-drowned in the Boston Harbor. The bar is set too high for you to play the sympathy card."

Deming's hastily grabbed pizza slice hung inches from her mouth as she processed the news. When she finally took a bite, Vivian cringed.

"That pizza's been sitting there since lunch," Vivian said.

"I don't care. I'm starving." Deming took another bite, talking around the food. "The harbor, huh? Nice day for a swim." She glanced at the bandage on Jack's forehead, lifting her brows.

He touched it, having forgotten it was there. "I'm fine."

"Hmm." Deming swallowed, licking her lips. "How big was this explosion?" She took another bite of cold pizza.

"Big enough," Hannah said. "When Charlie hands in his report, you'll be one of the first to see it. Right now, we're looking for connections between the victims."

"Charlie again, huh?" Deming grumbled. "He's the only forensic guy this department has?"

"You got something against Charlie?" Ferguson asked.

Deming shook her head. "Never mind." She waved her hand, dismissing the topic. "After this morning's revelation, we have more important things to talk about."

"What revelation?" Hannah said.

"You thought Special Agent Benton was dead," Deming said, scanning the faces of everyone in the room. "That's big." She frowned at Jack. "And I shouldn't have to tell you that, Benton. You should have said something immediately. At least, given us a heads-up."

"I only discovered it this morning." Jack fought the urge to squirm under everyone's censure. "Why do you care?" It was none of anyone's business as far as he could tell.

"*Because*," Deming said. "She *loved* you and thought you'd *died*. She was in mourning. *Deep* mourning from all appearances." There was an implied *you louse*, but Jack ignored it as Deming took another bite of cold pizza. Jack tried to catch Hannah's gaze, but she was looking everywhere but at him. *Love*, Deming said. Neither he nor Hannah had ever exchanged words of love.

Jack shook his head, feeling persecuted. "What the hell are you trying to say, Deming?"

"Yeah." Gilroy frowned at Deming. "What the hell are you talking about?"

Hannah's face had lost its color. "She's saying Twoomey lost his wife a year ago."

"And that Stone's fiancée died in Afghanistan," Vivian said.

Jack studied the murder board. "And Zelezny lost his wife four months ago."

Deming nodded. "Broken love. The perp thinks he's putting his victims out of their misery."

"Bingo." Gilroy smiled, wiggling his brows at Deming. "I knew you weren't just a pretty face." Deming batted her eyelashes at Gilroy and playfully preened.

Ferguson stood, as if his frustration could no longer allow him to sit still. "By having them mauled by dogs, drowned, or frozen to death?"

"Or blown up," Hannah said. "We have a connection that makes sense. Good work, Deming."

Deming lifted her pizza slice in salute. "You're welcome."

"But he made a mistake," Hannah said.

"You can thank me later," Jack said. She was alive because he was there to hustle her off the yacht before it blew up. Gilroy nodded, and sent Hannah some disgruntled side-eye.

"This guy doesn't make mistakes." Hannah looked right at him.

Gilroy frowned at her. "What are you saying? That the perp wasn't targeting you?"

Hannah shook her head. "Jack's not dead," she said. "Maybe the perp figured that out and changed his mind about me."

"I'd say you were giving the perp more credit than he deserves, but it fits with the theory he's being tipped off by someone from inside the department." Gilroy exchanged weighted glances with Jack.

"I no longer fit his ritual," she said. "So maybe I'm safe?"

Hannah looked hopeful, and Jack wasn't sure if that was a good thing or bad. He preferred her scared. A scared Hannah meant she wouldn't take so many chances. Especially since Jack's conclusion was exactly the opposite of Hannah's. This information meant the perp knew Hannah had loved and lost, which meant the perp *knew Hannah*. Intimate details of her life. Her hope that this meant she was safe could only get her killed.

Chapter 11

Her case was breaking wide open. No, *Jack's* case was breaking wide open. She'd lost control of this case because she'd become a target. Apparently, because Jack pretended to die. The repercussions of his mistake kept hitting *her*. It wasn't fair.

Hannah consoled herself that she was still on the case, not sidelined because of her impatience at the yacht, so that was good. Still… Life had become a game of give and take. Jack was alive. Yay! Hannah wanted to kill him. Boo. New leads coming in fast and furious. Yay! But she wasn't leading the case. Boo. Jack was alive and seemed happy to be an instant dad. Yay! Try as she might, she couldn't find a boo to counterbalance that yay.

"So, Deming." Hannah rubbed her face, trying to wipe stress from her expression. "What now? The killer failed. Will he escalate or back off and regroup? Or am I right? Jack's alive. I'm safe."

Ferguson bristled with impatience, pacing behind his desk. "She doesn't have a crystal ball, Hannah. Charlie's report on the bomb should tell us about this guy's intent. Maybe we're looking at a prepper, a vet, maybe a disgruntled ex-cop."

"Who likes poetry?" Vivian said.

"Charlie's report"—Ferguson stopped pacing to scowl at Vivian—"will be based on measurable intel, will lead us in the right direction with facts, not voodoo psychology. Sorry, I hate to be the bearer of bad news, but the last thing Hannah should do is assume she's safe."

"Hear, hear," Gilroy said. Hannah scowled at the bald man. She didn't know much about him, but from what she'd gleaned from the short time she'd been around him, he was a stick-in-the-mud. Gloom and doom.

Hannah caught the profiler's attention. "Deming?"

"Vivian," Deming said, "the perp is using poetry. Doesn't mean he likes it." Then she shrugged. "I agree with Gilroy."

"You mean me." Ferguson narrowed his eyes at her. The profiler ignored him.

"Our guy lacks a signature," Deming said. "To conclude that you're safe, Hannah, would be insane. The way he kills is different every time. Odds are we're looking at two possibilities. He freaks and comes at you with everything he's got—"

"Not what a planner would do," Jack said.

"No, but he's never failed to kill his intended target," Deming said. "Not that we know of, anyway. It might push him into doing something rash. That's my point. We don't have enough information to predict his behavior." Deming wrapped her hair into a scrunchie. "I'm beat and my brain isn't working anymore, but having said that, yeah, you're right. If you don't fit his guidelines for a kill, you're safe."

"If," Gilroy said, "she's right. We can't know for sure what motivates this guy until we catch him."

"Poetry." Ferguson sneered, kicking his desk before sitting down again. "Why couldn't it have been a good Grisham book? Are you sure the perp isn't a chick?"

"The poem was written by William Blake," Hannah said. "A man. Men have written most poems in existence."

"If we don't include Anonymous." Deming winked at Ferguson. "And female serial killers are rare. That means it doesn't happen often."

"I know what the word rare means. What is this?" Ferguson scowled. "Pick on Ferguson Day?"

"Do we need to choose just one day?" Gilroy smiled at the detective, leaning back in his chair.

"Enough," Jack said. "Deming, he's getting something out of killing these people. You said he's asexual. If not sexual gratification, what?"

Jack pulled at his collar, which brought Hannah's attention to his hair. It had grown longer than she was used to. Unruly. She wondered if he'd grown it for his last undercover posting. It brought back memories of when she'd first met him. He'd been unrecognizable from the man he was now. Hair down to his shoulders, unshaven, leather and jeans, he was sex on a stick. His tight, faded black T-shirt had been ripped across his chest and belly, showcasing a six-pack. The knife that caused that damage had also sliced his skin enough to make him bleed, but not enough to cause more than discomfort. He'd been bloody, though seemingly unaffected. And *damn*, he'd rocked her world. She hadn't known he was undercover at the time, so she'd only allowed herself to fantasize about him. When he caught her looking, she'd nearly died from embarrassment, but consoled herself that she'd never see him again. It was only the first of many wrong assumptions she'd made about the man since that day.

"There has to be video of the perp near or around the crime scenes." Ferguson caught the IT tech's attention. "Vivian, any news?"

"We have a uniformed officer watching surveillance videos, looking for leads," she said. "It's been underway for weeks now. Gilroy was with them for most of the day."

Gilroy nodded, absently drawing his hand over his shaved scalp. "I'm supervising the techs. It's a lot of feeds. Nothing so far."

"This guy is watching," Jack said. "Somehow. He can't be that different from every other serial killer."

"Agreed," Gilroy said. "The rush of the kill is why they do it."

"Jack, you bring up a good point," Deming said. "There is no real typology. The emails, the stanzas, sure, but the actual deaths are totally different. That could mean we're dealing with more than one killer. Many killers, in fact."

"How likely is that?" Jack said.

Hannah shook her head. "If more than one person knows a secret, it's no longer a secret."

"It's rare," Gilroy said.

Deming nodded. "My point is behavioral science is based on statistics, and if we have nothing to compare these crimes with—" She allowed her words to hang in the air.

Ferguson grimaced. "We're screwed."

"If we're dealing with a cabal of psychopaths," Hannah said. "So how would it go? They divvy up Blake's poem and become creative with their kills?"

Deming grimaced. "Statistically speaking, it's unlikely, but it would explain a lot."

"Yeah, well, so we do our jobs." Ferguson stood. "We interview the families of the victims again and see what we shake loose." He opened his desk drawer, took out his wallet, badge, and Glock. "Special Agent Cambridge, would you accompany me on the interviews?"

It sounded as if he were asking her on a date. The only things missing were flowers and too much cologne. Hannah's first inclination was to say, "I have to get home to Ellen" but she stopped herself in time. Then she caught sight of Jack's angry expression, and she wanted to say *hell yeah*. But Jack stared her down, silently willing her to abide by their agreement.

Attached to his hip. Also, this was a perfect opportunity to have Jack's back, and prove to him that she wasn't attempting to subvert his authority.

"That would be up to Special Agent Benton." She lowered her gaze to her desk, waiting, swallowing the bitter taste of being sidelined in her own case.

Jack didn't hesitate to take up the mantle of team leader. "Deming, go with Ferguson. I want Gilroy hounding the techs on the security feeds."

Gilroy stood, nodded, and was out the door by the time Deming also stood. She poured herself a coffee and headed out the door. "Ferguson, you're driving. My spare is barely inflated and I don't have the patience to break down again today."

Ferguson didn't look happy about the substitution, but Hannah refused to care. She wasn't a ball to be passed between these men. She was exhausted, and they still had to generate a report for Pepperidge.

Ferguson was out the door moments later, with Deming chasing after him. "And I want a meal! Do you hear me, Ferguson? I will be fed!"

* * * *

Two hours later, Ferguson and Deming still hadn't checked in, so she assumed they uncovered nothing new in their interviews, and Pepperidge, newly finished report in hand, ordered the team home. The lieutenant walked with them to the elevator, a bouquet of roses in hand.

"Nice," Hannah said. The elevator door opened and they stepped on.

"Romantic." Vivian smiled. Gilroy smiled, but it didn't reach his eyes. He looked uncomfortable.

"What did you do now?" Jack said. Hannah slapped his arm and turned to Pepperidge, about to apologize, but Pepperidge laughed.

"I have a date with Jolene at Jimmy's Restaurant, and Jolene likes roses," he said, "so I bring roses."

The elevator arrived on the ground floor, the doors opened, and with an unapologetic shrug, the lieutenant walked out of the elevator whistling, with a spring to his step. Eight o'clock at night, after the day they'd had, Hannah thought it a miracle anyone could have a spring to their step. She was impressed.

Vivian reapplied her lipstick using a compact mirror while they followed the lieutenant down the hall to the exit. With a snap, she shut it and hung her purse over her forearm. "I'm beat. A nice glass of wine and a Jane Austen movie, I think."

"Sounds good." And it did, but Hannah didn't see her night ending so sublimely. Not with Jack underfoot. Not with the coming interrogation about Ellen. He'd probably been honing it all afternoon. She gave him side-eye as they followed Vivian outside, thinking all she wanted to do was go home, hug Ellen, and lick her wounds. Odds of getting that without a bunch of drama was nil.

"Have a good night," Jack said. Pepperidge went one way and everyone else went the other.

"You, too." Vivian waved and walked toward the parking lot and her older model beige sedan.

"Wait up," Gilroy said. "I'll walk you to your car. My rental is there, too."

Vivian pressed her hand to her chest and blinked at Gilroy, as if surprised, but she nodded and waited until he stepped to her side before continuing to walk toward the parking lot.

Then Hannah was alone with Jack. Again. It made her heart race as she slid into the passenger seat of his Camaro. Thanks to ample security lighting, she could see the federal building's parking lot even at this time of night, and could see Gilroy stop with Vivian at her car, chat a bit, then wait until she got behind the wheel and drove off before he walked on, presumably toward his car.

Hannah thought about asking Jack to drive her to *her* car, maybe take two cars home. The Camry had Ellen's infant seat in the trunk. It would be a perfect excuse to delay the inevitable. But a niggling fear of the perp maybe tampering with it, despite security, stopped her request. She couldn't think of anything that would be more of a tempest than a car blowing up.

Like Jack's had last year.

Memories of the charred body that was supposed to be Jack's pressed against her consciousness. She hated the memory, especially since now she knew it was a stranger. The poor guy. Whoever he'd been, she knew there had to be someone out there, mourning him, even if they didn't know what had happened to him.

She settled deeper into the seat and rested her head back. The soft leather was cool to the touch and was so comfortable, she could have slept then and there, but for the worry of Jack's inevitable questions and how she'd answer them. Now that she knew he was alive, she wasn't sure what she wanted to do with him!

Hannah buckled in and waited for the onslaught of questions. They were coming. She was sure of it. Five minutes later, as he drove through the city streets, and he remained silent, she began to feel as if she'd dodged a bullet. She relaxed so much her eyelids grew heavy. Then she remembered something relevant to the case, and a jolt of adrenaline had her sitting up straight.

"Hey," she said. "Did forensics get us that report on the brownstone garden?"

"The pathologist called an hour ago with his report," Jack said. "His team found lots of footprints and BPD officers spent all afternoon canvasing the residents' footwear. No leads."

"Charlie Foulkes," she said.

Jack nodded. "Right."

"Deming knows him. Do you know how?"

"She never said. Deming keeps things close to the vest. Separates her work from her private life." He put the car's directional on and changed lanes, speeding ahead. "Not a bad thing in a coworker. Makes things easy."

"Unlike us?"

Jack frowned, but kept his eyes on the road. "Why do you care if Deming knows the guy?" He glanced at her. "Have you been seeing him romantically?"

The idea that she had time for romance was laughable, and none of his business, so she ignored his questions. "Every time his name is brought up, Deming practically flinches."

"Doesn't sound like her." Still frowning, he kept glancing at her as if waiting for an answer to his question about Charlie. Well, he could wait forever. Jack died on her. She owed him nothing.

"Forget it," she said. "Probably nothing." Turning her head, she stared out the window but barely noted the passing scenery. There was too much going on, and her thoughts were a jumble. "I wonder how the residents of the brownstone took all the commotion in their lives."

He merged the car into traffic, looking disgruntled. "I don't know. I didn't ask."

"Just curious." Hannah pictured Mrs. Branaghan and her cribbage club drinking tea, tittering over the day's activity, Ellen being passed between the women. "I'm sure they're eating it up with a spoon. Mrs. Branaghan is proud of their crime watch group. This must be the most excitement they've seen in forty years."

"Charlie delegated the brownstone shoe canvasing to uniformed police officers."

Hannah nodded. "I know he spent the day at the marina."

"His forensic team is working in shifts, round the clock, pulling personnel from other precincts to help out. When this case is over, we'll have to send them a case of Jack Daniels." She nodded, feeling her consciousness play with the idea of drifting off.

As the silence lengthened and her eyelids fluttered closed, she heard him say, "Can we stop talking about the case for a while? I've waited all afternoon, and now I can't wait any longer. I need to know. Tell me what happened when I left."

A jolt of panic forced her eyes open, and sleep became the last thing on her mind. She didn't want to talk about it, but she knew he deserved to hear the truth. Hell, she deserved him hearing it...to comprehend what he'd done to her. "My birth control failed. I got pregnant. As I was...trying to figure out how to tell you, we fought, and then you were...gone. I didn't know what to do."

He shifted in his seat, apparently composed, his gaze fixed on the street, but she could tell he was upset. Yeah, well, she was upset, too. She remembered finding out about his murder at work, receiving the news in a daze, then making it to her apartment before she came unglued. Being surrounded by his stuff, his scent, made everything worse, not better.

"It was hard," she said. "I was afraid Murtagh would come for me next. I kind of skated through the days, transferred to Boston. I had complications that sent me to Brigham and Women's Hospital on bed rest. Every time they thought I could go home, they'd take a test that would change their minds. I was there for a month, mid-March until she was born. I spent my days on my back, worrying I was losing our baby. It was horrible and—" She suffered from PTSD. The death, the traumatic pregnancy—she'd only recently been able to sleep through the night. She had nightmares and panic attacks, but telling him that might give him the excuse he needed to kick her off the team, so she kept it to herself. "I went into labor right on time, and she came out perfect. Ellen was perfect."

His grip on the steering wheel tightened as he took a turn onto Storrow Drive. "How did you keep it all a secret? Even now. No one knows."

More easily than she could have hoped. "I worked from home when I couldn't hide the pregnancy any longer." She shook her head. "And now, I have no life. Just work and Ellen. Separate. No one comes to the apartment. When I was in the hospital, people assumed I was on assignment. I allowed them to think that, and the Special Agent in Charge doesn't gossip. Remember, I'm new to Boston." She could see his confusion, and realized he still didn't understand what his death had done to her. "I was in mourning, Jack, with a new baby. It's a miracle I knew my own name."

He seemed baffled. "Who took care of you?"

"*I did.*" She wanted to slap him. Who the hell did he think would take care of her? He knew her parents were dead.

"Okay, okay. Don't yell." He took his eyes off the road for a moment, frowning at her. "This is a lot to take in. I'm trying to do and say the right things—"

"Good luck with that."

"—but it's not easy."

"You had easy. This is what happened." She folded her arms over her chest and glared unseeing out the side window. "I had the baby. Mrs. Branaghan babysits while I'm at work. That's it. The whole story."

"I have a daughter." His tone had her looking at him. He seemed worried. "I don't know her, but I want to. I want to do the right thing for my benefit, as well as hers and yours. I was an ass. I get that. I'll make it up to you if you'll let me, but I need to be in Ellen's life. You have to see that."

She did, and wanted that, too. It's just that Hannah hadn't planned that far in advance. "It's a lot to process."

He snorted. "Understatement of the year."

She studied him, and saw a lot to admire. He'd gotten more attractive since she'd seen him last. She wouldn't have thought it possible, but he seemed more confident, maybe a little more self-aware. That realization made her sigh, frustrated, because Hannah felt more vulnerable since last they'd been in each other's lives. Parenthood had humbled her. It ripped the scales of ignorance from her eyes and forced her to see how alone she was, how easy it was to be distracted by friends, work, college, whatever. Bring a baby into the world? Everything else takes a back seat, leaving a person *humbled*. And vulnerable.

Parenthood was exhausting. She couldn't remember the last time she wasn't worried, but even she had to admit, it was worth it. Ellen made everything worth it.

"I'm glad you want to be in her life," Hannah said, but couldn't help thinking, *let's see if he has the stomach for it.*

Chapter 12

When Jack pulled up to the curb outside of the brownstone, he felt a knot solidify in his gut. He was going to see Ellen again. It distracted him, so when Hannah spoke to him, he merely nodded, unable to have a conversation when he was feeling this level of anxiety. His heart was racing and his damn hands were sweaty.

"Jack." Her impatience cut through his distraction.

"Hmm?" He stopped at the front door, impatience to get inside clawing at him. "Yeah?"

"I asked if you would have stayed if you'd known about the baby." She jangled the keys in her hand, looking irritated.

"Yes." No hesitation. He knew himself. A child would love him no matter what. He'd never turn his back on that opportunity. He saw Hannah's face fall, and knew she was taking it the wrong way. She thought he was saying Ellen was more important than her. "You'd never have left me if you were carrying my child."

She gasped. "Left you? You left me!"

He shook his head. "You can't understand." And he refused to explain. He'd look like a fool, and sound like a coward. Hannah averted her eyes, hiding whatever thoughts her expression might have revealed.

Once inside, he beat her to Mrs. Branaghan's door, knocking harder than he'd intended. He stepped back, glancing at Hannah, who looked a bit shell-shocked. He sympathized. He was feeling a whole hell of a lot shell-shocked. Father. He was a father. Ellen was his daughter. Shell-shocked described him perfectly.

The door opened and there Mrs. Branaghan stood, holding a cooing Ellen. Jack took her from Mrs. Branaghan's arms and wandered down the hall, up the stairs to Hannah's apartment. He'd waited all day for this moment, and now that it was here, his breath came a little easier, his heart beat a little slower, and his mind was at rest. She was safe. He had her. Everything was going to be alright.

"You're mine," Jack whispered into her tiny ear. "And I'm going to make sure nothing bad ever happens to you."

"Then keep my secret." Hannah had followed at a slower pace, but caught up with him, and then opened the apartment door. "She'll never be safe otherwise."

"Secret for now," Jack said. "With a killer on your tail, it makes sense." She nodded, then stepped inside the apartment. Jack kissed Ellen on the forehead, and then followed Hannah, kicking the door closed behind them. "As much as I want to shout to the world I have a daughter, I'll wait." He saw her shoulders relax, presumably with relief. "For now, Hannah. For now."

"Thank you." She gave him a sad little smile.

"I'm starving. Do you know if Ellen ate?"

Hannah's eyes narrowed. "Of course she ate. She's a baby. She eats all day," she said. "Do you think I starve my child?" She took Ellen from his arms.

He followed her into the kitchen, disappointed that she'd taken the baby. "I'll make supper."

Hannah snorted, humor lightening her expression. "You only know how to make eggs."

"I'm *making* eggs." What had she expected?

Hannah laughed, surprising him. "Fine. I like eggs."

* * * *

An hour later, fed and sleepy, Hannah was trying to ignore Jack surveilling the neighborhood out the living room window. It was impossible. "Stop it, Jack." He was freaking her out, and she wanted to sleep, but she still hadn't prepared the couch for him. "There are two patrol cars out there, a camera mounted on the back porch, and Natalie is on the clock." She carried Ellen into her bedroom, every muscle in her body aching from her dip in the Boston Harbor. "The perp already has his photos of me. Why would he come back?"

"Because they do." He'd followed them into the bedroom. "What are you doing?"

"It's Ellen's bedtime."

"Are you sure?" He had way more energy than anyone had the right to this late at night.

"Yes, I'm sure." Three hours ago, she'd have taken offense at his questioning her parenting, but she'd figured out it was more a reflection of his lack of confidence than any lack of confidence in *her* skills. Been there, done that, she thought. Jack was discovering the learning curve of parenting was steep and unkind. "It was Ellen's bedtime at eleven o'clock yesterday, the day before, and now today. It will be her bedtime tomorrow, too." She changed the baby's diaper under his intense scrutiny. He was watching her like he was cramming for a test. It was adorable. "If you're looking for more time with Ellen, you can be the one to wake up and hold her if she cries tonight. There are prefilled bottles in the refrigerator, and the warmer is easy to use. You plug it in, slip the bottle in the device, and it turns off when the bottle is the correct temperature."

"Why don't you just use the microwave?"

"*Don't* use the microwave."

"Why?"

"Jack." Hannah was exhausted. "I don't have the energy to give you a crash course in keeping Ellen alive. Time for due diligence is over. You spent it on assignment doing whatever you were doing while I was poring over every baby book in existence. You're just going to have to take my word for things. For now, anyway. Okay?"

"Okay." He seemed eager enough. "What do we do if she cries?"

"Make her stop."

His face fell. Ellen yawned and smacked her lips. Though Jack looked properly chastised, she could see the light of challenge in his eyes. Hannah suspected she'd just triggered Jack's ambition to be the first man to get a graduate degree in parenthood. The thought had her smiling, which seemed to confuse the hell out of him.

"I'm glad you find this so amusing," he said, disgruntled.

"I'm punch-drunk, not amused. Don't mind me."

After snapping Ellen's onesie, then her terry cloth pajamas, Hannah leaned down and kissed her daughter. Ellen was nearly asleep, so she held her out for Jack to hold. He took Ellen in his arms as if she were glass filigree and he feared shattering her into a million pieces. It was a marvel to watch his gentleness. His *reverence*. Jack kissed Ellen, and that did it. It nearly brought Hannah to tears, because it reminded her that Jack lost something, too, when he'd died. Something precious. And nothing could bring Hannah's pregnancy and Ellen's first four months back.

Then Jack stepped closer to Hannah, offering her Ellen, bringing their faces close. She took her daughter from his arms, as his breath warmed her lips, and it made her wish things had been different between them. She'd loved Jack with all her heart and soul, but didn't trust he reciprocated her feelings, so kept them secret. Was that Jack's fault? No, she thought. It was hers. And the repercussion was Jack had thought she didn't love him.

Jack held her gaze, and whatever he saw there had him leaning toward her, slowly, giving her a chance to pull back and shut him down. Hannah didn't suffer so much as a hesitation, and met his lips halfway to their kiss. It was a gentle pressure, over too quickly to deepen. Then Jack left the baby's room in a rush, even before her eyes opened again.

Hannah put the sleepy baby in her crib, quietly closed the door behind her, and found Jack standing in her darkened bedroom, his back to her, staring out the window. She knew he was looking for signs of their perp.

"Tell me it's going to be okay, Jack." She lingered at the doorway, not wanting to turn the light on until Jack moved from his position at the window.

"It will. I won't allow anything to hurt you, Hannah. Or the baby." He kept his gaze directed out the window, and his tone was as close to emotionless as a person could manage and still say the word "baby."

"I'm afraid for Ellen."

He shook his head. "Worrying is wasted effort. Let's work the case. What's the next stanza?" He tugged the drapes closed. "You can turn the lights on now."

Hannah flipped them on, dispelling the intimacy of the darkened room, and then stepped inside. "I don't have it in me to think anymore. It's your turn to think."

"The next stanza, Hannah."

Her shoulder's sagged. "Don't pretend you think the perp will move on to the next victim. Gilroy's right. It's wishful thinking. We're stuck on 'tempest' like a skipping record until I'm dead or the perp is caught."

"You don't know that." He glanced at her, but when their gazes met, he looked away. "What's the next one?"

She sat on her bed's edge, trying to ignore that Jack was in her bedroom. She'd yet to call him on that kiss, and knew she wouldn't. He would see it as an invitation to do it again, and she didn't have the willpower to say no. And she *should* say no. There was no way she could just pretend the last year didn't happen.

"Do you want me to recite it?" She could. She had the damn thing running in a continuous loop in her head.

"No. Give me the highlights, or whatever could be construed as a weapon of choice."

"Torches, tombs, and talk of couches," she said. "I wouldn't mind that last one. I'm so tired. Death by couch might be a restful ending."

"Not funny." He paced the floor, brooding. "Recite the whole stanza."

Hannah flopped back and sank into the mattress. It felt heavenly. Eyes closed, she dredged up the poem from memory. "'Seven more loves weep night and day, Round the tombs where my loves lay, And seven more loves attend each night, Around my couch with torches bright.' Like I said," she yawned. "Death by couch." She heard him stop pacing but didn't have the energy to open her eyes to keep track of him.

"Still not funny. I'm beginning to agree with Ferguson."

Admitting that Ferguson said something right was a big leap, worthy of note. She opened one eye, because two eyes would have taken too much energy. She peered at him. "About what?" Hands on his hips, he seemed deep in thought, scowling at the floor.

"I wish this guy had obsessed on a John Grisham novel. Are you sure that's the next stanza? I don't think it is."

"Hmm." She closed her eye again and cautioned herself that if she fell asleep in this position, she'd wake in the middle of the night fully clothed with a mouth that tasted like sock. She needed to brush, at least. "I'm too tired to think. We have a scholar from UMass to do all the poem heavy lifting."

"Yeah. Vivian's working on bringing him into the precinct room, but the professor, apparently, is getting antsy now that he knows it's a serial killer case. Doesn't want his family targeted."

"Don't blame him. He doesn't know what we know." Her yawn was long and her mouth stretched so wide her jaw clicked.

"What little we know. Move your feet." Suddenly she felt his hands on her calves, and then he tossed her legs aside. Hannah curled into a ball on the mattress, her lower lip jutting out. He opened the hope chest at the foot of her bed, taking out a blanket and sheets. "I'll make up the couch. Do you mind sacrificing a pillow?" She told herself not to be surprised. He might not know her apartment, but he knew what she stored in her hope chest. They'd lived together for almost two years. She kept linens in there. Her mother had stored her wedding dress in hers. "Hannah. Wake up. A pillow?"

Hannah blinked past images of Jack sleeping on her couch, his head on her pillow, using bedding they'd bought together when things had been good. She just wanted to go to sleep and forget. *But*...she had things to do first.

"Sure. Fine. Go for it." Hannah dragged herself off the bed and peeled off her suit jacket, replacing it on its hanger in her closet. Intent on not thinking, and readying herself for bed, she'd stripped down to bra and panties before noticing the room had fallen silent. She turned around and saw Jack staring, one of her pillows hanging from his fist. Poised on the balls of his feet, the man looked like a predator about to pounce on his prey, and she was the prey.

She recognized that look, and it triggered a jolt of adrenaline, and a reciprocating need. Caution demanded she dispel the potency of the moment, but it felt too good. Jack was alive. Her emotions must have betrayed her, because he, as if about to speak, took a step toward her. Without thinking, Hannah quickly stepped back, tripping on her shoes and falling into the closet, dragging silk blouses off their hangers on her way down. She landed hard, and then all she saw were hanging suits obscuring her view. Exhausted, she sat there, feeling mortified. Her suits parted and then she saw his beautiful face. His smile was kind as he extended his hand, offering an olive branch she didn't hesitate to take.

He was alive. Her prayers were answered.

Jack tugged her into his arms, hugging her, blending their bodies' heat. Oh, how she'd missed this. *Missed him.*

He cradled her cheeks and kissed her with such tenderness she forgot everything but how he made her feel. Then he gathered her close, moving his hands down her back, pressing her close, cupping her ass, squeezing. The thrill of his touch had her knees buckling. His embrace tightened. Then his kiss deepened, and Jack moaned deep in his throat, like a growl, and she welcomed the surety of his tongue caressing hers. Light-headed, feeling a bit frantic, she suddenly couldn't touch him enough, kiss him enough. He cupped her breast, sliding his thumb over her nipple until she gasped with the pleasure of it. She wanted to be closer, so she dragged her foot down his calf, wrapping her leg around his. His arousal pressed against the apex of her thighs, sending a shiver through her. She reached for him, cupped the hard ridge straining against the fabric of his pants. He was ready for her and eager.

He sucked in a breath as she gently squeezed him, and then his hands were on her panties, pulling. The delicate lace ripped, and he laughed, sounding sexy and excited. He unsnapped her bra, and her breasts popped out. Jack was on them, bending so he could kiss their tips. Then he fell to his knees, his lips on her belly, kissing his way downward. When he reached the center of her, she lasted mere moments before her knees failed her again and she was kneeling before him, face-to-face, kissing him.

"Jack!" She wanted him more than she'd ever wanted any man before.

He lifted her into his arms, and suddenly she was on the bed, he was grabbing a condom from the side table and she was pinned beneath him, his heavy arousal pressed to her thigh. She wrapped her legs around his hips, arching toward him, needing him inside her, but he resisted, moving down her body, kissing, lingering, and when he reached her wet heat, he covered her with his mouth and supped until her hips moved upward, and waves of blinding arousal had Hannah melting under his touch.

Her patience broke. She needed him inside her. "Jack." He lifted his head.

Tearing open the condom, she was relieved when he moved closer, allowing her to gently roll it over his arousal. One swift thrust later, Jack had her body surrendering. Her eyes fluttered closed, her breath left her body as she climaxed almost instantly. Squeezing him with her thighs, arching up, clutching at his ass, she rode waves of pleasure as a long, drawn out moan escaped her lips.

Jack laughed low, and husky, showing no indication that he was done with her. The man teased her nipple with his tongue, watching her face, as if her reaction fed him in some way.

She broke into a sweat, forgot to breathe, and soon Jack had her cresting with her second climax. It slammed her, and wave after wave of delicious ecstasy had her lingering on a plateau of pleasure.

By then, only a sliver of her consciousness remained, tethering her to reality. She heard Jack gasp deep in his throat as his body grew taut. His arms flexed as he hovered above her, and then Jack's body tensed as he found his own release.

The world seemed good again, and everything seemed possible. Even happiness.

When their breathing slowed, and Jack's weight grew heavy, Hannah nipped at his shoulder, marveling at his strength. The absolute size of him was a turn-on. Jack took her nip as his cue to roll off her, only he took Hannah with him, keeping them connected, Hannah draped over his chest. She listened to the pounding of his heart beneath her ear, and relished the smell of sweat and pheromones.

Jack was alive.

Tonight, that was enough. Come tomorrow? She was a realist, and Ellen had to be her priority. She'd enjoy this time they had together, cherish it, and worry about the rest later, when things made sense again.

Jack either loved her or he didn't. She refused to ruin this moment with fear.

His hand caressed her back, once, twice, and then settled on her ass. "It's late," he said. "You're exhausted."

Hannah didn't understand what he was saying until he sat and grabbed a fresh T-shirt and briefs. "You're sleeping on the couch?"

He nodded, retrieving his holstered gun and cell phone from the floor. He put them on the side table. "I'm another line of defense, and if the baby wakes, I can get her without disturbing you. You've had a shitty day. You need your sleep."

She didn't know what to say. Was Jack making an excuse for a strategic retreat, or was he telling the truth? "Really?" Or was this a *wham, bam, thank you ma'am?*

Jack crawled back into bed and gathered her in his arms, then he pulled the covers over her. It did a lot toward calming her down, but she still felt disgruntled. "You need to sleep, Hannah. I'd like nothing more than to sleep by your side all night long. Hell, who am I kidding? If I stayed in this bed, we wouldn't be sleeping. It's just…you've been under a lot of stress, for an extended period of time, and today was hard. We both know odds are tomorrow will be harder. You need to sleep."

She nodded. "Haven't slept more than a few hours a night since you died. What makes you think tonight will be any different?"

He dropped kisses on her forehead. "I'll lay here until you fall asleep, then I have to radio the officers guarding the brownstone's perimeter, make sure they're doing their job. I don't want to wake you coming and going from bed."

"Don't be silly. I already I told you. I don't sleep. I'm a parent, remember?" She yawned and pressed her face to his neck, burrowing deeper into his embrace. Two minutes later, she was fast asleep.

Chapter 13

Jack woke the next morning with scratchy eyes and his head aching. Every muscle of his six-foot, hundred and eighty pound frame protested a night sleeping on a five-foot, four-inch couch. He'd tossed and turned, using the time to worry about how the killer intended to attack Hannah again, and when his mind wandered from envisioning one horrendous scenario after another, he'd strategized how to win Hannah back.

He still loved her. A year's separation didn't change that, though he'd be lying if he didn't acknowledge he'd hoped it would. What sane man would *want* his pride at the mercy of another person? But facts were facts. His pride was long gone and his heart needed her.

He had a family now, Hannah and Ellen, and he wanted in. Yeah, he was fully aware there were obstacles in his way, primarily him being an ass for leaving the way he did. Hannah had every right not to want him around. It was Jack's job to convince her otherwise, and no strategy or trick was off the table. This was war.

His cell phone rang, vibrating on the coffee table at eye level. Six a.m. and Ferguson was calling. "Benton here." He tossed the sheet off his body and swung his feet to the floor.

"We have another body."

Damn. "Text me the address. We'll meet you there." He hung up and walked into Hannah's bedroom. Still asleep, though sun streamed through the drapes, she was pale and had dark circles under her eyes even while sleeping. Hannah looked exhausted.

Loath to wake her, he contemplated leaving without her. She'd be safe here with Ellen, protected by the stationed police officers and her friend, Natalie. But Hannah would kill him if he did that.

"Honey." Not wanting to startle her, he kept his tone quiet, hoping to nudge her from sleep rather than startle her awake. Despite the prediction she wouldn't sleep, Hannah had barely moved all night. He knew, because he'd checked on her twice when Ellen woke for feedings. Hannah had slept through all of it. He, however, had barely slept.

"Jack?" she whispered. He used his palms to rub his eyes, yawning. "Jack?" He saw she wasn't yet awake, and seemed to still be dreaming. Cocooned in the sheet, naked as a jaybird, Hannah was all things sexy. He smiled until he saw the tears streaming down her temples. "Jack." Quietly sobbing, her head lolled to the side.

He scooped her into his arms, cradling her as he sat on the bed's edge. "Shh. Hannah, honey. I'm here."

Moments stretched on as Hannah lay draped on his lap, slowly waking. Then she wiped her eyes with the back of her hand, and pushed her bangs aside, blinking up at him. She forced a small smile. "Sorry. I should have warned you."

Holding her made him feel a little bit better. Not much, but a little. "Warn me about what?"

"The ten-second heartbreak." Her self-deprecating laugh held little humor, and was short-lived. Though still tearful, he could see she was struggling to move past it. "I'd hoped for a reprieve now that you're alive. No such luck."

"I don't understand." He wiped a tear she'd missed.

"Lucky you."

He gave her a little squeeze. "Hannah. Talk to me."

She sighed, pressing her palm to his naked chest. "I get ten seconds. That's it. Then I'm fully wake."

"I still don't understand."

"And then I remember you're dead, Jack. Ten seconds of blissful ignorance, and then I remember. It's like losing you all over again. Every morning."

His hands crumpled the crisp cotton sheets still tangled about her body. Focusing on the coolness of the material, on her firm body beneath it, he struggled to keep his clawing guilt hidden.

"I'm alive, Hannah. Very much alive, and I'm here with you. I'll always be here if you allow it." She grimaced.

"Did I hear your phone? Or was that a dream, too?" Hannah pushed off his lap, forcing him to release her as she grabbed her robe and shrugged it on. Her familiar shield was in place. Jack envied her that. *His* heart seemed always glaringly on his sleeve.

"Ferguson said they found another body," he said.

Hannah shook her head. "That's not right."

"They found a note. An email. He's sure."

She scrubbed her face with her hands. "But I'm not dead. It's my turn."

Her adamancy unnerved him. "Maybe you were right. You don't fit his fantasy anymore. Or the killer doesn't know you're alive, so he's moved on."

"The timeline, Jack. If what you say is true, we'd have a month before the next kill. But they found another body. Something is off. One call to the precinct would have told the perp I was alive. He's a planner." Jack wanted to argue, but Hannah flashed her palm. "The explosion made the news yesterday. He has to know he failed." She opened the closet door and grabbed clothes off their hangers.

Jack curled his toes into the plush carpeting of the area rug, thinking of coffee, of killers, of wanting this case closed. "Maybe Deming is right. Maybe it's multiple killers. Maybe the next guy on the list went after his assigned target because whoever was assigned your kill failed. Let's see what the evidence at the crime scene tells us. Ferguson texted me the location."

"Where did it happen?"

"Copp's Hill Burying Ground."

He could see her growing excitement. "Freedom Trail," she said.

"Yeah," he said. "The Freedom Trail. It's looking more and more likely that Deming is right. The marina is an outlier." He grabbed fresh clothes from the closet. "Do you want to shower first or eat first?"

"Eat. I'm starving."

Jack tossed his suit and shirt on the bed. "Let me wake the baby." He'd never woken a baby before.

"You don't wake babies, Jack, and if you're lucky, they return the favor and don't wake you." Hannah's smile softened her features as she stood in the center of the room, watching him. "Hurry up showering. She's due to wake any second." She rushed out of the bedroom, but not before checking out his ass. His body's response was instant, and had him contemplating chasing after her. Just like old times.

It was the quickest and arguably the *coldest* shower he'd ever endured. Ten minutes later, dressed and anxious, he walked into the nursery. Ellen was awake and cooing. When she saw him, she kicked her feet and stuck her hands in her mouth. If he had to guess, he'd say she was happy. Jack's heart melted. He was no expert, but indications were this baby liked her dad.

He could smell coffee brewing and heard the toaster popping as he lifted Ellen out of her crib. Then she instantly filled her diaper with an unmistakable smelly explosion. Holding her away from his clothes, Jack didn't know what to do.

"Hannah." He didn't want to yell, lest he startle Ellen, so he carried his daughter into the kitchen at arm's length. Somehow, he managed to maintain a calm expression, though panic had set in. Hannah sat at the kitchen table, her coffee before her, smearing strawberry jam on toast. "She filled her diaper," he said. Even to Jack's ears, his tone made the words sound like an accusation.

Hannah's smile was sublime. "Is that my girl? Yes, it is. Who is my girl? You are. Yes, you are. Did Daddy get you this morning?" Her attention was a hundred percent on his daughter, but Jack was a hundred percent reacting to her words. Daddy. Yeah, he was Ellen's daddy.

She took Ellen, enfolded her in an embrace and kissed her sweet head. Then they were gone and Jack was alone. He thought about following her, lending a hand, but the coffee's aroma called to him, and it smelled better than Ellen's diaper. He wandered to the counter, just in time for the toaster to pop.

She'd put in two pieces of wheat bread for him. Considerate. He saw butter, jam, and peanut butter on the table. She'd remembered his preferences. Jack liked this new reality, much better than the undercover life he'd been living in New Jersey. Yeah, the Coppola syndicate knew how to do an amazing breakfast spread, but they were also sociopathic murderers. This was better.

* * * *

Half an hour later, eager to get on-site, Jack and Hannah delivered Ellen into the care and protective custody of Mrs. Branaghan and Natalie. They arrived at the crime scene soon thereafter, Copp's Hill Burying Ground. Though Deming predicted it, Jack knew his profiler would be racked with frustration and anger at this news. She'd spent the better part of yesterday in the area, interviewing local merchants and then repairing her flat tire, yet the murder apparently took place right under her nose. Seemed impossible.

He saw Deming ahead, chatting with Detective Ferguson inside a taped-off crime scene. Copp's Hill Burying Ground was a historical cemetery in the center of old Boston, and looked much the same as most cemeteries in New England. A sea of granite slab headstones with etched writing, weatherworn and barely legible, with a smattering of grand marble monuments and some flags marking veterans' graves. The difference between this cemetery and most other revolutionary-era cemeteries in Massachusetts was that this one was one of sixteen historically significant stops on the famous Freedom Trail, a two-and-a-half-mile-long walking path through downtown Boston. Marked largely with brick, it wound its way from Boston Common to the Bunker Hill Monument in Charlestown.

Ferguson waved them over. Sergeant O'Neil was milling about, talking with his men. Jack gave him a nod of acknowledgment as he passed. O'Neil nodded back, but found the energy to wave and smile brightly at Hannah when she called out a greeting.

Jack caught Deming's gaze. "It's not all bad news," he said. He ducked under the yellow tape, approaching the profiler. "Your projections were correct. The killer used the Freedom Trail again. Stone's murder is still an outlier. It's not a consolation, but we know more than we did yesterday, and that's because of you."

Deming shrugged. The muscles along her jawline tightened reflexively. Jack knew she was upset, but knowing Deming, she was banking the emotion, using it to buckle down and work harder. "The perp's timeline is blown to pieces." She scanned the crowd. "And I don't see BPD footing the bill for round-the-clock surveillance of the Freedom Trail." She shrugged again. "But you're right, this kill does follow our projections. Copp's Burying Ground is on the Freedom Trail, and that means Stone is still an outlier. She was the killer's first mistake. Not killing Hannah was his second. We'll get this guy."

"Small consolation for this man." Ferguson nodded toward the grave. "*Freedom.*" He scowled at the corpse in the desecrated tomb, and then at the crowd straining against the crime scene tape. "What freedom does the perp give his victims by killing them so...spectacularly?"

Jack donned latex gloves. "Who found the body?"

Ferguson pointed to two teens smoking cigarettes and texting on their smart phones. "I told them to contact their parents. Liquor on their breath, so whatever they say might be a little off. Looks like they got trashed before school, found the victim, ditched the booze and then contacted 911."

"That's what they said?" Jack gave the teenage boys a good looking-over.

"No," Ferguson said. "But that's probably what happened."

"We'll take their phones soon. See who they contacted. See if they deleted anything. I don't see them as perps, but I don't want to take any chances, either," Deming said.

Ferguson indicated the tomb using his notepad. "Eight feet long, four feet wide, gray inscribed granite. The victim's fingertips are bloody, nails ripped off. He was alive when he was buried and tried to get out. The plastic bag over his head was spiked with chloroform-soaked cotton balls, so he didn't suffer long. There's that, I guess."

"I can smell the chloroform from here," Jack said. One of the teens put his phone away, catching Jack's attention. "How did they find the body?"

Deming wrinkled her nose. "They say the cover to the tomb moved when they sat on it."

"They called the cops, though it meant getting in trouble." Hannah crouched next to the tomb, looking, but not touching.

Deming smirked. "They came here to get wasted, then vandalized graves in a historical site."

Hannah snapped on a latex glove and searched the pockets of the victim. She found a wallet. "The plastic bag over his head is torn, by him, most likely. So why is he dead and not just unconscious?"

"Hey." Charlie Foulkes ducked under the crime scene tape, wearing a Hawaiian shirt and khakis. "You messing with my crime scene, Special Agent Cambridge?"

"Just trying to ID the vic." Hannah held up the wallet. "Requisite pictures of the crowd again, Charlie, please. I find it hard to believe our guy doesn't watch."

"They usually do, and stop telling me my job." The beefy redhead pointed to one of his team photographing the crowds. "Already doing it." He dropped his case, did an admirable job of not looking at Deming, while Deming acted as if Charlie didn't exist. Jack made a mental note to ask his profiler about that bit of weirdness. There was something going on between her and the case's forensic pathologist, and he wanted to know what.

"Why is he dead?" Jack said. Hannah was right. With the torn plastic bag over his head, the guy should have been unconscious, not dead.

Charlie squatted down next to the open tomb, peering at the victim. "Petechial hemorrhaging. Cyanosis."

"Yeah, we noticed," Ferguson said. "So, he's blue. What else?"

"Suffocated. Most likely, the duct tape around his neck restricted blood flow sufficiently to make the lack of air in the tomb, combined with the chloroform, a deadly combination. Autopsy will confirm." Charlie pulled latex gloves from his pocket and tugged them on. "Or not. Look." He pointed to the victim's legs. "He was paralyzed."

Jack studied the tomb. "The lid has to be two hundred pounds. In the best of circumstances, it would have been problematic for this guy to move it."

"They said they sat on the cover and it moved." Ferguson turned toward the teens who were giving up their cell phones to the uniformed officers interviewing them.

"No way," Deming said. "Those kids were trying their hand at grave robbing." Jack saw her glance at Charlie, and when the head of forensics met her gaze, she looked away quickly.

"Kids these days." Hannah flipped through the vic's wallet. "Gary Buntle. He lives"—Hannah pointed to the right—"Hull Street. South of here. He's a local."

Deming grimaced. "Our victims are loners. He'll be like the rest of them. No one will know anything about him."

"Maybe," Jack said. "Check the NCIC index."

Deming typed Buntle's name into her iPad, accessing the National Crime Information Center's database. "Not listed. No record. Hannah, how old is he?"

Hannah peered at his license. "Twenty-nine."

"Maybe a vet," Ferguson said. "Try the VA database."

She typed it in. "Yes. He is. I got him right here." Deming patted her iPad. "See? Not all technology hates me. Three tours in Afghanistan. He was a lifer. Lost use of his legs a year ago when his armored vehicle drove over an IED. Oh, geez." She winced. "Seven months ago, his wife died in a car accident. He fits the killer's target demographic."

"Broken love." Jack glanced at the crumpled copier paper pinned to the victim's shirt. It was the fifth stanza. Same font, same paper. This one, however, was covered in blood.

Charlie unpinned the paper from the dead man's shirt. "'Seven of my sweet loves thy knife Has bereavèd of their life. Their marble tombs I built with tears, And with cold and shuddering fears.'" He frowned, arching a brow at Jack. "The perp chose to kill with a tomb? Knife seems like it would have been easier. Maybe easy isn't what he's after." Deming bit her lip, nodding.

Ferguson smirked. "Charlie, your voice was made to recite poetry. Maybe you chose the wrong profession."

"Stop flirting," Charlie said, absently. The detective barked out a laugh as Deming stared at the body.

"Poor guy," she said.

"Suffocation isn't so bad," Charlie said. "You just sleep. There are worse ways to go."

For whatever reason, his words upset her. Deming lifted her iPad. "Benton, VA files on Buntle verify the local obituary on his wife. Another grieving victim."

Jack dialed Vivian at the precinct. "Yeah. Hi, Vivian. Please contact *Boston Globe*'s obit manager and have them provide obits for all our vics' spouses, lovers or whatever. I'm coming in." He hung up.

Hannah was searching the growing crowds on the outskirts of the burying grounds, no doubt wondering if the perp was watching. Jack wondered also, and he hoped Charlie's forensics team photographed the bastard if he was here.

"Nothing more we can do until Charlie's team is done." Jack turned toward the detective. "Ferguson, were you able to interview the victims' families again?"

"Yeah. Nothing new," Ferguson said.

"The perp's escalated," Deming said. "A kill a month to a kill a day." Deming glanced at Hannah. "Well, an attempted kill, anyway. Either way, this is bad news. Serial killers have rituals. They can't just stop them." She shook her head, clearly upset.

"Cynthia, you okay?" Charlies said. Jack thought his frown revealed great concern. Care, even.

Deming glanced at the team, and then at Charlie, and then shook her head, as if she was irritated Charlie spoke to her at all. Then without another word, she stormed off, ducking under the crime scene tape toward Buntle's address.

"What?" Ferguson's gaze trailed after her. "What was that about?" He turned to Charlie for an explanation, but the forensic pathologist shrugged, ignoring him.

Jack waved Ferguson after her. "Help Deming check out the victim's residence. Maybe he's living with someone." Nobody thought that likely, but Jack didn't want Deming alone.

After the barest hesitation, Ferguson obeyed, though he gave Charlie a thorough side-eye. Jack felt for the detective. Women were complicated. He glanced at Hannah.

"What?" she said.

"Nothing. Let's go," he said. They left Charlie and his team, hopeful they'd find something to tie the killer to the crime scene.

On the drive back to the precinct house, they brainstormed possible directions the case might go, and when they stepped into the incident room, they saw Vivian taping obituaries of the vics' loved ones under their corresponding pictures.

"They weren't all in the *Boston Globe*," Gilroy said. He waved to Hannah, before pointing to the obits. "Some were posted in different papers, different parts of the country, on different days, some different months, but all were within the last year."

"That's good," Hannah said.

Gilroy grimaced. "It's something."

"What about the security tapes we gathered in the crime scene areas?" Jack said. "Any leads at all?" When Gilroy shook his head, Jack couldn't hide his disappointment.

The four of them spent the next hour conferring about possible next moves. A lot of time was spent coming up with arguments to convince Lieutenant Pepperidge to spend money on surveilling Freedom Trail sites. They were all positive the next crime scene would on the trail.

Later, when Deming and Ferguson arrived back at the incident room, Jack read them into what they'd discovered. Ferguson wasn't impressed. "Random. The deaths of the vic's significant others couldn't have been more random if they'd tried. How is this information helpful?" he said.

"Put enough leads together," Jack said, "and we have a case, a conviction. I don't need to tell you that this is how it works, Ferguson." Jack studied the murder board. "What are we missing?" Hannah stood at his shoulder, also staring at the board.

"Evidence." Ferguson sat at his desk, not hiding his frustration.

"You are missing," Vivian said. Everyone turned toward the IT specialist, who was looking at Jack.

"*My* obit," Jack said. Hannah was the only person that might have submitted one. He had no living family. "Hannah, did you send my obituary to the paper?"

"I was only your partner." Hannah shifted her weight from one foot to the other, not meeting his gaze. "It wasn't my place." Her explanation stumped him. If it wasn't Hannah's place, then whose place was it?

Humility doused his anger almost instantly, because Hannah was right. He'd never admitted that he loved her…and that was his fault. It reminded him that he was more alone than Hannah. He'd designed a life where he'd always be alone. Safer that way. For his heart. Damn. His picture could just as easily be on that murder board as hers.

Hannah turned from the group, keeping her face hidden as she sat at her desk, futzing with manila files. "No one knew we were," she glanced around the room, "dating."

Jack stepped to her side. "The other victims loved the ones they lost." He sat on her desk's edge, noticing that her expression tightened, her cheeks flushed. "Somehow the perp discovered you loved me." She had loved him. Maybe still did.

"I was careful to hide our relationship," she said. "We both were. No one knew what we were to each other." She'd used the past tense. From the angry look in her eye, she'd done it on purpose. "I'm certain of it."

"Well, I'm not," Jack said. "How can you be?" He felt bad to press this point, but it was important to the case. Her hand shook as she nudged a lock of hair behind her ear. "When you thought I'd died, you gave yourself away, Hannah. Somehow."

"Leave her alone, Benton," Ferguson said. The detective seemed moments from physically coming to Hannah's defense.

Hannah, for her part, seemed moments from clocking Jack in the nose. "I lost my partner," she said. "Is there an appropriate amount of grief to show? If so, I don't know it. I was upset. What do you want me to say? Someone *might* have noticed."

He shook his head. "You told someone you loved me." Hannah sent him a repressive glare. "The perp knows about us, or else our only connection between the vics disappears. Think. Who did you tell?" She turned from him, breathless and trembling. Oh, *damn.* Jack peered closer, and saw he'd triggered one of Hannah's panic attacks. He waved everyone toward the door. "Give us the room, please."

Ferguson didn't move. He kept his eyes on Hannah until she nodded to him, and then he followed everyone else out of the room, as if Jack had just discharged a starter gun. Gilroy waited at the door, keeping it open for Vivian, who'd lingered to grab her purse. Then they were all gone, into the hall and the door closed behind them.

Hannah pushed her chair back from the desk and put her head between her legs. She was sucking in air, holding her breath, and then slowly releasing it. Jack waited, not wanting to interrupt what was evidently a routine. A few minutes later, when her breathing slowed, she sat up, though her eyes remained closed, her body unmoving, Jack still hadn't figured out how to force Hannah to tell him the truth.

"Crap," she mumbled, her expression strained. "I'd hoped they were behind me."

"Panic attacks?" He weighed the value of keeping quiet, but didn't have the patience. "How long have they been hitting you?"

"How long have you been dead?" She opened her eyes and as soon as they focused, she turned toward him, glaring. "You rise from the dead, but the attacks remain."

That was a battle he'd never win. "Are you going to be okay?"

"I always am." She took a deep breath, held it for a moment, and then released it slowly. "I will be." She took another breath and held it.

As he watched her struggle to control her emotions, the question she refused to answer hung over them. "Who knew you loved me?" Her eyes welled with tears as she released her breath with a burst. It sounded like a sob.

"No one. Not even you."

"Hannah—"

She glared at him. "Jack, if you didn't figure it out, how could anyone else?"

Ouch. She was right, and he'd been searching for a sign, any sign, that she'd loved him. How could he have missed it? What sort of man couldn't see when someone loved him? Worse yet, he'd interpreted her behavior to mean she *didn't* love him. Some investigator he'd turned out to be.

Hannah gave herself a little shake, wiping tears. "There's one thing, maybe—" She shook her head again. "But no, it's not possible. No way could anyone have known it was me."

Still reeling from the latest revelation, it took Jack a moment to hear her words. "Let me decide."

"I wrote anonymously to an advice column in the *Boston Globe*. Late March."

"Like…Miss Manners?"

"No. I wasn't asking which fork to use at a dinner party, Jack. I was terrified I was about to lose our baby."

"So…like Dear Abby."

Her shoulder's slumped. "Isn't that sad? I had no one I could tell my problems to but Natalie, and I was beginning to feel guilty for putting it all on her shoulders, so—" She rubbed her face of tears, blinking new ones away. "It doesn't matter. Like I said, it was anonymous, no return address. Only Natalie knew we'd lived together, that I'd loved you." Jack didn't miss that she'd used past tense again. "Believe me, when you'd died, I wanted to tell people, but how could I declare *after you're horrifically murdered* that we were a couple? It would have been weird. *I* would have been weird, so I said nothing. Then the panic attacks persisted, I became desperate. I left D.C. I couldn't go to the bureau's psych department. They'd slap PTSD in my file and it would affect my career."

"Hannah, you're textbook PTSD."

"Whatever. I found a way to make things work. I couldn't risk my job. I was going to be a single mother soon." She pushed her bangs out of her eyes. "One day, one of the many days I lingered in my hospital bed, I was reading the *Boston Globe*'s advice column and had the idea to write in, *totally anonymously.* They published free advice, and that's what I needed." Confusion colored her frown. "Jack, there's no way anyone could know I wrote that letter. The things I wrote about...no one knew was happening to me. My problems with the pregnancy. Ellen."

Jack shook his head. This had to be the connection. "You gave yourself away somehow. What did you write?" Her expression shut down.

"I told you," she said. "There's nothing in that letter that would tie it to me."

"You used my name? Gave details?"

"No. It wasn't like that. I'm telling you, it was nothing."

Jack pulled her to her feet, holding her, kissing her forehead. He waited for her to resist, but she didn't. "I'm sorry, Hannah. I can't drop this. I need to know." She trembled in his arms.

"I don't want it to be true." She pressed her face to his chest. "If you're right, if my letter is the cause of me being targeted, then someone close to me is trying to kill me. So close, they could see what I was hiding from the rest of the world." Hannah wiped her tears. "I can't stop crying. You're alive, so why am I still crying?"

"I'm sorry. I can't begin to tell you how sorry I am." Pressing his lips to her temple, he closed his eyes and squeezed her more tightly. He promised himself he'd make it up to her—to both Hannah and Ellen—but he was also realistic. He couldn't tell her everything would be all right, because no matter how this case shook out, her life had been shredded already.

If she knew the perp, it would be one more betrayal to add to a list that was already crushing her. It killed Jack to know he was the first to betray her, making her vulnerable to this latest punch to the gut. He understood it was why she hesitated to forgive him. He got that. It's why Hannah hadn't trusted him enough to reveal that she'd written a letter to the advice column.

"I love you, Hannah." He felt her stiffen in his arms and forced himself not to protect himself from rejection. That led nowhere. He felt what he felt, no matter how Hannah might feel in response. It was time he started owning up to that. "I've loved you almost since the moment I met you, and there wasn't a day I was away from you that I wasn't kicking myself for leaving. When my assignment came to an end, I picked up the phone, searching for you. That's how I discovered you'd moved out of D.C., transferred here. I made *more* calls, twisted a few arms and used up all my IOUs to come to Boston. Then yesterday I discovered you'd been targeted." He gave her a squeeze, kissing her temple. "In danger or not, Hannah, I need you to believe I would have been here anyway, hat in hand, trying to win you back. I know you don't trust me. I know you have reasons not to, but I'm telling you the truth. I love you."

He kissed her and hoped she wouldn't pull away. He hoped a lot of things, but the way events were playing out, neither were looking at a happy ending.

Chapter 14

She kissed him back and felt relief mix with pleasure. She'd been waiting for him to kiss her. She hadn't known that until this moment, but now that it was happening, it felt right. It was glorious. It was a gift to escape reality for this precious moment and enjoy his body against hers, his lips, his tongue caressing hers... Jack could always make her forget the pain and ugliness in the world.

When he broke their kiss, she pulled him back, not wanting the feeling to end, but then caught his glance toward the door even as their lips met again. Any moment, someone could bust in and catch them unaware. He was right. This was not the time for kisses, it was time to think, to reason out her problems. So she stepped out of his arms, heart racing, thoughts muddled.

He'd told her he loved her, and she believed him. Hannah had been waiting years to hear that, but it came *after* he'd learned of Ellen. Fear of not being enough, *that it took having his child* to make her enough filled her head. She didn't want to think like that, but couldn't help herself. She wanted his words of love to be true, to mean everything would be all right, that Ellen's father wanted them, loved them. But Jack had hurt her too much already to trust him now. What if he hurt her again? What if he discarded Ellen this time around?

She squared her shoulders, attempting to focus on the case. "We need to let everyone know about the advice column. I know. I understand, though I don't like it." A glance at Jack told her he wasn't thinking about the case. His eyes were on her lips. His hands were fisted at his sides, as if he were forcing himself not to reach for her. "More grist for the gossip mill," she said.

"Hannah—"

"No." She knew he wanted her to tell him she loved him, too. She did, but…didn't want to. "I need to process what you said. I'm sorry—"

"It's okay." He took her hand and squeezed. "I didn't tell you to force your hand. I just thought you deserved to know." He ran the tip of his finger down her cheek and then cupped her chin, stepping closer. "We have a lot to talk about, but I know I can't be your priority right now. Hell, I'm not even *my* top priority now. It's you and Ellen. It's catching this killer. But don't for a second believe this conversation is over." He dropped a kiss on her lips, then met her gaze, searching for answers that she couldn't give.

Vivian poked her head into the room. Hannah and Jack separated, but Jack held up a finger, silently asking for a minute more. The tech nodded, then disappeared into the hall.

"Hannah, the perp is someone close to you."

"I know. I understand that we can't trust anyone." She didn't want it to be true, but she would be a fool to discount the mounting evidence.

"Pepperidge needs to be told," Jack said. "We have to trust him, and I can vouch for Gilroy and Deming."

"We'll need to interview the tenants at the brownstone again, but this time to ask if anyone's been asking about me." Hannah groaned. "They're going to love this."

Jack narrowed his eyes. "Someone who fits our profile. Who knows you well."

"You're thinking of Natalie." Hannah shook her head. "I trust her with my life. No…with *Ellen*, Jack. She'd never hurt me. And anyway, she just arrived in Boston, and I'm the one who brought her here." Jack folded his arms over his chest.

"Our perp knows things about you no one else does," Jack said. *Things she'd only told Jack, Mrs. Branaghan and Natalie.* "That you love me." He smiled, but she could tell he was teasing.

Hannah averted her gaze. "That I *loved* you."

Jack grabbed her hand and kissed the back of it, making her heart swell with emotion. "Well, we can agree I'm not the killer. So that only leaves Natalie and Mrs. Branaghan. This case might as well be solved."

She arched a brow, knowing he was *still* teasing her. "You *say* you were on assignment this last year, but I don't know that. Can you support your alibi?"

Jack narrowed his eyes. "I was undercover. Even the FBI won't admit where I was."

"You have connections in the bureau that directed you to my whereabouts. You're smart enough and strong enough to commit the murders and have information about me no one else does. The same can't be said for Natalie or Mrs. Branaghan."

"Not funny."

"Just saying." Hannah shrugged. "None of this is relevant, anyway, because I already know our perp isn't one of you three." She walked to the door, opening it and flagging the team back into the room. "Our killer's motive seems to be putting the victims out of their misery." She met Jack's gaze. "Mercy killing, so *definitely* not you."

"Yeah? Why?"

"In all the years I've known you," Hannah said, "you've never once shown me mercy."

Chapter 15

"Someone tipped off the media," Vivian said, frowning at her cell phone's screen as she stormed into the incident room. Before the door could swing closed behind her, Gilroy followed, his lips pressed tightly together, looking pissed.

"Local news. Open WCVB's website app, Benton," Gilroy said, striding toward his desk. Deming pushed through the door just behind him, her heels clicking on the tile.

Jack pulled out his phone, and sure enough, live footage of New Sudbury precinct's building, the Channel 5 reporter, and other venue's news crews were being broadcast from the sidewalk outside. All the incident room's desk phones began to ring, and everyone looked at Jack.

Deming stopped walking when she reached her desk, lips pursed, staring at her ringing desk phone. "What are the odds it's my poetry expert returning my call?"

"I dreamt of poetry last night," Jack said. Stanza after stanza of "Broken Love" had played in his head with Hannah cast as victim, always killed by the numbers. The phones continued to ring.

"What poetry expert will consult with the team if they know a serial killer might target them?" Deming said.

"More bad news," Gilroy said, glaring at his computer screen. "Forensics just sent me their findings on the footprints at the brownstone. They match tenants who are not physically agile enough to drop a woman into a marina or a full-grown man into a granite-lidded grave, or stuff a man into a freezer. All casts of footprints are accounted for. We got nothing."

"And we're running out of time," Hannah said, and then covered her mouth with her fingertips.

"Put these phones on mute," Jack said, reaching for his own. When the room was silent again, he caught Vivian waving at him. He nodded, and hoped she had good news.

"Lieutenant Pepperidge gave me access to the city's security software." Vivian moved her mouse across its pad, frowning at her computer screen. "I was able to access online all the cameras we use in Boston." She glanced at the door, as if fearing her next words might be overheard. "Unfortunately, video logs from those cameras were offline during the murders. Whether by vandalism, or design, I don't know. I took the initiative to send uniformed officers to check them out." She pointed to her computer's screen. "They've just gotten back to me. Nothing. No noticeable vandalism. They're not experts, of course, but I'd need authorization to take down the hardware and poke around inside, see what I can see."

"You have it," Jack said. "Talk to Charlie. I want a forensic tech doing the work."

"Tech. You can't rely on tech," Deming said, her lips thinned with irritation. "Vivian, what about software glitches?"

"I've requested a thorough malware scan done. I'm waiting to hear back from the department, and the security firm that sold us this software. I want to know if something like this has happened before." She shrugged.

Ferguson pushed through the incident door and slammed it behind him as he hurried to his desk. "I called the victim's families *again*. All of them." He sat, rubbing his eyes with the palms of his hands. After a few blinks, he focused on Jack. "No new information. They're as frustrated as we are, and they're angry that we haven't caught this guy yet."

"So am I," Jack said, glancing at Hannah. She was leaning against her desk, her expression giving nothing away.

"Do you guys know we have a ton of news crews outside?" Ferguson said.

"It's come to our attention," Jack said, grimacing.

"Keep up, Ferguson." Deming turned to Jack, holding up her phone. "I just received an email. FBI forensic accountants say the owners of the *Teapot* are still off the grid. That feels ominous." She stepped to the coffee machine, frowning as she poured herself a cup.

It was raining bad news, and Jack was sick of it. "We have a leak, and that leak is helping our killer whether they know it or not. Gilroy, I want you taking lead on finding who's behind it." His team dropped their eyes to the floor, their expressions grim. An internal leak meant one of the "good guys" had gone bad, and until they found them, they knew no one could be trusted. It wasn't a comfortable place for people whose survival relied on their support team.

"Will do," Gilroy said, turning back to his computer.

"We now have to worry about copycats." Jack didn't want to vent. Punching a wall never solved anything, but he was tempted. "The horse is out of the barn, but that doesn't mean we can't do better about keeping information in-house. No talking where someone might overhear." Ferguson stewed at his desk. Deming calmly assessed Jack, and Vivian nodded, futzing with items on her desktop.

"The reporters are calling the perp 'Mercy Killer.'" Gilroy arched a brow, reading off his phone even as his fingers were poised on his computer's keyboard. "The *Boston Globe* updated its site, and it's now breaking news. Our leak seems to know everything."

Hannah undid her clip and neatened her hair before reclipping it. "Gilroy? What's happening on the tip line?"

"I have uniformed police following up anything that looks credible. We'll be flooded now," Gilroy said, glancing at Jack. "What do you want to do?"

Jack grimaced. "Farm out the responsibility. If they find anything, have them contact you, but the leak is top priority, and..." He focused on Hannah. "Hannah has a lead."

Gilroy and the other team members turned to Hannah, hope coloring their gazes. Hannah shook her head, surprising Jack, and prompting him to scowl and take a step toward her.

"Vivian," Hannah said, "we need copies of the *Boston Globe*'s advice column. March's issues. Maybe April, too." Jack waited for her to continue with specifics, but she didn't, so he gave her another expectant look, making it clear he wanted her to say more. Hannah shook her head again.

Vivian seemed shocked. "March? Any reason why?"

"Please, just do it," Hannah said. When Jack opened his mouth, intent on explaining, Hannah glowered at him. "Don't prejudice her, Jack. Let's see what she finds." Vivian lifted her phone's receiver, watching the byplay between him and Hannah.

Jack knew Hannah's letter might have nothing to do with the case, but it also might be relevant, so for the next *three hours*—team members coming and going, doing their best to fulfill their assignments—he and Hannah reviewed case files and transcripts of interviews, and studied the poem, while they waited for the *Boston Globe* to gather and then transmit the requested advice column letters. By the time the tech had them printed out, Jack could see Hannah was wound tighter than a tick. They all watch Vivian as she scanned a few, her expression growing more alarmed by the moment.

"How did you know?" Vivian's cheeks had flushed and her hands shook.

Hannah squeezed her pencil so tightly it broke in her hand.

"What?" Ferguson said.

"What did you find, Vivian?" Deming approached the tech's desk, peering over her shoulder.

"Ten advice column letters and their responses. A week's worth. Last week of March." Vivian kept her gaze on Hannah's face, and was clearly upset. "Hannah found the connection between our victims." Jack's heart beat a little faster. Everyone leaned forward in their chairs, waiting for the tech to continue.

Deming read over Vivian's shoulder, and soon pointed to the top letter. "This could be Buntle's letter."

Vivian startled, as if she only now noticed she'd been staring at Hannah. Then she focused on the page Deming now touched. "Yes," Vivian lifted another page, "and this could be Zelezny's." She flipped through more. "Some are signed." She held up a page. "Look. Stone's letter."

Gilroy approached Vivian's desk. "Print us all copies, please."

Vivian nodded quickly, as if embarrassed she hadn't thought of that herself. Soon, the printer began spitting out the letters as Hannah slumped in her chair. Jack didn't like how she'd grown pale, and he feared she might faint. Stepping to her side, he handed her a water bottle from his desk's supply, and shielded her from the other team member's view.

Her fears had come true. If, as Hannah insisted, only someone who knew intimate details of her life could tie her to the letter, that's exactly what had happened. The team had to look more closely at the people in her inner circle. That meant all the cops she'd come to see as her friends here at the precinct. Anyone who could connect her to the letter she wrote to the advice column in the *Boston Globe*. *Even Natalie.*

Jack texted just that to Gilroy, minus any mention of Ellen. When he read Jack's text, he frowned, and then looked up, his unspoken questions written on his face, but after a nod, Gilroy stepped away from his desk and made a call. He was a consummate profession, and Jack knew he'd tie up this loose end, leaving Jack to follow this lead.

Late March. Ellen was born April 12. March was when Hannah had languished in the hospital, afraid of losing their baby, and now her letter was evidence. Admissible in court. It wasn't just the team who'd be reading this intensely personal letter. *Anyone* could, and it could be published again, but this time with her name attached to it.

No wonder she was upset. The moment she laid claim to one of these letters…

For the first time since discovering its existence, Jack was more worried than curious about its content.

"Hannah." Vivian leaned to the side, trying to see past Jack, but he refused to move. "I don't see any letter that mentions Special Agent Benton." Gilroy had his back to the room, his phone to his ear, but even he glanced over his shoulder to hear Hannah's response.

"Hannah?" Deming stepped to the side until she could see Hannah's face, waving Hannah over to Vivian's desk. "Is one of these letters yours?" When Hannah didn't move, the profiler gathered letters and silently read as she walked across the room to Hannah. "Oh, my, this is sad." She stopped walking when she reached Jack, then handed a packet of letters to Hannah. Jack knew Deming wasn't trying to be cruel, but the effect was cruel nonetheless. Hannah seemed moments from a meltdown, but Jack couldn't stop this, nor would he, given the chance. Identifying her letter might be the difference between someone else dying or not.

Jack leaned, whispering for Hannah's ears only. "We'll get through this. I promise."

"Promise, huh?" Hannah's voice cracked, and then failed. Clearing her throat, she sipped from the water bottle, and then dredged up a fake smile. "Well, if you promise." She lifted her chin, the image of defiance. Jack knew that her dismissive tone and words couldn't have been more carefully chosen to shut him out, or to remind him she wouldn't be in this situation if he hadn't left last year.

She was right, but this moment wasn't about the past. If he had his way, they'd have a lifetime to run an autopsy on what happened between them, but now wasn't that time. Whether she knew it or not, whether she welcomed it or not, he was here for her and here he'd stay.

But it was time for her to tell the truth.

Chapter 16

Hannah took the offered pages from Deming without a word. The top one was Stone's letter. Signed. The young woman had a distinctive, easily recognizable voice; her word choices romantic, sad, yet hopeful. The weight of Jack's gaze reminded Hannah her reactions were being logged, judged, and filed away in his highly analytical brain. He was good at his job, one of the best, and they needed him to catch this perp, but knowing her reactions were being entered into evidence made her reluctant to show any.

"The Stone letter suggests her death wasn't the outlier we'd supposed," Hannah said. "She was a planned kill."

Deming shook her head. "But she wasn't found on the Freedom Trail. She must be an outlier. Our *planner* messed up, or my profile is wrong."

"Fancy that," Ferguson mumbled. Deming glared at him, but then dismissed him with a turn of her head.

Hannah set Stone's letter facedown on her desk and moved to the next one. Zelezny's. Filled with tales of his late wife, his feelings of loss, talk of his job, the retired plumber revealed incapacitating loneliness and his struggles with despair. When Hannah finished reading the epistle, she felt overwhelming empathy for the man. He'd been grief-stricken. Like she'd been.

The next letter was Gary Buntle's. A veteran, he wrote about his brush with death in the Army, and his paralysis. When his wife died soon after in a car accident, he was pushed to the brink of suicide. Buntle wanted to know if his grief would lessen with time. This was a common thread to all the letters, so far. When would their suffering end? Hannah already knew her letter was no different.

"Vivian," Hannah said, hating the wobble in her voice. "We need a list of the other people who wrote in to the Globe's advice column. It's where he's picking his victims. Top priority must be preventing his next murder. Let's try to do this without tipping off the killer." Jack rested his hand on her shoulder.

"How many issues of the Globe are we talking about?" Vivian said.

"Seventeen stanzas?" Deming lifted her brows. "I say as many as we can. At least, from March until today."

"Do it, Vivian. Gilroy?" Jack waited until the special agent caught his eye. "We good?" Gilroy glanced at Hannah for a moment, and then settled his gaze on Jack, nodding. She had no idea what they were talking about, but she was so upset, she didn't have the mental space to inquire. She was too busy trying to project calm, like she was coping, though she wasn't.

"I'm on it," Gilroy said to Jack. "Waiting for a call."

Jack grimaced, nodding. "Then coordinate with Ferguson while you wait. Arrange officers to escort the potential vics to the precinct. I want to question them, and I want this kept quiet, so pick the officers carefully. Ferguson should be able to help with that, too."

Vivian was biting her lip, deep in thought.

Hannah lifted a page. "This letter says the writer is a salesman. Twoomey's."

Deming glanced at Twoomey's letter, but quickly turned back to the one in her hand. She cringed. "Oh, my heaven," Deming said. The longer the profiler read, the more Hannah knew it had to be her letter.

Jack was watching her, his show of sympathy so strong it hit her like a wave, but instead of making her feel better, it made her feel weak, and had her throat closing. She couldn't handle that right now, so she did her best to pretend this was happening to someone else.

"Ten years ago, this lady's fiancé," Deming said, "left her for another woman. She's never gotten over him. It ruined her life." She dropped the letter in front of Hannah, moving on to the next letter. "Someone should have told her men aren't worth that kind of heartache," the profiler mumbled.

"You'll get your chance to lecture the woman when we track her down," Jack said, "and save her life."

Vivian was reading a letter instead of giving Gilroy the names he needed, but the special agent seemed patience personified, unlike Hannah. "Vivian," Hannah said, with more sharpness of tone than she'd intended. "Gilroy needs the names the *Boston Globe* gathered for us." The tech ignored her, and continued reading.

"Poor lady." Deming was reading, too, shaking her head.

"How do you know the writer is a woman?" Ferguson was reading, too, a pained grimace in place.

Deming's expression was colored with sadness. "She's in the hospital, lover dead, losing their baby." Deming turned toward Hannah. As did Vivian. The room went silent, and it was clear that everyone had figured it was Hannah's letter.

Her deepest wound was exposed, and she wanted to die.

Vivian was the first to recover. "We have all but two return addresses." Vivian handed Gilroy a stack of papers. "The...ah, the author of the letter Deming just read, and the letter about...the unrequited love." She held another paper out to Gilroy, who didn't look at it before hurrying from the room. "I'll contact the Globe about the other writers." She glanced at Hannah, and then stared at her phone, but made no move to lift the receiver.

Jack clapped his hands twice, catching everyone's attention. "Saving these people is our top priority. Ferguson, go chase Gilroy down. He should have waited for you." Ferguson glanced at Hannah before he left the room, but she couldn't meet his gaze, so she had no idea what he was thinking. In fact, she didn't want to know. "Vivian," Jack said, "when you talk with your contact at the *Boston Globe*, make sure they understand this information is *not* for publication, that lives are on the line. Then brainstorm ideas with them on how we can track the missing letter writers' identities without tipping off the killer that we've found his kill list. If we can't find the names quickly any other way, we'll just have to give the Globe a scoop like they've never seen before."

Vivian lifted her phone's receiver, but didn't dial yet. "Hannah? Did you lose the baby?" Hannah's throat spasmed closed, making it hard to breathe. It took her a moment to find her composure as the room fell silent, everyone staring.

"Yes." Eyes averted, Hannah did her best to sell the lie. Though it was for a good cause, it was still hard lying to people who cared. Deming's sympathy tore at her, and Vivian seemed devastated. She could only hope they'd forgive her when this case was over and the truth known.

Jack rested his hand on her shoulder again, squeezing gently. "Good work, everyone." Then he stepped to the murder board and wrote Mercy Killer on the top. "Our perp is putting his victims out of their misery. Chalk one up for behavioral science."

Deming folded her arms over her chest, frowning at the board. "Our perp can't handle his victims' pain, but has no problem with their suffering while he kills them. What a sick bastard."

"William Blake is rolling in his grave." Vivian dialed, putting the phone's receiver to her ear

Jack held Hannah's gaze, not saying anything. He'd allowed her lie about Ellen to stand, supporting her decision to keep their daughter's existence a secret. That's all that mattered. Her team's support was gravy. It humbled her, filling her with gratitude and *relief.* One less thing to worry about.

An hour later, Jack's phone pinged and he glanced at its screen. "Vivian, your contacts at the *Boston Globe* came through. Gilroy just texted me that patrol cars have picked up the targets now. All writers are accounted for except the one. Any progress on tracking down the unrequited lover?"

Vivian shook her head and opened a small bag of chips, munching away. "They want to reprint it and ask the writer to contact them. I told them no." She shrugged. "If they can't find the target, can the killer? I think we should inform the *Boston Globe* about the poem. It will protect any future victims and the information that we have the kill list."

Jack nodded. It was on his list of things to discuss with the lieutenant.

Charlie Foulkes walked in holding a manila folder, scanned the room and his gaze lingered on Special Agent Deming before zeroing in on Jack. "The toxicology report on Buntle." He lifted the file shoulder height. "Test confirms what we already knew. It was chloroform. He was drugged. A first for this killer. Maybe Buntle, though paralyzed, wasn't such an easy mark." Charlie stepped up to Jack and gave him the file.

"Thanks, Charlie," Hannah said.

He glanced at Hannah and nodded. "No discernable wheelchair tracks around the site, and though we can't completely rule out that he was in his chair up until he was put in the tomb, we're thinking Buntle was carried, so the perp is strong enough to lift a hundred-and-thirty-pound person."

"The burying ground was dry and packed that day," Jack said.

"Which is why the wheel chair can't be ruled out. The chloroform rules out the victim lowering himself into that grave on his own steam, so the perp touched him one way or the other."

"But no DNA? How'd he manage that?" Jack said.

"He knows forensics," Charlie said. "Buntle was awake when he died… the torn plastic around his head, his bloody nails, and the blood on the lid's interior. He tried to loosen the tape around his neck." He indicated both sides of his neck. "Claw marks here, and here. Blood on his hands. His own. No secondary DNA."

Hannah sighed, feeling depressed. Another manila folder filled with their poem expert's notes sat on her desk. UMass had it hand-delivered.

She picked up the folder and opened it, seeing a paragraph flagged with a yellow sticky note.

"The best poems are 'distillations of pain, grief, love. Intense.' It says so right here," Hannah said, "so it must be true." She dropped the file on her desk with a resounding thud.

Charlie shrugged. "A poem never spoke to me unless it said, *memorize me or you'll flunk this class*." He glanced at Deming, but she was looking at her nails. "I've a ton of work on my desk to wade through. If I find anything new, I'll deliver it."

"No need," Deming said. "Just send it up with someone you trust." Still, she studied her nails. Charlie looked as if he were about to respond, but then turned and left without a word.

"*What is up with you two?*" Jack said. "How do you even know him?"

Deming bit her lip. "He used to be best friends with my brother." Jack's frown disappeared, and he nodded as if that explained everything, but everyone else continued to stare at Deming.

"Vivian?" Hannah said. "Can you put the next stanza on the murder board?"

Vivian complied, just as the incident room door opened again. Mrs. Pepperidge, carrying a bright purple clutch, rushed in. Her impractical purple heels clip-clopped on the tile and her white A-line dress swayed about her calves.

"I just heard. Where is Cooper?" Clearly upset, Mrs. Pepperidge looked toward her husband's office. "How could you people let me walk around Boston willy-nilly *knowing* there's a killer on the loose?" She hurried into her husband's office.

Jack exchanged glances with Hannah. Neither knew what to say.

Deming shrugged. "Killers are always on the loose in Boston."

Vivian frowned. "She's scared."

Even behind the closed door of the lieutenant's office, they could hear Mrs. Pepperidge's voice rise and fall, though Hannah couldn't make out the words spoken. Hannah didn't blame the lieutenant's wife for being upset. If Hannah's husband had information a serial killer was on the loose and didn't warn her, she'd skin him alive.

"Deming," Jack said, "I need you and Vivian to work up a preliminary report on where we're at with this case. I need to present it to Pepperidge by end of day. Give me enough time to review it first, please." Deming nodded. "Hannah. You're with me." Jack waved her toward Pepperidge's office. "We've waited too long as it is to read him into our findings."

Hannah wanted to wait until the Pepperidges' marital spat died down, but Jack was knocking on the door and the lieutenant shouted "Enter" before she could have her say. Jack opened the door. The Pepperidges *both* seemed relieved to see them. Then the lieutenant kissed his wife's cheek.

"Honey," he said, "we'll talk more on this when I get home tonight."

Mrs. Pepperidge, still upset, nevertheless nodded and silently moved to leave. Hannah saw her chin quiver and couldn't help but extend her hand for a sympathetic touch. "Try not to worry," Hannah said. "Our perp works from a list, and you're not on it."

Mrs. Pepperidge couldn't hide her surprise, but recovered quickly, patting Hannah's hand. She mouthed "thank you," then hurried away.

"Lieutenant, we need to talk," Jack said.

Pepperidge's genial expression disappeared when the door closed behind his wife. "Who the hell leaked this information to the press?"

"Your guess is as good as mine." Jack handed him a folder. "I had Gilroy check every one of my team's alibis himself, so my team is cleared." He glanced at Hannah. "Natalie checked out, too. You didn't tell me she was special ops."

Hannah narrowed her eyes. "You didn't ask."

Pepperidge dropped the file on his desk without even opening it. "I'll be lucky if I have a job tomorrow. Hell, I'll be lucky if I have a marriage tonight." He glanced at a tin of cookies on his desk, and then pressed his palm to his belly, sighing. "I could have told you none of them were suspects. The killer must be someone at your brownstone, Cambridge. How many people live in that building, and how many people go in and out every day visiting them? Your time would have been better served investigating them."

"Ferguson did." Hannah placed another file on Pepperidge's desk. "Another dead end. All had alibis or they are clearly incapable of the kills. Some are on walkers."

"Really?" Pepperidge grimaced, and then absently opened the cookie tin, grabbing one, and biting into it. "Maybe it's time to get fresh eyes on this." He offered the tin to Jack and Hannah. Both declined.

"With all due respect, Lieutenant," Jack glanced at Hannah, "I'm the fresh eyes here. I've been on the case two days and we're close, and getting closer."

"Horseshit. You didn't tell me that you and Cambridge were lovers." Pepperidge glowered. "If the DA had known, you'd never have been okayed to replace her, and you know that. We need someone who can see things clearly."

"My life is the bureau," Hannah said. "All I ever had was Jack, and when he'd died, I was alone, except for my job. No one knew of my troubles, and no one could have tied me to the letter I sent to the newspaper. None of that changes because Jack knew me a year ago."

"Someone knew what was going on in your life," Pepperidge said. "Someone knew you wrote to the *Boston Globe*." He turned to Jack. "Figure this out."

Then Pepperidge offered Hannah a cookie again. He couldn't hide his concern.

Hannah and the lieutenant had something in common. A stillborn baby. Or so the lieutenant thought. Her letter had to have triggered painful memories for him, and for that she was sorry. Ellen didn't die, but the lieutenant and Mrs. Pepperidge's babies did. There was no correcting the impression without admitting the truth, and Hannah refused to do that, so was forced to stand there and accept the lieutenant's sympathy, even though she didn't deserve it.

Hannah grabbed a cookie and bit it, needing a distraction from her quivering chin.

"Our perp knows Hannah and is local," Jack said. "Hannah transferred from D.C. last November. Everyone she's become close to here has been vetted. I saw to it."

"You're missing something." Pepperidge closed the cookie tin. "Do better, Benton. Special Agent Cambridge's life depends on you doing better." Jack nodded, lowering his gaze. "Tell your team they've been investigated and cleared. I don't want this coming up later, blindsiding anyone."

She and Jack both had their marching orders. *Read the team in.* Not long after they stepped out of Pepperidge's office, they saw Mrs. Pepperidge walking into the incident room holding bags of sodas and leading a delivery guy who carried multiple pizza boxes from a restaurant a block down from the building. Jack hurried to help Mrs. Pepperidge carry the bags.

"I'm sorry for causing a scene," Mrs. Pepperidge said. "Please accept pizza as my way of apologizing. Food is love!"

The lieutenant trailed from his office into the incident room. "Jolene? That was quick." His wife hurried to his side, gave him a peck on the lips and whispered something in his ear. His answering smile said all was right in their world.

Hannah's heart swelled as she watched the couple. Even deep in the chaos of this case, they managed to keep their priorities straight. They loved each other, and worked every day to make that their world. Hannah saw it from their scheduled date nights, his buying bouquets of roses, and his wife's frequent visits to the precinct bringing pizza, cookies, and kind words.

Hannah wanted that. She glanced at Jack, wondering if he saw what she saw; a couple who worked through their problems, trusting in the other to have their back, to be there when times became tough.

Jack was glaring at a report on his desk, his mind *where it should be*, she supposed. On the case.

Hannah sighed as the Pepperidges ensconced themselves in the lieutenant's office, closing out the world, and them in. Her envy was a familiar thing, but now it served a purpose other than depressing her. She knew what she wanted. To be loved, to give Ellen a father. And now that Jack was back, she had a choice to make. Did she want Jack to be that person? Could she trust him to be there for her when times became tough? That remained to be seen.

The case was taking a toll on him, on them, but when they were at home with Ellen, all that melted away. He was happy when he was with Ellen. Happy in a way he'd never been when it was just her. More content, less anxious. It was good for Ellen, but Hannah wasn't sure what that meant for Jack and Hannah's relationship.

Vivian handed out a packet of information to every team member. "Six months of *Boston Globe*'s advice column. Everyone gets a copy. They've discontinued the column until further notice, and are waiting on Special Agent Benton's okay to reprint our last anonymous writer's letter." Vivian bit her lip, distracted.

"The jilted lover letter," Deming said, nodding. "It's risky. It would definitely tip off the killer, but we can't use that person as bait. It would be unconscionable."

"The *Boston Globe* is going above and beyond," Vivian said. "They want this guy caught, too."

Hannah grimaced. "The Globe reported what little information we had on the perp. He's feeling safe, and I don't want him feeling safe. I want him anxious and scared. I need him making mistakes. There's a leak in the department reporting to the news media and it's hurt our investigation. The paper didn't care about that."

"They're doing their job. Free press, remember?" Vivian taped the next stanza onto the murder board. "'Seven more loves weep night and day, Round the tombs where my loves lay, And seven more loves attend each night, Around my couch with torches bright.'"

"That's a lot of sevens." Jack wasn't hiding his unease. The killer's clues were proving useless to prevent the next kill. "Are we even sure there will be another kill? We've taken away his targets."

"I don't know," Deming said. "Our perp would need to break his pattern to continue. He'd have to find new victims, or he could stop. Let's hope this puts him off his game and he makes a mistake."

"We have to assume he'll try to kill again," Hannah said, "so we have to assume the next stanza will guide him."

Mrs. Pepperidge exited her husband's office like a butterfly bursting from its chrysalis. "Did I hear you right? All the killer's targets are safe? I can't tell you how that relieves my mind."

Lieutenant Pepperidge nodded. "I'll see you tonight, Jolene."

Mrs. Pepperidge waved good-bye. "Once again, sorry about earlier."

"We totally understand," Hannah said. "In our line of work, it's easy to get used to things that should never become commonplace."

They all thanked Mrs. Pepperidge for the pizza and soda, and then watched her leave. The lieutenant settled his gaze on Hannah, who shook her head. "We haven't told them," she said.

"Told us what?" Ferguson walked into the incident room, with Gilroy trailing behind him. "We just saved a slew of potential victims, and instead of coming back to a hero's welcome, Gilroy and I are greeted with more problems. Why am I not surprised? What did Deming do now?"

"Oh, blow me, Ferguson." Deming picked up a slice of pizza, and moved to her desk, looking exhausted.

Gilroy sat heavily on his chair, and used his palm to rub his eye. "All the targets are in police protective custody as we speak," he said.

"Tell them," Pepperidge said.

Jack nodded to Hannah. She knew he was right. There was no putting this off. "The killer knows me. Enough to have guessed I wrote one of the letters," she said.

Reactions were all over the place, but embarrassment ruled. Deming was the first to speak. "You kept this from us because...?"

"You know why." Ferguson grabbed a slice from a pizza box. "We're suspects."

"No. You're all cleared." The lieutenant stared them down. "If you have a problem with our investigation, take it up with someone who cares. Get to work. Find this guy. There are seventeen stanzas to that damn poem and I'm sick of it. Sick of poetry, of secrets, of people dying in weird ways. I want this case solved." He went back to his office with a slice of pizza in his hand.

Deming tossed her crust in her waste bin and licked her fingers. "You know what we have to do." Hannah had no idea. Jack seemed interested, though. "Hannah was lured to the yacht. The other victims were presumably lured to their deaths. Our killer is smart enough to make it look invisible. Now that we've robbed him of his victims, he has few choices; abandon his ritual, alter it, or target the one person on his list not in hiding."

Hannah smiled. "Are you suggesting we set a trap?" It nudged aside the weight of hopelessness. Deming didn't appear as enthusiastic as Hannah was, but it was a good idea.

"We'd finally be in the driver's seat," Gilroy said, "instead of all this damn waiting around."

"No," Jack said.

Ferguson scowled. "It would put Hannah in harm's way. So, I vote no, too."

"Ferguson, if our places were reversed, you'd jump at this chance. And you." Hannah glared at Jack, who glared back at her. "You're pulling rank," she said.

"Damn right. That's what rank is for." Jack smiled, but it didn't reach his eyes.

"Benton, just think about it." Deming winked at Hannah, making her believe maybe, if they worked on him, they might push this idea down the road.

"We have two bad choices right now," Hannah said. "The perp either kills again, or he fades into the ether. We can't just wait around hoping."

"She's right," Gilroy said.

Hannah's gaze clashed with Jack's, but what she saw in his eyes stopped her cold.

Jack was scared.

Chapter 17

He could lose her again.

She'd been pregnant when he left her. *Pregnant.* Oh, how he wished he'd known. It would have given him the excuse to stay. Instead, he'd run, all to protect his pride. Jack blamed his screwed-up childhood, but found no consolation in the excuse. Discovering he was a father was triggering old fears. What if he became *his* father? Who would protect Hannah and Ellen from him?

Jack didn't know what to think, but he held onto the one thing he knew was true. He loved Hannah, and wanted to be a good father to his daughter. He clutched that truth like a talisman and hoped it would lead him to make the right decisions.

That night, their drive home was silent.

As they passed the uniformed policemen guarding the entrance of her brownstone, Jack exchanged pleasantries with the officers, but was distracted. He was too busy castigating himself, worrying that Hannah's silence on the drive here meant she'd decided her future didn't include him. When Mrs. Branaghan answered the door on the first knock and they collected the baby, he was still worrying. Then he and Hannah trudged upstairs to their apartment, exhausted and hungry, and it became impossible to worry about anything but his daughter.

Ellen was fussy and screaming. Tiny little screams of misery. Jack's mind cleared of everything but that. Walking down the hall, he held the baby out to Hannah, panicking, thinking he'd somehow broken her, but Hannah shook her head, refusing to save him.

"Babies cry," she said, smiling softly, pulling the apartment's key from her pocket. "Being a parent means weathering the storm." She opened the door and stepped inside.

Jack quickly followed, sensitive to the other tenants hearing little Ellen's cries. It wasn't that she was loud. She was *maybe* twenty pounds, so basically *tiny*, as was her voice box and lung capacity, but the *pitch* of her cries set him on edge. It made stopping her cries paramount to any other priority. *Any other priority.* He kicked the door closed behind them and lifted Ellen up and down, careful not to strain her little neck but desperate to distract her.

"She's not happy," he said, and hated the uncertainty in his tone.

Hannah threw her jacket over the back of the couch and approached them, her expression one of unconcern. "You're doing fine, Jack. She's tired, like us. If I don't sleep soon, I'm gonna start crying, too."

"Not funny." He didn't think he could handle two women crying.

Jack draped the baby over his shoulder, and watched as Hannah disappeared into her bedroom. He thought to follow, but didn't want to come across as stalkerish, or give the impression he wanted to hand off this screaming child. *Now.* He didn't. It's just…he didn't know what the hell he was doing here, and wanted Hannah's moral support. She was the expert.

His daughter's cries escalated.

Hannah came back quickly enough, having changed out of her work clothes into sweats. She'd tied her pale hair into a messy bun, so she looked like a college kid, except her sweatpants had the FBI logo on them, reminding Jack she'd been out of Quantico and in the field for seven years now.

"I think she wants her mother," he said. Jack held Ellen out again, but Hannah shook her head *again*. "Her diaper is dry, she's fed, so that means she's tired, but she has an hour before bedtime, so she can't sleep."

"Why?"

"She'll be up all night otherwise. Just distract her, Jack."

"How?" He lifted Ellen so they were eyeball to eyeball, but it didn't lessen Ellen's tirade. He blew on her face, and other than blinking a few times, and kicking her feet a bit, it had no effect. She was pissed. "Her cries are freaking me out."

"Yeah." Hannah stepped to his side, smiling serenely at their daughter. "I think that's a biological imperative thing. Mother Nature didn't take anything for granted. She wants us to care about our babies, so she designed them that way." Hannah's lower lip jutted out, and she made cooing noises to Ellen. "Will you listen to her? She's acting like the world is coming to an end."

Jack could relate. He'd broken into a sweat and no matter what he did—jostling, pacing, cooing like a fool—Ellen kept crying. Out of options, Jack kept pacing, though at this point, it was more about calming himself down rather than any response he was receiving from Ellen. In fact, all his efforts seemed only to affect the quantity of air pushed through her voice box. Bouncing her on his shoulder made her cries come out in oscillating waves, so he swayed in place instead, though it didn't lessen her cries.

Hannah seemed sympathetic, and from the looks of her, Ellen's cries were wearing her down, also. She winced when Ellen hit a particularly strident note, yet she remained sitting on the couch, looking half dead with weariness.

Hannah pulled out a leather-bound scrapbook from under the coffee table, and set it on top. Then she patted the couch's cushion next to her.

"Sit. I want to show you this." She raised her voice to be heard over Ellen's cries. Jack sat, laying Ellen between them. Only after he loosened his tie and stripped off his suit jacket did he feel as if he could breathe again.

"What's that?" He indicated the book.

It was as if they were starting their relationship from scratch. Which felt beyond odd, because here they were, living together again, and they shared a baby. Yet times like this made him feel as if they were strangers.

He studied her, sitting there, smiling at their daughter. She was different. Not completely, but… He kept coming back to her earlier confession, when she said he'd broken her. He believed her, and it was as if she'd been put back together differently than her original model. Stronger in some places, but more delicate in others. He couldn't, in all honesty, say he *knew* Hannah anymore, though Ellen's existence made that somehow unimportant. Whoever Hannah was now, he wanted her and she got a blank check from him, because without Hannah, nothing else made sense in Jack's life.

"It's a photo album." Hannah leaned over and kissed Ellen's forehead. "Hey *pookie*, sweetie pie, did you miss Mommy today? I missed you. Yes, I did. I did." She kissed her again and Ellen's crying settled to discontent.

"I knew she just wanted her mother." Jack was relieved, but felt a bit disgruntled, wondering how long it would take Ellen to love him, too.

The baby scrunched up her face and there was a rumble in her diaper. "Oh, you had a bellyache?" Hannah chuckled. "Guess who is about to change his first diaper?" She gently tapped Ellen's nose. "Daddy. Yes, that's who. Daddy."

Daddy.

He was a special agent in the Federal Bureau of Investigation, trained at Quantico, an expert in hand-to-hand combat, knives, and a variety of handguns and other weaponry, yet this bundle of joy might as well have been an IED that was about to blow. Jack was ashamed to admit it, even to himself, but Ellen scared the hell out of him. Hearing himself referred to as Daddy, though, gave him the courage to tackle the dreaded diaper, because daddies change diapers, they hold crying babies, they're loved unconditionally. He wanted to be Ellen's daddy in a big way. He wanted Hannah to be his wife.

Hannah reached under the couch and pulled out a quilted changing pad, diaper, and a pop-up wipes dispenser, and arranged them on the coffee table next to the photo album. Then she looked at him. When he just looked back at her, she laughed, shaking her head.

"What are you thinking?" he said.

Her amusement reminded him of the Hannah he'd known before, and for a moment, he wondered how she'd react if she knew what he had planned for her. What would she say if he knelt on one knee, right now, and confessed his dreams of their future? Would she clam up, or be embarrassed *for him*? Would she be confused? Or would she accept him and agree to a life together as a family? He had no idea, and knew a smart man would wait until he had a better idea of her response.

"Jack." She pressed her hand to his thigh, as if consoling him. It was ridiculous. Consoling him because he was changing a diaper? He wanted to scoff, and discount the difficulty of the task, but he didn't want to denigrate this moment, either. "You can do this," she said, referring to the diaper change, he was sure.

When he opened his mouth to explain he was okay with the diaper change, he instead felt a confession press against the back of his throat, so he shut up and swallowed it whole. But he *wanted* to tell Hannah how he felt. He *wanted* to take the chance that she'd embrace him and his hopes for their future. The only thing stopping him was that he was mid–diaper change. Not a romantic choice for a declaration of love and commitment.

Ellen was wiggling, kicking her heels. Hannah opened the wipes dispenser and turned to him, expectant. "Jack?" she said.

"I'm ready," he said, wondering if some part of her understood he was talking about more than the diaper change. *I'm ready to trust you with my heart, Hannah Cambridge. Are you ready to accept it?*

Hannah smiled, her heart on her sleeve, looking at him like she used to. Like she loved him. "Prove it," she said.

Challenge accepted. Jack rolled up his sleeves, and took a moment to brace himself.

Hannah snorted in amusement, and then outright laughed. "The diaper isn't getting less ripe, Jack."

"I'm doing it. I'm doing it." He unsnapped the onesie and wished he'd paid more attention to how they'd been snapped, because it occurred to him that he'd have to put this outfit back together when he was done. The diaper came off quickly enough, but he learned too late that he should have wiped Ellen's tiny bottom before putting the replacement diaper under her. Hannah's warning came too late. By then, he'd soiled the pad, her onesie and the new diaper. Ellen eventually had to be stripped to the skin, and the whole process started all over again.

Ellen was not happy.

She howled. Hannah struggled not to laugh, so much so her eyes teared up. She cooed to Ellen, telling her to cut her daddy some slack, but Ellen remained unsympathetic. By the time the baby was changed, a new outfit donned, both she and Jack were inconsolable. He'd sweated clear through his shirt.

Hannah picked up the infant and paced the living room, cooing and singing sweetly into Ellen's ear while Jack recovered, slumped on the sofa. A few minutes later, the baby was asleep in her arms, and Jack was relieved beyond measure. Impressed, but mostly relieved. Hannah, however, was not pleased.

"I don't have the heart to wake her up," she said.

Jack took the news with a wince. "Why would you do that?"

"It's too early. She'll wake in the middle of the night. No one will get any sleep."

"I'll get up with her," Jack said. "I'm trained to go without sleep."

He could tell Hannah wanted to laugh, but was refraining. He wished she wouldn't. He'd take her laughing any day, even if it was at his expense. He followed her into Ellen's nursery, enjoying the cheerful decorations of white and yellow. It was girly, and adorable, and assured him that Hannah had done right by their girl.

After she laid Ellen in the crib, she turned on the sheep-shaped night-light, then turned off the overhead light. Neither spoke again until they left the room. "We were interrupted and I didn't get to show you something," she said.

"The photo album," he said.

She nodded, and then climbed on the couch, tucking her legs beneath her as she pulled the leather photo album onto the couch between them.

The album was filled with pictures of them, mostly selfies, mostly in D.C. in the apartment.

"I wanted Ellen to know her father, so I've been slowly putting this together." She flipped through the pages, smiling, and pressing a finger on this photo or that. There weren't many of them, reminding him that their relationship had been a secret, so there had been few photo ops. At the time, he'd told himself it was to protect Hannah and his relationship, but he now knew it was more about protecting his pride. If she left him, people would know, and from the moment she'd said yes to their first date, he knew she'd leave him eventually.

"Here it is." She drew her fingertips over a grainy black-and-white ultrasound photo. "This was taken at eight weeks gestation. I should have told you then, but... Well, I didn't. This one," she pointed at another photo to its right, "at eighteen weeks. This one was tough, because you were..." She glanced at him. "Not there." She ran her finger over the outline of Ellen's little jaw. "She looked like you even then." She smiled. "I have a lot of ultrasound photos because Ellen had a tough time inside me. They had to keep checking her."

His baby in vitro. Speechless, Jack suffered a wave of regret that he'd missed so much. It had him struggling to keep his composure. Hannah put the scrapbook on his lap so he could get a better look. From her expression, he could tell she was so caught up in the joy of sharing, that judging his reaction was the last thing on her mind, so he did his best to get over himself, and just apologize. Again. She'd earned it a million times over.

"I'm sor—" His voice broke. Clearing his throat, he tried again. "I'm sorry. I didn't know."

She nodded, keeping her attention on the photos. "I tried to tell you that night."

"The night I left."

"Died."

His stomach sank. "Died. I'm sorry." He traced his finger along the outline of his baby's photo. "Is she sucking her thumb?"

Hannah smiled, nodding. "They say it's pretty common." Her smile faded as she met his gaze. "I had a lot of time to think in the hospital. Being pregnant has a way of prioritizing life. Rumor has it Mrs. Pepperidge suffered four stillborn babies. That she named the ones who made it past twenty weeks. They even have birth certificates, death certificates, too." Hannah chewed on her lower lip, not meeting his eyes. "I was lucky. I got Ellen instead."

Jack stood. "I need a drink. You?"

She nodded absently, returning her attention to the photo album. "There's beer in the fridge."

He wanted something stronger, but wasn't about to complain. Jack escaped to the kitchen, struggling with his guilt, desperate to see a way past his mistakes. It was as if the woman he loved, the life he wanted, was behind a wall, and the wall was made up of stuff he didn't want to deal with. He grabbed two beers from the refrigerator and then went in search of a bottle opener, tugging drawers open until he tugged one drawer with too much force and it fell to the floor, spilling everything. He spied the bottle opener among the fallen.

He saw Hannah leaning against the kitchen door's casement as he gathered everything, and then slid the drawer back in place.

"You okay?" she said.

He grimaced, shaking his head. "I want to howl," he said, "pound the snot out of someone, or at the very least destroy some furniture. I have a ball of rage or fear in the pit of my stomach—not sure which—and my head is in a place I can barely stand."

She approached him, touching his arm. Jack saw her worry, and immediately felt bad for laying his crap on her shoulders. She had enough going on. "Why?" she said.

"I screwed up, Hannah, and I don't know how to make it right." He pulled her into his arms, grateful when she returned his embrace. "How can you ever forgive me?"

Hannah snuggled deeper in his arms, rubbing her face against his chest. "I already have."

He leaned back, searching her face. "Excuse me?"

Her smile was sad, and she looked tired. "I don't have the energy to stay angry at you. Parenting an infant takes everything. I've got nothing left for grudges." She leaned against him again, reaching up and wrapping her arms around his shoulders, burying her face in his neck. "Jack, a part of me died when I thought you'd been murdered. Now I'm…I'm confused, I guess. I don't know what to think."

He kissed the top of her head. "I can't even imagine what you went through."

He felt her head nodding, rubbing against his jaw. "I want it in my past. I can't wait until this part of my life is a faded memory."

"Yeah?"

"Yeah," she said. "Because it means I've survived. You, too."

He cupped her cheek and kissed her lips, gently first, and then he became more demanding, sweeping his tongue inside her mouth. Hannah arched against him, moaning sweetly, clutching at him. Her ardency triggered his, then Jack was cradling her in his arms, never once breaking their kiss, hurrying out of the kitchen into the bedroom. He didn't stop until he had her on the bed, struggling out of her clothes.

He stripped off his shirt, unbuckled his belt, searching her expression for signs of hesitancy; afraid to see it, but more afraid to miss a cue to stop. Hannah seemed as eager as he, though, stripping quickly, making it hard to concentrate on anything else. She was the one who pulled his boxer briefs down, allowing him to kick them to the side before joining her on the bed.

"Hannah." Naked, body and soul, he lay next to her, hovering, caressing her body as he searched her gaze. "I can't get enough of you." He kissed her neck, inhaling her scent, feeling his hunger grow. "I touch you, and always want more. I kiss you, and never want it to end."

He caressed her belly, imagining her pregnant with Ellen. She must have picked up on his thoughts, because she covered his hand and smiled.

"Even when I thought you were dead," she said, "I had a part of you inside me. I had Ellen. It devastated me when I thought I'd lose her, because it would have been like you dying all over again." Her chin quivered, and tears were poised on her lashes.

"Please don't cry, Hannah," he whispered, kissing the tears that spilled over on her cheeks. "I'm here, and I'm not leaving again."

Hannah took a deep, shuddering breath. "I'm not looking for pity, Jack, and I'd never keep Ellen from you, so don't feel as if this needs to be more than it is."

"Pity? What?" Confusion and surprise fought for dominance, but then she pulled his head down to her, kissing him with gusto. Then he wasn't thinking at all.

Her hands were hot, running over his chest, down his belly, cupping his arousal. Her lips were warm and wet, and he wanted them on him. Jack deepened their kiss until she was moaning and pulling him over her, wrapping her legs around his waist. He entered her slowly, drawing out the experience until she was the one arching her hips upward, seeking more of him. And then they were one, moving inexorably toward the same goal, but as far as Jack was concerned, he had it all. Hannah. She'd never make love to him like this if she didn't love him. *This had to mean she loved him.*

He cupped her breast, drew his lips down her neck, tasting the spot where her racing pulse revealed her emotions. His need demanded he take her hard and fast, to possess her completely, but he forced himself to move slowly, to gentle Hannah's frantic movements that threatened he'd find his release first. He didn't want this moment to end that soon, because making love with Hannah was not something he could ever again take for granted.

He ran his tongue along her delicate earlobe, teasing her nipple with his thumb, nipping at her lips. He felt her fingers caress the hard ridges of muscles down his back, and they sent a cascade of tremors through his body. She moaned, as if she'd lost control, which made Jack lose it. Then suddenly he was thrusting hard, sheathing himself deep inside her wet heat, pulling tiny gasps of pleasure from her lips.

Then Hannah shouted his name, tipped him over the precipice toward orgasm, and they crested together. It seemed to last forever, and all the while, Hannah whispered his name.

The moment felt like heaven, a vindication of his hopes. She still desired him. She'd had his child. Maybe that would be enough for her to take a chance on him again. He wouldn't ask her for more, but he could hope more was in their future. One day. Until then, he'd take what he could get.

"Dammit!" Hannah hadn't even caught her breath before she pushed away from him and jumped off the bed.

She was mad. Jack's heart sank as he prepared himself for rejection.

Chapter 18

"No, no, no, no," she moaned. She raced into the bathroom, trying to control her fear. They hadn't used a condom this time.

When she stepped into the shower, she told herself the odds of becoming pregnant were practically nonexistent, but it didn't slow her racing heart. She'd heard stories of people having sex *once* and greeting a newborn nine months later.

She stepped under the spray and thoroughly washed herself, struggling to calm down. When Jack surprised her by stepping into the tub, embracing her, she froze, and then she wanted to hit him, but he was holding her so tightly she couldn't move. Then his kiss pressed against her temple, and her whole body sagged against him.

"I know I should stop trying to keep you, Hannah, but I can't. Please, don't regret this," he said. The warm spray trailed down their bodies, making them slick to the touch.

She realized that Jack didn't understand why she was upset. He wasn't thinking about the life they might have just created. She shook her head, sighing. He was talking about something else, something equally as important. "Jack, we had sex. Sex between us has always been off the charts, but desire didn't stop you from leaving last time." She lifted her chin, meeting his gaze. "I have to protect myself. Protect Ellen." Yeah, she understood the irony of her words. She'd just failed to protect herself from this man, and risked pregnancy. She was afraid protecting herself from Jack would always be impossible.

He lowered his head and pressed a tender kiss on her lips, then readjusted his arms and pulled her more intimately to his body. It made her feel safe, loved, and wanted. "I promise I'll be better," he said. "I'll be a better man."

"Oh, Jack." He broke her heart.

"I'll share my feelings more."

She tasted the water on his chest, kissed his neck, licked the saltiness off him. "You have no feelings."

Jack laughed, but there was pain in the sound. "I wish." He caressed her back, lowering his hand to cup her bottom. The warm water sprayed down on them, soothing her tired muscles and overwrought nerves. "It's because I loved you that I ran."

"Excuse me?" She pushed out of his arms.

Jack wouldn't release her, so she leaned back, studying his expression. The shower's spray only covered Jack now and she was getting cold. "I was afraid," he said. "There. I've said it."

"Why would loving me make you run?" None of this made sense, but she was cold, so she leaned against Jack again, sharing his warmth as she blinked against the water's spray. "You drive me crazy."

"You were the one." Jack rubbed his lips against her temple, dropping kisses here and there. "And that scared the hell out of me. I thought I could never have you."

"Why?" Hannah pushed off from Jack and told herself not to care that she missed his touch already.

Jack turned off the water and threw open the shower curtain. He wrapped her in a towel and tugged her back into his arms. "I knew what we had couldn't last. You were already losing patience with me. Admit it, Hannah. The weeks before I left, all we did was fight."

"I was scared. I was pregnant. I wasn't sure you'd want a baby, or would stick around if you'd learned I was pregnant, and I knew I would show soon." Hannah had already been three months pregnant when he'd 'died.' Shivering in the arms of the love of her life, waiting for a truth she wasn't sure she could handle, she felt as if she were dangling over a precipice of sharp stakes, holding onto a shredding vine.

"I didn't know any of that," Jack said. "And you know running is my MO. You knew that. It's not something I'm proud of, but truthfully, I thought I was doing you a favor, giving you an out."

Hannah glared at him. "Well, you made sure we didn't last when you ran off, you jerk." She stepped onto the chilly tile and hurried into the bedroom.

"Do you think I don't know that? I get it. I'm an ass, but admit it, Hannah. You had been thinking about leaving me for weeks by then." He secured a towel around his hips. "You never told me you loved me and I was crazy for you—"

"*Your leaving is my fault?*" His towel was riding low, and any moment Hannah expected it to fall to his feet. It was disconcerting—and arousing. She dried off and slipped her sweats back on, hoping clothes would serve as a barrier between them, maybe deter her from doing something stupid. She noticed the rumpled bed. Something stupid *again.*

"*No.* It wasn't your fault," he said. "It was my baggage getting in the way of my life again."

"I never gave you any indication I was anything but deeply in love with you. Sure, I never said it, but I was waiting for you to say it. You're the guy. Guys are supposed to say it first."

Jack threw his hands up. "Well, how am I supposed to know that?"

Hannah was speechless. Then just as quickly, she had more to say than air in her lungs. "Have you ever watched a movie? Read a book? The guy *always* says it first!"

"You can't be serious!" He looked flummoxed.

"Jack, you wouldn't even admit we were living together! No one at work even guessed!"

"Because I had to work there! How exactly was I supposed to show my face after you dumped me?"

She couldn't believe what he was saying. "But I wasn't going to dump you. I loved you, you idiot!"

Jack's expression crumpled. "As soon as I boarded the plane that night, I saw my mistake, but it was too late. I'd committed to the job. I'd assumed Goodwin had said my good-byes, and that you'd never forgive me. I ran and didn't look back."

"A phone call, Jack. All it would have taken was a phone call and I would have waited for you forever." Betrayal burned sticky and hot, and try as she might, she couldn't return to the feeling of peace she'd had when they'd had sex. He held his palms up, appearing to want to placate her. Hannah felt that moment had come and gone.

"I came back for you, Hannah."

Maybe. She couldn't hold him responsible for taking her job; someone had to, so it might as well be him, but she had her doubts about everything else. "Remember what I said about holding grudges?" she said. He nodded. "Well, I'm revisiting that decision." Jack's shoulders slumped. "Don't think sex changes anything either, just because we, well, *you know*, doesn't mean everything else goes away." She'd have sex with him. Hell, she'd live for sex with him, but it was suddenly clear to her that she couldn't take him back. Too much had changed. She wasn't the Hannah he knew.

He stood up straight, strode toward her with such purpose, she took a step back. When he was mere inches in front of her, he leaned in until his breath warmed her face. "Don't think sex *doesn't* change anything." His gaze dropped to her mouth. She licked her lips, and lifted her chin to meet his kiss halfway.

Their phones beeped. Hannah blinked, saw Jack's gaze cloud over with speculation. They hurried to their phones. A text from Charlie Foulkes. "There's been a break in the case," she said.

Jack threw his phone on the bed and grabbed clean clothes out of the closet. "Foulkes said he wants to meet with the lieutenant, too. Did he say anything else to you?"

"No. All the text said was to meet him in the incident room." She glanced at the clock. "Do you think they found DNA evidence on Buntle?"

"Pray it's not another body. Hurry up and get dressed." All traces of humanity were wiped from Jack's expression. He was a machine. An FBI investigator.

And that's how it's done, she thought. Compartmentalization. The train wreck of her life was on hold, would always be on hold, when there was a break in a case.

Hannah called Mrs. Branaghan and Natalie, asking them to come upstairs. By the time they'd arrived she was dressed, her wet hair clipped back, but she was still feeling disgruntled. They noticed. Mrs. Branaghan's and Natalie's curious stares went unanswered, however, though Hannah didn't fool herself into thinking they couldn't figure it out on their own. She had man troubles.

And she and Jack had that *just had sex* look. It was embarrassing, especially since she probably came across as pathetic in this scenario. The guy abandons her, and as soon as he swings back into town, she's going at it with him like they're rabbits. Her pride was stinging as she opened the apartment door to leave.

"I'm ovulating," she said, loud enough to be heard by all. As soon as the words left her mouth, she realized she wasn't sorry she'd said it. It was time for Jack to understand a few things, too. Like unprotected sex creates babies. "So there's a chance you just knocked me up again, *Jack*." Mouths dropped open and then clamped shut, and one of them was Jack's.

"Good," he snapped, then hurried out of the apartment.

Now it was Hannah's mouth that dropped open. Natalie and Mrs. Branaghan's laughter followed her as she hurried after him, past the smiling protective detail, and out onto the sidewalk. By then, her face felt beet red as she realized *everyone* in the precinct would soon hear the news.

When they were on the curb, he seemed repentant. "Okay, I deserved that."

"Damn right." She wasn't sure how to react to his parting shot that he was happy she might be pregnant, so she left it hanging there, promising herself she'd revisit it when she gathered her courage.

That she found herself smiling during the whole drive to New Sudbury precinct made no sense. That she was still smiling as she entered the incident room made even less sense. Her smile died when she saw Charlie hovering by Lieutenant Pepperidge's office door. Pepperidge poked his head out and waved her and Jack into the room. Neither man seemed happy. In fact, they looked downright disturbed. Whatever the news was, it wasn't good.

Chapter 19

"Tell them." Pepperidge pulled out a bottle of scotch from his top drawer and poured an inch into four half-pint mason jars, like the ones his wife sent in with candies, all wrapped up in bows.

Charlie Foulkes was the first to imbibe. He appeared to be taking a moment to gather his thoughts, making Jack believe whatever the news was, it was a bombshell. "We found new forensic evidence in the Buntle case."

Jack didn't know much about the forensic pathologist, but he seemed a straight shooter, and if he'd been best friends with Deming's brother, it was as good a reference as any man could ask for. Deming's brother died years ago, and from all accounts he'd been a saint.

"*And*?" Jack said. When Charlie hesitated, he forced himself to be patient. His scotch went down quickly and smooth. "Enough foreplay, Foulkes," he said. "Spill it." Hannah sat in one of the two chairs before Pepperidge's desk. She eagerly received the report Charlie handed her.

"It's a shocker," Charlie said, shrugging. "Can't pretend that it isn't. We found Ferguson's print on the stanza in Buntle's grave." Charlie allowed them a moment to process his news.

Boom. Jack couldn't believe it, and Hannah's features reflected her shock, too. But evidence was evidence. Denial would only waste time. They had to follow it where it led them.

"He finally made a mistake." Jack licked his lips, tasting the scotch. When he thought about it, Ferguson did hit all the perp attributes. He knew Hannah well, maybe better than anyone else in the precinct, and he was the one who discovered the email on her computer. He had extensive connections within the department, was local. So, yeah. He seemed good for it.

"You can't be serious." Hannah glared at Jack. "Test the paper again." She dropped the file on the desk in disgust. "It's a mistake. Has anyone spoken to Paddy?"

"Paddy?" Jack frowned. He was "Ferguson" yesterday.

Pepperidge shook his head. "No."

"I made a point of asking him if he'd touched anything at the crime scene when I got the tests back," Charlie said. "He said he didn't, so his prints got there prior to him arriving at the crime scene."

Hannah searched the forensic expert's eyes. "This is Paddy, Charlie. You can't think he did this." It was obvious to Jack she didn't want to believe the evidence.

"Charlie is just doing his job, Cambridge," Pepperidge said, as Charlie shifted from foot to foot, clearly uncomfortable.

Pepperidge exchanged weighted looks with Jack, and it was obvious the lieutenant was putting Hannah's behavior on his shoulders. After all, Jack kept her on the case. Well, Jack was about to ask Ferguson what the hell was going on. And he couldn't wait.

"He's home with two plainclothes officers watching his place," Pepperidge said. "If he makes a move, we'll know it and bring him in." He saluted Jack with his glass before upending it. "This is your case. A fingerprint isn't a conviction, so it's your call how you want this to play out."

Hannah grabbed her jelly jar off the desk. A big swallow had her coughing and grimacing. She put the glass back on the desk, spilling the scotch in her haste. "We need to talk to him."

Pepperidge glanced at Jack. They all knew if they made it official, it would go into the detective's permanent record. "IA will want in on this, too. We move on him now, it's going to be a damn circus."

"You're ignoring the real problem." Hannah glared at them all, forgetting they weren't the ones who put Ferguson's print on the evidence. "Paddy Ferguson isn't our guy, and while you're throwing our resources at him, the real killer is still out there. Whoever is leaking our intel to the press will get ahold of this, too, and the public will let down their guard." Hannah leaned toward the lieutenant, her face flushed. "You know him better than any of us, Lieutenant. You saw our reports. He's clean. He alibied. You said it yourself."

Jack's mind whirled with whys and wherefores for Hannah's defense of Ferguson, all of which he wanted to dismiss, but found he couldn't. "We can't ignore evidence, Hannah, no matter how much you like the guy." Yeah, that was jealousy tinging his words, and he hated it, not that he thought Hannah was interested in the guy. Not anymore, anyway. But the detective certainly gave the signal he'd be receptive to a relationship with Hannah. Or *anything* with Hannah.

"Charlie." Hannah seemed intent on ignoring Jack. "How many prints were found on the page?"

"All we need is one." Charlie put his empty glass on the desk. "And one is what I found. A perfect thumbprint." He turned to the lieutenant. "I don't know if this means anything, but it's also the first stanza altered by a victim's DNA. Something to think about. It had Buntle's bloody fingerprints all over it." Charlie made motions that he was about to leave. "I'll have an official report on your desk in the morning. Right now, though, I have to go home. I'm finishing a twenty-hour shift and need a shower. Some sleep." He left without another word.

Jack felt sick. Personally, he barely knew Ferguson, but the people he'd interviewed about him, his record in the Army, at the BPD, all of that didn't lie. Hannah was right. Something was off. Ferguson couldn't have fooled them all. But the evidence couldn't be ignored, either. "He's strong enough to have lifted Buntle into the tomb. He had inside information on the case as liaison detective. It was his thumbprint, Hannah. Right now, short of new evidence coming to light, he's looking good for prime suspect."

"No. This is a chain-of-evidence mistake," Hannah said. "I know it. Or something equally stupid that we haven't figured out yet."

Pepperidge nodded. "We'll investigate. That's what we do. But we have a responsibility to put aside loyalties and seek out the truth, Cambridge. If this is a mistake, we'll find out."

"Except," Hannah said. "He's innocent and we're wasting time."

"You don't know that," Jack said. "You hope it, but don't know it. Keep that in mind, please." He hated that he sounded unfeeling, but she had to stay on task. "He's the first real suspect we've had since the killings began, and he's looking good for it. He knows you enough to recognize your letter to the advice column. Do you remember confiding in him? Or if not confiding, maybe letting slip some information? Maybe over drinks after work?" Just the idea of that hurt, but Jack needed to know.

"What the hell are you suggesting?" Hannah stood, meeting Jack's suspicion head on.

"Maybe he followed you home." *Saw you with Ellen* was the implication. Jaw set, looking for a fight, Hannah was furious. He refused to back down. These were all reasonable conjectures. "Should we really ignore this evidence because you like the guy?"

Pepperidge sipped his scotch. "Other than the obvious reasons, Hannah, why do you think he's innocent?"

"Poetry." She spit the word at Jack, and made him feel like he'd done something wrong. "Ferguson hates poetry, hates the idea of it. He's not our guy, but someone wants us to think he is. I want to know how the perp got Ferguson's print on the page." Hannah took another sip of scotch and slammed the glass back on the desk, sloshing the remaining liquor.

"Maybe the perp got careless," Jack said, still not willing to abandon hard evidence over hope. "Maybe Ferguson got careless."

Hannah scowled. "Screw you." She turned her back to him. "Lieutenant, bring Ferguson in, but don't tell him what's going on. He's a good man. If he knew what you two were thinking, we could lose him, and we need him on this case. He figured out we had a serial killer. Remember?"

Pepperidge frowned. "You know that's a strike against him, Cambridge. Right?"

"And if Ferguson is half the detective I think he is," Jack said, "he'd be agreeing with me." Hannah was completely blind to even the possibility of Ferguson's guilt, but she was right about one thing. They needed Ferguson here, in interrogation, and he could care less if the detective was offended. Jack wanted to know how his fingerprint got on the killer's note.

Chapter 20

A half hour later, feeling warm and sleepy from the scotch, Hannah was relieved to see Ferguson walk into the darkened incident room. She'd convinced the lieutenant and Jack to allow her to speak with the detective alone first. They'd agreed to wait in Pepperidge's office. If, and this was Jack's requirement, *if* she had her gun drawn and hidden, but at the ready. They'd agreed having the Glock in her top drawer was adequate *only* if she left the drawer ajar.

"Ferguson." She waved him over. Her desk lamp illuminated his face, giving his pale skin a ghostly hue, which made her think she must be quite a sight with her pale hair and even paler skin. Ferguson's smile was soft, and his eyes inviting. If Jack hadn't come back to her, Hannah could see a world where she would have dated him, maybe made a life with him. The detective was a good man, and she refused to believe he could kill in cold blood.

"Hey, Hannah. What's up?" He looked around the room, peering into Pepperidge's office. "What are those two talking about?" He sank into the chair next to her desk and folded his hands on his belly. "It's late." The implication that this had better be good was there, but she knew it was all show. He was a smart guy. Something was going down and he knew he was in the middle of it.

"There's been a development. Charlie found forensic evidence linking the murders to a suspect."

Ferguson's stress faded in a blink of the eye. He leaned toward her, his eagerness pushing aside his earlier unasked questions. "About time."

"It's your fingerprint. They found it on Buntle's stanza." Not a flicker of anything. Just stillness. Then his body relaxed into his chair and his expression grew guarded.

Without turning his head, he glanced over his shoulder toward the lieutenant's office. "Whose idea was it to make you point man?"

"Mine." He nodded, as if he agreed with the decision in a purely academic way.

"If I'm your perp, what's to stop me from leaping over this desk and killing you?" He didn't hide his hurt, or his anger. Hannah lifted the gun from her drawer and placed it on the desktop.

"Let's not play games. Talk to me," she said. This was his chance to clear up any misconception so they could continue the search for the real killer.

"And say what? That I have no idea how my print got there?" He shook his head. "I didn't touch the paper. I'm not a rookie. And I'd have to be three sheets to the wind to touch a piece of solid evidence linked directly to the perp."

He didn't touch the paper. Crap. "Forensics says otherwise, so unless you're thinking someone stole your prints and transferred it to the paper, we have a problem."

"Doesn't seem like a problem from where you're sitting," he said. "You have a prime suspect now."

"It's a huge detour, Paddy. I'll have to figure out how the perp framed you before I can get anyone to look for someone else, so spill it. Did you touch the evidence?"

"No. I didn't." He waved Jack and the lieutenant into the incident room. "You two might as well come out so I don't have to repeat myself. The answer is *no*," he said, "I am not the Mercy Killer. I'll take a polygraph, whatever." The lieutenant and Jack approached. Hannah discreetly holstered her gun.

"I don't think you're our perp," Hannah said.

Ferguson indicted the lieutenant and Jack. "Who gave the order to watch my house?" He smirked when he saw Jack's surprise. "This is my turf. Those patrolmen have my back. Did you really think I wouldn't find out?"

"I gave the order. Would you have done anything differently?" the lieutenant said. Ferguson shrugged.

Jack stood next to Hannah. "How'd your print get on the stanza?" he said.

"I don't know." Ferguson exchanged glances with Hannah.

She nudged the stanza toward the detective. It was in its plastic evidence bag, logged and signed out from the evidence locker. "I want you to look at it, really look at it, and tell me if you recognize the paper." Ferguson acted as if he didn't want to touch the bag. He glared at it, as if the paper were the one framing him, and not the perp, who was too connected for all their peace of mind. "Pick it up, Paddy. Look at it."

Jack gave her a look, which she supposed meant he didn't like her using the detective's first name. After a repressive glare, Hannah ignored him and opened the clear plastic evidence bag herself, using a Kleenex to prevent leaving prints behind. It smelled of dried blood and had grown brittle.

Grudgingly, the detective peered at it. Then he tugged Hannah's wrist to the side to put the paper directly under the desk lamp. After a moment, he released her and sat back in his chair. "It looks like regular copier paper to me. The type I see every day coming out of Vivian's printer."

Pepperidge leaned, peering at the paper, and slipped on his reader glasses to peer some more. After a moment, he sighed. "This is getting us nowhere."

Hannah wasn't willing to give up. "We need Charlie to tell us where this paper came from. There must be *types* of copier paper. Maybe we could—"

"Stop," Jack said.

Hannah wasn't willing to be put off. "No, I'm right on this. We need—"

Ferguson shook his head. "The only copier paper I've touched in the last year has come from that printer." He pointed toward Vivian's desk. Hannah blinked, her mind racing in a million directions. She exchanged confused looks with Jack, who figured it out first.

"Our perp has access to this room," Jack said. "It doesn't clear Ferguson, but it widens the suspect list. A list we've already alibied."

"Ferguson's alibi checked out, too, but here we are," the lieutenant said. "He's the only one whose print is on the paper. Other than the victim's. Does this mean we're supposed to add Vivian to our suspect list?"

That never occurred to Hannah. "Of course not." Then suddenly she wasn't so sure. All the circumstantial evidence that damned Ferguson now damned anyone who had access to Vivian's printer. "It could be the cleaning staff. The mail room people. *Anyone* who has access to this room."

"This is bullshit. Our perp is playing us," Jack said.

"Finally," Hannah said. "You're seeing reason." If they couldn't trust each other, there was no way they'd catch the killer.

"We need the team on this," Jack said. "I'll call Deming and Gilroy." He glanced at Ferguson, his mind made up, but his reluctance evident. "You call Vivian." Everyone exchanged worried glances while the calls were made. Jack got through to Deming and Gilroy quickly. Ferguson kept getting Vivian's voice mail.

"She's not answering," Ferguson said.

Pepperidge swore. "Find her and get her in here. Keep it quiet. This has the potential to blow up in our faces."

"Hannah and I will go to Vivian's house." Jack indicated the exit, trying to rush her out of there. She instinctively wanted to oppose his high-handed attitude, but she was anxious to find Vivian, too. She had a bad feeling in her gut, so she handed the evidence bag back to the lieutenant, and caught Ferguson's glance. He was watching her, revealing more regret and longing than she was comfortable seeing. It didn't take a genius to see he'd written her off as a lost cause, and she wished she could argue the point.

But she loved Jack. Dammit. She did. For better or worse, she loved Jack.

They left the building quickly. The chill of the night air got her trembling. Rather, that's what Hannah blamed it on. She was nervous, and everything felt off. Maybe it was the scotch. Maybe it was the meeting they'd just had. Whatever, Vivian AWOL was making her nervous.

She kept calling Vivian, and reached her voice mail again and again. She called her again when she hopped into Jack's Camaro, and again when they were blocks from her apartment. The tech didn't answer her doorbell, or their repeated knocking. Close neighbors didn't know where she was, so Hannah's unease grew stronger. It was late. Jack was scowling as they got back into his car.

"Where the hell is she?" He didn't put the keys in the ignition, so it made Hannah think he was willing to wait for Vivian's arrival.

"She's the type to stay home watching chick flicks, or read a book. This late, she should be home." *Something was wrong.* "Maybe we should go back," she glanced behind her, studying Vivian's front door through the car's rear window. "We should break into her apartment. Maybe she's unconscious." Or worse.

"Not without a warrant."

Hannah adjusted herself in the passenger seat to face him, uncomfortable with his tone. "A warrant? Why?"

"What's the next stanza?" he said.

Hannah shook her head, irritated that he was changing the subject. That's when she noticed more than a few drapes pulled aside, revealing residents watching them from nearby apartment windows. "My life is insane," she mumbled.

"The stanza, Hannah." They were both allowing the obvious to remain unsaid. It was paper from Vivian's printer. If Ferguson looked good for the perp, why not Vivian? Was her ladylike attitude a ruse hiding the evil of a serial killer? Hannah didn't want to believe it.

"I refuse to believe she's the perp." She sank deep in the car's seat.

"Hannah." He shook his head in amazement. "You have to separate your feelings from the evidence. She is, or she isn't. The evidence will

decide this, not our feelings. Recite the stanza, word for word, please. If she *is* the perp, she's probably using it right now to kill someone."

At first, she thought she'd misheard him. Then she slapped his arm. "You're crazy!"

"Hannah. The stanza."

"*Fine!*" She was so upset, she couldn't access the stanza from memory, so she pulled it up on her phone and read it. "'Seven more loves weep night and day, Round the tombs where my loves lay, And seven more loves attend each night, Around my couch with torches bright.'" She dropped her phone to her lap, and glared at Jack. "You can't think Vivian is our killer. She's skittish, romantic, couldn't hurt a fly."

"Our perp is skittish, romantic and doesn't watch as the victims die. She uses a poem to dictate their deaths."

Hannah scowled. "You thought Ferguson was the killer no more than a half hour ago."

"He's still a suspect. They all alibied at the times of death, but the perp isn't at the crime scene at the time of death, so we've been alibiing them for the wrong time frames."

Hannah folded her arms over her chest, glaring out the car's windshield. "Vivian isn't the Mercy Killer."

"Let's find her and prove it." He obviously wasn't in the mood to argue, and Hannah was overwhelmed with the possibility that he might be correct. The perp knew her, and there wasn't anyone in her life who she'd look at and think, *yeah, you could be a serial killer.* She was beginning to think Jack was correct. She had no business being on this investigation, because of all the team members, Vivian knew her the best. If she *was* the killer, Hannah should turn in her credentials.

The drive back to the precinct seemed to go on forever as Boston's streetlights cast ominous shadows over parked cars lining every curb. It was a sea of cheap Fords, Chevys, and a smattering of Hondas rusted by harsh New England weather.

"Try not to allow this to upset you," he said, glancing at her. He seemed angry, but she knew that was just how Jack acted when he thought she was upset. It upset him for her to be upset, so *he* got angry. Ugh. *Men.*

"Do you know what your problem is, Jack? You lack faith in people. You left me because you couldn't believe I loved you. You didn't trust me or my feelings."

He nodded, making no attempt to deny her accusation. "You never said you loved me."

"Would that have made a difference?" She watched his expression closely, but he kept his eyes on the road, his hands white-knuckling the steering wheel. "Well, Vivian will be cleared. Ferguson, all of them. They'll all be cleared. Again. I have faith." Jack needed to have his head shuffled. He was so wrongheaded about the simplest things, and if they ever stood a chance of having a future together, he needed to *change his ways*.

"Until then," he said, "we need to find Vivian, so recite the poem again."

Hannah repressed a primal scream at his obstinacy, but decided that in his tiny, messed-up way, she kind of saw how he was right. Kind of. Clearing Vivian freed them to find the real killer, so clear her they would. She opened her notepad on her phone and read the stanza aloud. "'Seven more loves weep night and day, Round the tombs where my loves lay, And seven more loves attend each night, Around my couch with torches bright.'" Hannah bit her lower lip, worrying the symbolism, struggling to see how it could help them. "'Around my couch with torches bright,'" she repeated. "Seven."

"'Seven more loves weep night and day.' What the hell does seven have to do with anything?" Jack said. Hannah thought the poem sounded strange coming from Jack's mouth. He had such a masculine tone and clipped cadence, he made it sound as if he were reciting Ikea instructions.

"'Round the tombs where my loves lay.'" Hannah arched a brow. "Sounds like us, doesn't it? You were dead, as dead as someone in a tomb, and I wept night and day."

"This is not about us." Jack took his eyes off the road long enough to throw her an anxious look.

"Isn't it? I was targeted because of you." As soon as the words left her mouth, she knew they weren't true. No one had known about her and Jack. It was the baby she'd feared losing, her and Jack's baby that put her on the killer's list. That's what her letter had focused on. She'd been positive she was about to lose her baby.

Jack didn't argue, and Hannah wished he would. She was in the mood for a fight. Her phone rang. "It's Ferguson." She hit Accept, and put it on speakerphone. "What have you got?"

"We pinged her phone. She's at Pomodoro's Bistro on Hanover Street. Hannah—"

"Oh, what a relief!" Hannah smiled at Jack, who frowned, shaking his head. "What?"

"It's midnight," Jack said. His grimace dampened her relief, as did his implication. It was unlikely Pomodoro's was open this late. "Ferguson? Where is Pomodoro's Bistro?" Jack said.

"That's what I'm trying to—Benton, Hannah. It's on the Freedom Trail," Ferguson said. "Cruisers are on-site and reporting the restaurant is on fire. You better hurry and get there. Hanover Street. The rest of us are en route."

Hannah's hand was shaking by the time she hung up. "'Around my couches with torches bright.'" She shook her head in a daze. "Pomodoro's Bistro is on fire." Hannah was thrown back in her seat as Jack hit the gas, driving the streets of Boston like the devil was on his ass.

They arrived fifteen minutes later. Hannah didn't wait for the car to come to a complete stop, but hit the ground running. EMTs were caring for victims. Patrons and servers wore reflective blankets and oxygen masks. She saw a gurney being wheeled into an ambulance and recognized Vivian's tweed suit jacket and skirt. Covered in soot, her purse resting on her stomach, she was unconscious.

Hannah flashed her credentials. "Special Agent Cambridge. Will she live?" They ignored her as they secured Vivian's gurney in the ambulance. Hannah jumped inside with them. "I'm coming." She saw Jack running toward the ambulance as the EMT closed them in, driving off. Her phone rang. She picked up and immediately pulled the phone from her ear. Jack was shouting.

"What the hell are you doing? Ferguson just pulled up with Deming. I'm getting reports that witnesses are saying the fire started at Vivian's table. She was with a man. I'm looking at him right now."

Vivian looked as if she was dying, and Hannah wanted to touch her, but the EMTs were hooking her up to IVs and monitors. It was frightening. "What's he saying?"

"Nothing, Hannah. He's dead. You have to know this means she could be our perp."

She shook her head, not willing to believe it. "She's unconscious, Jack. She's a victim here, too. We have to give her a chance to explain before we derail the investigation like this." Hannah ignored the irritated glances from the EMT.

Jack was silent for a moment, and then she heard his impatient sigh. "Which hospital are you heading to?" Hannah asked the EMT. The guy moved Vivian's arm to get better access to the IV. That nudged Vivian's purse to the ambulance's floor, at Hannah's feet.

"Mass General. We're five minutes out," the EMT said.

"Did you hear that? Mass General." She heard Jack's "yes" as she grabbed the purse. She rifled through it without a moment's hesitation, and quickly found a letter. "Hurry, Jack." It didn't take long to read it, and as every word processed in her mind, Hannah's heart beat a little slower. It broke a little more. When she finished, her hand holding the letter dropped to her lap. "Jack, I'm holding Vivian's confession. She's our killer."

"Read it to me."

Hannah wiped a tear with the back of her wrist, and forced herself to read. "'Dear Hannah, I am the Mercy Killer. I didn't intend to be. It just happened. I was the last, unknown submitter to the *Boston Globe*'s advice column. Mine was the broken heart, the jilted bride. The gentleman I'm dining with tonight is the man who destroyed my dreams. Is it wrong of me to make him suffer, too? Such a splendid death I designed for me. A flaming torch. The Freedom Trail. A serial killer. Much print will be expended dissecting my efforts. I don't begrudge those who went into hiding, but wish them well. You, also, Hannah. This is something I had to do. Please try to understand. "Seven more loves weep night and day, Round the tombs where my loves lay, And seven more loves attend each night, Around my couch with torches bright." I am seven. And I'm finally free. Sincerely, Vivian O'Grady.'"

There was silence on the line, and then Jack swore. "No, she's not. She's the sixth stanza."

"Maybe she's counting the guy that jilted her? Seventh victim."

Vivian's body began to shake, and then progressed to seizing. The EMT checked her vitals, then pumped a syringe of drugs into her IV bag. Then Vivian went still.

"She's crashing!" The young EMT straddled her chest.

"What's going on there?" Jack's shouts hurt her ear as the EMT performed chest compressions on Vivian.

"She's dying, Jack. I have to go." The letter was evidence, but now it had Hannah's tears on it. Carefully placing it back into its envelope, she gathered Vivian's belongings and put them back into the purse. Vivian flatlined twice in the next five minutes, but had a heartbeat when the ambulance arrived at the trauma entrance. EMTs wheeled her gurney into Mass General.

Hannah was the last person to leave the ambulance, and when she climbed out, she stood in the parking lot, feeling overwhelmed and faint. How had she missed the signs? Vivian had fooled her and the rest of the team. People had died because Hannah had been so blind, and those deaths were on her now.

Chapter 21

Hannah had said little to Jack since he found her in the ER waiting room. When the doctors declared Vivian stable, but unconscious, he put uniformed policemen on her door and convinced Hannah it was time to leave.

"Let's go home to Ellen," he said.

"No," Hannah said. "Ellen is safe with Natalie and Mrs. Branaghan. Take me back to the precinct."

It was late when they met up with the rest of the team in the incident room. Jack was worried about Hannah. She was beyond exhausted, pale, and distracted. He felt shell-shocked himself, and humbled. They looked like amateurs, because Vivian had fooled them all.

The ride up the elevator to homicide was silent, but when the doors opened, the department was lit up and noisy. Detectives and patrolmen mingled around a makeshift buffet table in the hall outside of the incident room. He recognized Sergeant O'Neil in the back, and wondered why the guy was here. This was homicide. Then Jack saw Deming, who noticed him. She held a cup in one hand, and in the other balanced a plate filled with a variety of finger food. He and Hannah approached.

"Mrs. Pepperidge took pity on us." Deming lifted her paper cup in salute, before taking a sip. Jack could smell the wine. "Food is love, she said. Apparently, alcohol is, too. We're supposed to view this as a celebration. A victory meal, of sorts. Not feeling it." Deming grimaced, peering at the laughing faces and jovial officers. "None of this feels right."

Hannah was avoiding everyone's gazes, keeping her thoughts to herself. He wanted to hold her and whisk her off to hide somewhere, but she was acting distant, and he was afraid this case ending had pushed her further away from him. She seemed to be second-guessing everything. Maybe even him.

"I'm heading to my desk," Hannah said. "I have things I need to do."

Jack didn't stop her, afraid what she would say if he tried. Instead, he watched her disappear into the incident room. From the looks of Ferguson and Lieutenant Pepperidge, they were also taking this news hard, but homicide's night shift wasn't hiding their good cheer. Nobody here knew Vivian well. She'd always kept to herself. It explained why the whole damn department had turned the occasion into a party. Yet he and his team just wanted to grieve.

"Hannah found the note in Vivian's purse," Jack said.

"I want to see it." Deming frowned. "Does Charlie have it?" She asked as if that possibility made her less likely to pursue it. Jack had to suppose that whatever was going on between those two went deep. Deming didn't normally care about people enough to avoid them. She sipped her wine, put it down, then popped a chicken nugget into her mouth.

"Yes. Charlie is running it for DNA and prints right now. He wasn't happy to get the call, but he came in, along with his team."

"And Vivian? Any news?" she said.

"She's under guard in the ICU. She's not going anywhere."

"I feel stupid." Deming pushed her food around on her plate. "Some profiler I turned out to be."

"You did great," Jack said. "You pegged her completely. We investigated her, Deming. She was clean, had an alibi. But we have her confession now. Answers will come later."

"Ferguson kept saying it was a woman. I should have listened."

"We all should have. Seems obvious now." Jack caught a movement near the incident room door. It was Ferguson. He was looking through its glass pane, probably at Hannah inside. He seemed torn between entering or not. "We all dropped the ball."

"What's Hannah doing?" Deming sipped more wine, watching Ferguson *not* enter the incident room.

"Punishing herself." He was almost positive she was going over the case from beginning to end, listing all the places she'd missed a clue. He couldn't allow that. Jack watched as Ferguson pivoted and walked away from the door, a scowl on his face. It triggered Jack's need to see Hannah *now*. "Enjoy the food and wine while I go talk my partner off the ledge." Deming delayed his departure with a touch on his sleeve.

"Is that what she is?" Her smile was sad, but it was encouraging.

"She's more," Jack said. "Always has been." Deming's smile blossomed to a hopeful one. And for the first time since he stepped off the plane at Logan Airport, *he* felt hopeful. The case was over. It ended badly, but it was over and it was time to look toward the future.

He strode down the hall, nodding to those he recognized, and by the time he'd pushed through the doors to the incident room, Ferguson was nowhere in sight. Jack found Hannah at her desk staring at a case file, her head in her hands, just as he'd predicted.

"Stop," he said.

"Stop what?" She leaned back in her chair, grimacing at him, as if he'd done something wrong.

"Stop beating yourself up. We caught the perp. That's all that matters."

"Tell that to Gary Buntle. Or the guy with half his face smoking in the morgue right now."

"That's not on you. You didn't kill them." Jack towered over her. "Tomorrow is time enough to second-guess. After you've slept, had some food. There's a huge spread out there. We should be eating it."

"Go," she waved him off, returning to her file.

"It's time to move on, Hannah."

She shook her head. "It's time to mourn, Jack. That's what you do when you lose something."

"You didn't lose. You won. The case is solved."

"I lost my confidence. I worked with Vivian nearly twenty-four seven this month. How did I not see the evil in her? And look at you." She lifted her hand, indicating him. "I thought you loved me, but you left me in such a spectacular way. I can't be trusted to see the truth, and now people are dead because I wasn't good enough."

"That's insane, Hannah. I love you, it's just—"

"If you loved me, you never would have hurt me like that. What I feel for Ellen is love. What you feel for me is something else."

His stomach tightened. "You're wrong." *She was going to leave him.* This was her way of preparing him for the big good-bye. "I do love you. My pride got in the way and I left. I'm not excusing my behavior. I was a fool, yes, but who isn't when it comes to love?"

"Me," she said. "I asked one thing of you." Tears fell from her eyes. "To be with me. And you left."

He took her hand. "I'm sorry. I do love you, Hannah. I always have. You have to give me another chance. Give us a chance."

He heard someone enter the room, and thought it must be Ferguson finding the courage to approach Hannah. Frustrated, a sharp word hovering on his lips, he turned and saw the lieutenant's wife. Politeness forced him to say the right words. "Hello, Mrs. Pepperidge. Thanks for the nice spread outside."

"Jolene. Please call me Jolene." Carrying a bottle of wine, she seemed put out to find him with Hannah, making him wonder if she'd overheard his and Hannah's conversation. She presented the wine and two paper cups. "Jack, you remind me of my husband. All work, no play. My husband, by the way, I'll get back now that this nasty case is over." She uncorked the red wine, set the two cups on the desk next to Hannah's file, and poured until it approached their brims. "When you get a win, you celebrate."

Hannah shook her head. "But it's Vivian, Mrs. Pepperidge. I…I just can't."

Sadness flickered in Mrs. Pepperidge's eyes, but then she forced a smile. "I know. Life sucks. That's why we drink." She offered Jack the other cup.

Jack wasn't much of a wine drinker, but didn't want to be rude. He lifted his cup in salute. Hannah lifted hers. "Am I taking your cup?" he said. He held it out to the lieutenant's wife, but she shook her head, showing him her palm. Even so, he got the feeling that he was intruding on a moment she'd intended to share with Hannah.

"No, sit, sit." Mrs. Pepperidge's eyes twinkled as he sat on the chair next to Hannah's desk. She made him feel like a schoolboy. "Believe me, I've had my fill. Please drink. It's very expensive. I wanted Hannah to get her share before it was gone. Of all of us, she deserves it." She chuckled. "Not to take anything away from your involvement in the case, Special Agent Benton." She indicated his cup. "We wouldn't be here without you."

They gently tapped paper cups and managed not to spill the wine. Hannah was playing along, drinking, but he could see her impatience and knew she wanted both him and Mrs. Pepperidge gone. To brood, no doubt. Well, *too bad*. He wasn't about to allow that—blaming herself—and he would not be discarded with the case.

"Cheers," he said.

"Cheers," Mrs. Pepperidge and Hannah echoed.

The expensive wine went down easy, but he didn't like the bitter aftertaste, so he put the cup back on the desk and hoped Mrs. Pepperidge wouldn't be insulted if he didn't finish it.

"What do you have there?" Mrs. Pepperidge stepped to Hannah's side, peering over her shoulder. She narrowed her eyes, reading a copy of the advice column letter attributed to Vivian. It was in its plastic evidence sleeve, typed, anonymous—only it wasn't anonymous now. "'My heart is broken.' Yikes. This lady cuts to the chase." Mrs. Pepperidge pressed a palm to her chest as she continued to read. "'The one I loved left me long ago, betrayed me, and I should have moved on, but can't. I've tried to forget, but the hole in my heart won't allow it. Every morning I wake and remember what I lost. It tortures me. I feel like a fool and don't know how to make this pain go away. Please. Someone help me.'" Mrs. Pepperidge exchanged an awkward glance with Jack, and then pursed her lips. "If that doesn't break your heart, nothing will. Have you figured out who she is?"

"What makes you think it's a woman?" Jack said. He saw Hannah blinking, as if trying to clear her vision. He wondered if she were staving off another panic attack. She sipped more wine and cleared her throat. She didn't look good. Jack decided to take her home. "It could just as easily be from a man." Men got their hearts broken, too. Hannah was breaking his right now.

Surprised, Mrs. Pepperidge looked between him and Hannah, as if only now reading the undercurrents in the room. Nudging the wine toward Jack, the lieutenant's wife gave him a look that said, *here, drink, you look like you need it.* And she was right. Hannah was going to leave him. He downed the rest of the wine and grimaced at the bitterness. This high-priced wine sucked.

"I just assumed it was a woman. I'm showing my age, I guess." Mrs. Pepperidge leaned forward, peering at Hannah. "You're looking a bit pale, sweetie. Don't you agree, Jack?"

He did, but didn't say anything because he was feeling a bit queasy himself. "It's been a long day." Scrubbing his face with his hands, he gave his head a little shake to stave off his growing lethargy. He just wanted to take Hannah home and know that the two people he loved most were tucked away safe, near at hand. She hadn't left him yet. Jack would think of something to convince Hannah they belonged together.

"Jack?" Hannah touched his arm, leaning heavily on the desk. "Jack, what's happening?" She seemed afraid, and confused.

He reached out to her just as his vision narrowed and the strength left his body, and then he slid to the floor, unable to move, eyes fixed and unblinking.

Chapter 22

Hannah leaned forward to catch him, but fell forward onto her desktop instead, scattering folders to the floor. Mrs. Pepperidge walked around the desk and took Jack's now vacant seat.

"Finally. Alone at last." The lieutenant's wife seemed pleased. "Hannah, my dear. You're the one that got away." She nodded toward Jack. "You still love him, don't you? Despite what he did to you? What he took?"

Words failed Hannah. She didn't recognize this woman. *This* Mrs. Pepperidge was fierce and frightening.

"I was there," Mrs. Pepperidge said. "At the hospital last March. I saw you miserable, bedridden. I was in the hall when you handed your letter to the nurse to mail and overheard your explanation about what you were doing. It broke my heart." Her chin quivered. "Because while you were waiting for your baby to die, I was mourning the loss of my child. I kept an eye out for your letter in the Globe, and when I found it, *read* it, I knew what I had to do. Help people. *See* their pain, as no one saw mine." She covered her mouth with her fingertips, and her eyes lost focus. "We called her Winnie." Mrs. Pepperidge's smile was wobbly, her eyes misty. "My little girl… So delicate. It's my fault." Her gaze hardened as she dropped her hand, bitterness corrupting her expression. "We kill our babies, Hannah." She glanced at Jack, supine at her feet. "Did you name yours? They don't give you a birth certificate if it dies too soon."

Hannah's mouth wasn't working anymore. Poison. The wine. *And seven more loves in my bed Crown with wine my mournful head, Pitying and forgiving all Thy transgressions great and small.*

Mrs. Pepperidge seemed disappointed Hannah was unable to respond. She glanced over her shoulder as if to make sure they were alone. Lowering her voice, she leaned in, and said, "There are things a person shouldn't be forced to survive, but your pain should be seen. Immortalized. It's as if Blake's 'Broken Love' was written for my people. And the Freedom Trail tours will have to add the notorious Mercy Killing victims to their scripts, telling the story on every tour. I made sure of it." She smiled, coquettish. "Meet your department's leak." She bowed her head, as if accepting accolades. "The *Boston Globe* loves me."

"Please." Hannah's could only manage a whisper, and it was getting more difficult to keep her eyes open and focused. Jack, on his side on the floor, weakly clenched his fist and then relaxed it. *He was alive, but for how long?*

Mrs. Pepperidge nudged the empty wine cup with her manicured finger, looking between it and Hannah. "Don't look at me like that. I couldn't just do nothing. And Cooper helped me, the dear, though he didn't know it. He was there if I had any questions. My little helper."

Hannah pulled her arm off the desk by agonizing degrees, until it dropped to her side, her hand inching toward her gun's holster. Jack's leg twitched on the periphery of her vision.

"They wanted to die. Like you." All of Mrs. Pepperidge's smoothness, and cavalier tone faded. "Like me," the woman whispered.

Hannah was *nothing* like Mrs. Pepperidge. She wanted to live, but could feel the drug *killing* her as she struggled to move. "My baby—" Hannah managed to tug her gun from its holster, but it dropped from her weakened fingers onto her lap.

"You'll see your baby soon." Mrs. Pepperidge smoothed Hannah's bangs off her forehead. "You and Carey should be on the Freedom Trail with the rest of them, but things keep getting…complicated. I'll be better next time. Smarter. Seven down, ten more stanzas to go. At least he won't get in my way again." She glared at Jack. "That bastard destroyed you."

Jack did destroy her, but he gave her so much, too. Ellen. And now he was back and she wanted it to stay that way. She loved him. Loved him enough not to give up on him now. With monumental effort, Hannah dragged her other hand to her lap. Now both her hands weakly gripped the gun.

Mrs. Pepperidge nudged Jack with her black heeled pump. "You were pregnant. He deserted you, and made you lose the baby."

"My. Baby. Didn't. Die." With agonizing effort, Hannah curled her finger around the trigger just as Mrs. Pepperidge leaned over the desk and stripped the gun from her hand with little effort. Out of the corner of her eye, she saw Jack move, slowly removing his gun from its holster. He aimed it at Mrs. Pepperidge.

"*No*," Hannah said. To Mrs. Pepperidge? To Jack? All Hannah knew was the killing had to stop.

"This is taking too long, and you're suffering." Mrs. Pepperidge aimed the gun at Hannah's head.

Boom! The gun's discharge preceded a pink mist that spattered Hannah and her desk. Mrs. Pepperidge crumpled to the floor, shot in the head. Blinking, struggling to focus, Hannah sobbed. Jack lay still, hand slack around his gun, his eyes closed. Her vision pinpointed to a white dot, and then there was nothing.

Chapter 23

Beeping. Crisp cotton against her skin. Bright light on closed eyelids. The smell of disinfectant. Something tickling her nose, which twitched in response.

"Oh my gosh," a familiar voice said. "She's finally waking up." Vivian? But Vivian was dying in Mass General's ICU.

Hannah blinked, wincing as the overhead fluorescents irritated her eyes. Her vision cleared. Someone cradled her hand in theirs. It *was* Vivian, sitting next to Hannah. She was in a wheelchair, smiling ear to ear. And Hannah was in a hospital bed. Her heart sank. In a hospital bed *again*. The familiar weight of suffocation came roaring back as if it were only yesterday that she'd been here, desperate to save her baby. She wanted to go home.

"You're alive," Hannah croaked, then cleared her throat. She and Vivian weren't alone. Most of the team was here. But…not Jack. Mrs. Pepperidge's wine killed him, but he held out long enough to save her. To save them all. *Jack*. Her eyes filled with tears.

"Right back at you." Tears spilled down Vivian's cheeks, too. She wiped them using her hospital gown.

"Hannah," Ferguson said. "This has been a long time coming. We were afraid you'd never wake up." He stood at the foot of her bed, his concern pulling at his features. Deming looked a bit misty-eyed, too, and was trying to hide it behind a coffee cup.

"We've been taking turns babysitting you," Deming said, "so when the staff called and told us you'd been showing signs of waking, we hustled down here. Mrs. Branaghan is on her way. Natalie is on a plane and will arrive this afternoon. You scared the shit out of us."

Hannah swallowed a sob. Work. Check. Ellen? Jack? Jack was dead. Check, check. Her ten-second heartbreak. Now it would haunt her the rest of her days.

Where was Ellen? And why was Natalie on a plane?

"Hey, hey." Vivian hovered, patting her hand. "You're going to be all right, I promise." She smiled through her tears. "Look at me. Died a few times, but I'm still here."

Everything was a muddle. "What happened?" Hannah said.

Vivian winced, as if the memories were still too painful. "Mrs. Pepperidge set me up. *On a blind date.* That alone should have tipped me off. Can you see me? On a blind date? Well, she gave me a letter to read afterward, and I thought it was a pep talk or something. I put it in my purse." She sniffed, smiling, though her pain was unmistakable. "I should have known it was too good to be true. When I saw Kent, the bastard who broke my heart, I knew something was up. Mrs. Pepperidge had a bottle of wine delivered to the table, but by then I was too embarrassed to stay. It exploded just as I reached the exit. Knocked me out cold. Charlie said the bottle was a chemical bomb." She lowered her gaze, biting her lip. "Kent's dead." Her voice sounded wobbly. "The restaurant was destroyed. Five dead, twenty-three injured. I was cleared when forensics found a partial print on the letter, my so-called confession. It was Mrs. Pepperidge's. But none of my prints were on it."

"But... But, how did she know you wrote that letter to the *Boston Globe*?" Hannah said.

Vivian's chin quivered. "I told her one night. Month's ago. It was late. We'd had some of the scotch the lieutenant keeps in his office and... I told her and never thought twice about it. There was something about Mrs. Pepperidge that made a person trust her."

Yeah. Hannah had trusted her. She closed her eyes, desperate and feeling hopeless. They'd been played by an expert. No. By a psychopath with all the access and knowledge to commit the perfect crime. So many people died because Hannah hadn't been up to the task. The love of her life...

"*Jack.*" Tears spilled from her closed eyes.

"Speak of the devil," Ferguson said. Hannah blinked in confusion.

Jack burst through the hospital door, out of breath, stricken. "Hannah!" He was holding Ellen.

Deming wheeled Vivian out of the way as Jack barreled on through to Hannah's side, but not before handing the wiggly baby to Ferguson, who tensed up, but got the job done.

Jack sat on the bed's edge and gathered Hannah into his embrace. "Never, never, never do that to me again! Do you hear me?"

"What?" Deming said. "Almost die?"

"Oh, the irony stings. Don't it?" Ferguson kissed the baby and walked to the other side of Hannah's bed. "I can't believe you kept her a secret for so long, Hannah. Benton's crash course in parenting would have been amusing if it wasn't so sad to watch."

Hannah sobbed against Jack's chest, eyes squeezed shut. "Jack, I thought you'd died."

He loosened his grip only enough to kiss her soundly. "Back at you." He kissed her again, but her oxygen tubing got in the way. She tugged it down, and lifted her chin for his kiss. He pressed his lips to hers, gently, lovingly.

Ellen cooed. Hannah smiled, breaking the kiss, exchanging a happy glance with Jack. "My baby." Jack arranged Hannah back onto the bed. She lifted her arms, seeking Ellen. Her daughter's arms reached for her, but they weren't the arms Hannah remembered. Ellen was older. "How long have I been unconscious?" Panic acted like a band of steel across her chest, making it hard to breathe.

"We'll leave you two to talk." Ferguson hustled Deming and Vivian out the door, but not before giving Hannah an encouraging wink. "Welcome back from the dead."

Jack lowered Ellen into Hannah's arms, and as soon as she held her daughter, everything calmed and seemed right with the world. No matter what happened, she, Jack, and Ellen, they'd get through it.

"Everyone knows about Ellen. Don't get mad," Jack said. "With you in the hospital so long, unconscious—"

"How long?"

"Three weeks." His grimace hinted at the worry he'd been put through. "I thought Ellen's presence might wake you up, so I brought her every day. Word got out quickly."

"I'm not mad." She kissed her daughter's cheek. "We nearly died because I kept her existence a secret. I'm chalking that up to one of my worst ideas. Mrs. Pepperidge admitted she targeted me because she thought Ellen had been a stillbirth."

"You were protecting our baby. That's all that matters."

Ellen lifted her head, gifting her mother with a toothless grin. "She can lift her head now." Ellen's pudgy hand grabbed Hannah's hair and stuck a blond lock into her drooling mouth.

"She rolls over, too," he said.

Hannah didn't know whether to laugh or cry. "I missed it."

"I missed you." Jack kissed her, lingeringly, and when he lifted his head, he searched her eyes for something. Hannah wasn't sure what. "I love you," he said. "I've been telling you every day since I woke and wheeled myself into this hospital room. They said you couldn't hear me, but I didn't believe them. Did you hear me?"

Hannah hadn't, or if she had, she didn't remember. But she knew she loved him. That was clear. She loved him with all her heart.

"Don't ignore me, Hannah."

"I'm not—"

"I've just spent three weeks being ignored by you and I can't take it anymore. When I tell you I love you, you don't have to say it back, but at least tell me you believe me!" He looked frazzled.

She sniffled, nodding. "I believe you. I think I always knew, but you kept confusing me, and then you died. You have to stop doing that."

He frowned, clutching her free hand. "I was a fool."

* * * *

Jack pressed his lips to her temple, needing to be as close to her as possible. "I woke the day after Mrs. Pepperidge poisoned us, suffering a hangover from hell. But you," he said, "well, you just didn't want to wake up." He kissed her neck, happiness and relief sapping his strength. "Everyone feared the worst. I thought I'd lost you again."

She cupped his cheek. "You've lost weight. Are you sure you're okay?"

"Parenting isn't for the weak." Jack thought of the late nights at the hospital, the lost sleep with Ellen inconsolably crying for her mom, and figured it was a miracle he hadn't lost more weight. "I'm okay. Now that you're okay." He turned his head to press a kiss to her palm, and stayed there for a moment, eyes closed, allowing the moment to sink in. She was going to be fine. He turned his head, pinning her with a fierce look. "And don't think I'm above taking advantage of this situation. I finally have you where I want you. You'll have to listen to me now."

"Honestly," she said, "I'm going nowhere. I feel weighed down with stones. Comas aren't for the weak either." She closed her eyes and took a deep breath, caressing Ellen's back. "But I'm good. You're alive and Ellen is here."

"About that," he said. "I want to make a deal with you."

That got Hannah's eyes open. "A deal, huh? What kind of deal?"

Jack knew he had issues, knew exactly how those issues screwed up his relationship with Hannah, but that didn't make it easier to show vulnerability. "Here's the deal. You love me. Spend the rest of your life with me, *marry me*—"

Hannah laughed, rolling her eyes. "And what do I get out of it?"

Jack was hoping he'd be enough. "A man who will love you and Ellen more than life itself." She was about to interrupt, but he feared she'd make light of his declaration when he was deadly serious. "I'm not expecting you to put your seal of approval on me. I'm messed up. I get it. My leaving last year was unforgivable. But love me anyway. I know I've been wrongheaded, I've made every mistake in the book—"

"And invented a few."

"—but love me anyway, Hannah. Love me anyway. I came back because I couldn't bear to be without you a moment longer, and now there's Ellen." He didn't know what else to say. She had to take him back.

Hannah rested her hand on his. "I've always loved you. Yeah, you're complicated, and sometimes I don't understand you, but you're the one I want."

He brought her hand to his lips. "You love me. You said it, so marry me."

Her smile beamed at him. "I love you. I'll marry you." She kissed the top of Ellen's head. Their daughter was wiggling, looking for attention. "Was it wrong of me to want you to say it first last year?"

Jack lay next to her on the hospital bed, encircling Hannah and Ellen in his embrace, keeping them safe. "Wrong? No. Problematic. You were dealing with me and my insecurities, after all." He found himself chuckling, ecstatically happy.

"We don't do easy, you and I."

"No. We don't." He dropped a kiss on her lips, noting her frown, and the sadness in her eyes. "What?"

"You've waited long enough, Jack. Tell me the bad news. What happened to Mrs. Pepperidge? I think I remember what happened, but..." Jack looked away, not wanting to talk about something so horrible when he was feeling so happy. When she sighed and said, "I was afraid of that," he knew he had no choice.

"It was her or you. I chose you, Hannah, and I'd do it again." He pressed his forehead to hers, trying to coax her out of her misery. "The lieutenant is on leave, trying to come to terms with what happened. IA is investigating."

"I'm sorry." She shook her head. "I can't begin to tell you how sorry I am that it happened this way."

"They found her stash. It contained a journal detailing her kills and next targets. The owners of the *Teapot* were her cousins."

"*Were?*"

"They weren't supposed to be in town during the Stone murder, so caught her on board, saw the kill chart. It forced her to dispose of Stone's unconscious body quickly, rather than stage it on the Freedom Trail. She detailed the whole thing in her journal. Her cousins' bodies were weighted down with items she found on board and we found the couple where she'd written they'd be; under water, directly under the yacht. She used the *Teapot* as a weapon against you to kill two birds with one stone. Kill you and destroy the crime scene evidence. But she miscalculated the water's depth. It was too deep for her plan. The very thing that prevented our people from finding the bodies when they processed the crime scene, is what protected the bodies from being destroyed by the blast."

Jack watched as Hannah took each piece of information to heart, using it like a cudgel to punish herself. "Stop internalizing this, Hannah. She was a serial killer."

She nodded, snuggling closer to him and Ellen. "Give me time." He nodded. "You've had three weeks," she said. "I still need to process."

"Well, there's other news." He smiled brightly, though there was a part of him worried she wouldn't take this news well either. "Even unconscious you've found a way to multitask." He saw her confusion and shrugged. It's not as if he could keep it from her forever. "You're pregnant. We're going to have another baby." Her shocked expression quickly made way for laughing, which lifted a weight of worry off Jack's shoulders.

She loved him. He loved her. Whatever the future held, they were willing and able to meet that challenge.

Hannah kissed Ellen's cheek and reached for Jack. "Wow. We really don't do things the easy way, do we?" Cupping the back of his head, she urged him forward, looking for a kiss. He obliged, happily.

"Tell me you love me again," Jack said against her lips. "Tell me you forgive me."

"I love you. I forgive you. Just never leave me again." More tears. He knew it had a lot to do with exhaustion. She could barely keep her eyes open. Afraid she'd drop the baby, Jack took Ellen, and held her next to her mother so she could still be with her, but not have to bear the baby's weight.

"So we'll marry," he said. "We'll marry as soon as you get out of this hospital." Jack waited, hoping she wouldn't fight him on this. "If you love me, you'll marry me as soon as possible."

Hannah smiled past her exhaustion. "I love you," she said, "and one of these days you'll believe me."

"Then marry me."

"In a heartbeat."

In a heartbeat. Jack laughed, because joy and exultation swelled his chest. Lifting Ellen into the air, he said, "Mommy and I are getting married. What do you think about that?"

"She's happy," Hannah said. "I'm happy." Hannah was the image of contentment, other than tears covering her cheeks. Tears of happiness.

Jack kissed them until his face was wet with her tears. "Weep no more, my love. Weep no more, I beg of you."

And she did.

Epilogue

Special Agent Cynthia Deming wheeled IT tech Vivian O'Grady down the hall toward her hospital room, and couldn't wipe the smile off her face. She was so happy for Benton. It wasn't easy to find the love of your life, and he had, and he was so damn lucky. She almost felt envious, until she thought about all that would entail. Making someone else a priority. Putting your life on hold to fill their needs. Relying on them to feel as strongly about you as you did about them... She shook her head, trying to push past the knot of anxiety such thoughts created.

Ahead, the elevator *bing*ed and opened. Special Agent Gilroy stepped off, looking harried and confused. When he saw her and Vivian, he immediately relaxed. He zeroed in on Vivian. "I went to your room first and saw you were gone, Miss O'Grady." He glanced at Cynthia and frowned. "What's this about Cambridge waking up?"

Cynthia nodded. "It's true, but don't go in there yet."

Vivian nodded and blushed. "They're having...a moment," she said.

Gilroy's expression softened even more as he approached, and Cynthia had to bite her lip not to rib the agent. He and Vivian had gotten closer these last three weeks. Opposites attract, she supposed. Vivian's softness to Gilroy's hardness. Vivian's overflowing emotionalism to Gilroy's... Cynthia struggled to describe Gilroy. He hated drama of any kind and was the first to run if something resembling an emotion was aired in his vicinity. Yet the man had glommed onto Vivian.

Gilroy tilted his head to the side and gave Cynthia a look. "I'll bring Vivian back to her room." Then he took the wheelchair handles and pushed Vivian on to the elevator. When Cynthia attempted to step on the elevator, too, Gilroy shook his head. "We're heading up." He widened his eyes, signaling he didn't want her to play fifth wheel, so Cynthia stepped back into the hall, no longer able to repress her laugh. She was face-to-face with a scowling Gilroy and a blushing Vivian as the elevator doors closed them inside.

And then she was alone. It felt weird.

Cynthia pressed the elevator button.

There were three elevators, and the numbered lights above them made clear that none were anywhere near her floor. Smoothing down her perfectly pressed Christian Dior suit jacket, she glanced left and right down the hall. There were uniformed police officers milling in front of Hannah's room. Now that she'd woken from her coma, Cynthia suspected there'd be a long stream of visitors checking in on her, needing to reassure themselves that she was okay. It was nice. Cynthia was happy for her. Happy for the couple.

She pressed the elevator button again, and then impatiently tapped her Louboutin pump against the floor. Benton was still on family leave, but Cynthia was supposed to meet Special Agents Modena and Gilroy after lunch, downtown at FBI headquarters. Apparently, an old case was rearing its ugly head again, and they were to be debriefed.

An elevator binged, she turned toward it and when the doors opened, Charlie stood front and center inside, a huge bouquet of flowers gripped in his right hand.

"Charlie." Cynthia's jaw dropped. Why she was surprised to see him was beyond her, but she was. "You brought flowers." That was sweet. And so like Charlie. She swallowed hard, pushing down the myriad of emotions that always swirled inside her when she was anywhere near him.

He stepped off the elevator. "I heard she'd woken up."

The doors started closing. She reached for it like a lifeline, then stepped on the elevator. "Yeah. I'd give the happy family a moment or two, or you might walk in on something you can't unsee."

Charlie frowned, taking a step closer until his large frame walled her into the elevator, trapping her. "Why are you doing this, Cynthia?" He seemed truly puzzled, and it drove her insane.

Why was she avoiding him? Why did she turn into someone totally different whenever he was around? Why did she take a job that ensured being away from Boston for long stretches of time? A normal man wouldn't have to ask. He'd *know*. But Charlie wasn't normal. He was perfect. Damn him.

As the elevator doors began to close again, Charlie seemed poised to reach for her to force a confrontation. Instead, his fist clenched around a bouquet he'd bought for another woman. They stared at each other, their gazes holding until the doors closed with a clang and she was alone again, the elevator moving down to ground level.

"Damn." Cynthia took a quick breath and looked up, blinking tears away. *She would not feel these things. She refused to feel these emotions.*

If Charlie found out she'd fallen in love with him, it would *ruin* what was left of their friendship, and other than her job, Charlie was all Cynthia had left.

Meet the Author

Kris Rafferty was born in Cambridge, Massachusetts. After earning a bachelor's in arts from the University of Massachusetts/Boston, she married her college sweetheart, traveled the country, and wrote books. Three children and a Pomeranian/Shih Tzu mutt later, she spends her days devoting her life to her family and her craft.

Don't miss the next book in
Kris Rafferty's wonderful series,
SECRET AGENTS.

DEADLY PAST
is about Cynthia Deming and Charlie Foulkes...and their
romantic, suspenseful story.
Coming to you in
December 2018!

If you enjoyed CATCH A KILLER
by Kris Rafferty,
make sure you read the first book
in the
Secret Agents series:
CAUGHT BY YOU
available at your favorite e-tailer

Turn the page for a quick peek!

Chapter 1

"Deming? Are you insane?" Special Agent Vincent Modena was in the back of the FBI's surveillance van, kneeling knee to knee with Special Agent Cynthia Deming, the task force's profiler. It wasn't Deming who was the problem; it was the five-pound flounder she held by the gills. It was staring at him, and smelled hideous.

"Your cover is a week-long fishing trip. You're too clean." Deming narrowed her blue eyes, and then slapped the fish against Vincent's chest.

"Stop!" He grabbed her wrist, processing the moment. Rich, blond, gorgeous Cynthia Deming, in a black Dolce & Gabbana suit and heels, was on her knees swinging a fish. Nope. He was living it and still didn't believe his eyes. Meanwhile, the flounder hung limp in the air between them. "I'm supposed to keep Avery Coppola *in* the diner, Deming. Hit me with that again, and the smell will chase her *out*." She broke his grip, seemingly teetering between agreeing and having another go at him with the fish.

Special Agent Jack Benton, FBI task force team leader, jumped from the van's passenger seat into the back. "What the hell?" He grimaced, glaring at the profiler and Vincent, as if Vincent had anything to do with the fish. He didn't.

"Exactly," Vincent said. "What the hell, Deming?"

"What's with the fish?" Benton's black hair hung in his face, obscuring the intensity in his blue-eyed gaze. His yearlong deep embed with Dante Coppola's syndicate crashed and burned yesterday, requiring the task force to extract him. His split lip hinted at the bruises and abrasions hidden beneath his conservative black suit and tie, but it was the banked rage that made his team nervous. Benton hadn't taken time off to shake his role of gunrunner, and some deep embeds needed more recovery time than others, but he'd escaped with a lead, so Benton wasn't going anywhere. The lead was, Coppola hired contract killers to find and kill his ex-wife and her little sister. Rumor had it, when she'd divorced him three years ago, the ex-wife left with incriminating files. Now, Coppola knew where the ex-wife was, and so did Benton. It appeared as if the task force lucked out and got here first.

"The fish is necessary for authenticity," Deming said. "Modena's too…" She waved a hand at him. "Handsome."

"Hey, Benton." Vincent held Deming gaze and then winked. "Deming thinks I'm handsome."

She shook her head, barely paying attention to Vincent. "Maybe *clean* is a better word. After a week of backcountry camping, he wouldn't be this clean." She used the back of her wrist to nudge a blond lock off her cheek. "No one sleeps outside for a week, lives off fresh catch of the day, and doesn't suffer from puffy face and bad hair. Avery's clever and distrustful. She's had to be to escape detection for three years with a sister in tow. With contract killers on her scent, she'll smell a rat if Modena doesn't commit to his backstory."

"She'll smell something." Special Agent Harris Gilroy was the task force's official driver. Blond hair cropped to his head, brown eyes, mid-thirties, he looked like an Irish bare-knuckle fighter, crooked nose and all.

"His backpack is enough of a prop," Benton said. "Get rid of the fish, Deming."

"Fine." She tossed it into a Styrofoam cooler, and then stripped off her latex gloves, throwing them inside, too. She seemed on edge. Yesterday's violent extraction of Benton had notably rattled her, rattled them all, as did the dead bodies the team left behind. And when Deming was rattled, she distracted herself with details—like Vincent's backstory and a fish—so Vincent tried not to take the fish assault personally.

"Our warrant is to surveil Avery Coppola's apartment," Benton said. "Unfortunately, I couldn't convince the judge that rumored files containing alleged evidence is grounds for a search warrant, so we watch and wait for Coppola's men to make their move. If the files are in her apartment, she either surrenders them, or we need probable cause to take them. If Coppola's men find her, maybe make a move on her at the apartment, we've got them and our probable cause, so cross your fingers. Modena, you keep an eye on her at the diner while we set up the cameras outside of her apartment. I want any potential attack on video. Let a judge and jury see who these monsters are, and if we're forced to bust into her apartment to save her, and happen to find evidence, they'll be forced to make our findings admissible in court. Time is short, folks. We have no idea when Coppola's men will show, but this isn't rocket science. If she has files, which my contact assured me she does, it's probably hidden in her apartment. Coppola's men have to know that."

"Yeah, about that, Benton," Deming said. "I think I should go in the diner instead of Modena. Look at him. He looks dangerous. She'll think he's a contract killer, maybe run, and ruin the whole operation. We can think of a different backstory for me."

"Deming, you'd be walking into a backwoods diner wearing Dolce & Gabbana," Vincent said. "Do you really think you'll get anywhere near her without making her suspicious? And Benton knows I have advantages you don't have." He allowed a slow smile to crack his lips. "Leave the ex-wife to me."

She shook her head, still not convinced. "But—"

"I know. I know. I'm handsome, clean, *and* dangerous." Vincent winked, trying not to enjoy Deming's annoyance too much. Being on the sidelines was twisting her in knots. She wanted in on the action, and he didn't blame her, but he'd waited too long to meet Avery Coppola to just give this moment away. "I think you're crushing on me."

"Blow me, Modena." She turned toward Benton, waiting for his decision.

"We stick with the plan," Benton said. "Modena, go."

Gilroy reached into a console between the two front seats and produced a bottle of Febreze. He aimed it into the back of the van and sprayed with no concern for whom he doused. Between the fish smell, and being gassed by Gilroy, Vincent found it a relief to spill out into the parking lot, backpack slung over his shoulder.

As the task force sped off in the van, heading down the street toward Avery Coppola's apartment, Vincent walked toward the diner, passing a multitude of beat up SUVs and trucks, listening to his hiking boots crunch gravel underfoot. The chirping of birds, the breezes rustling through maple and oak leaves, it was a nice change from the city. August in the North Country of New Hampshire, mountainous. Vincent was enjoying himself, and the diner's aromas wafting through the air. His stomach growled as he approached the door, but his thoughts were all on the woman inside.

Avery Coppola. *Damn.* Her name had been popping up in the Coppola case for a year now, but Vincent had only actively studied her for the last few months. He was a little ashamed to be this excited about meeting her... Dante Coppola's one vulnerability. Avery was the crime lord's ex-wife, so probably poison, without conscience. Totally his type. Vincent's ex-wife taught him a thing or two about women like that. On his second tour in

Afghanistan, she'd sent him a Dear John letter paper clipped to divorce papers. It had a way of changing a man's paradigm real quick. It certainly forced Vincent to see things more clearly. Women were mercurial at best, self-serving at worst. It was weird to know he had something in common with a murderous crime lord. Both he and Coppola married women who'd betrayed them.

He'd memorized Avery's pictures. She had the look of an innocent, red-headed imp, and seemed younger than her years. She certainly didn't look like someone who could inspired an ex-husband to hire contract killers to off her. Not a sterling personal recommendation, and yet, the contradiction tickled Vincent's curiosity. What would she be like? Or rather, how best to bend her to his will?

Benton wanted to try and flip her, see if they could convince her to give up the goods on her ex, rather than make the Feds slog for the evidence, but they didn't have enough intel to know how best to approach her. Deming, the task force's profiler, suggested they feel her out with some casual conversation. Benton had tapped Vincent, and he'd report back to the team after they'd finished installing security cameras around her apartment.

Just meeting her would probably answer most of the questions his team had. Then, if all went as planned, they'd find the leverage they needed to flip her, and she'd help break open the task force's RICO case against her ex-husband. If *that* went south, she'd either face jail time or risk a bullet between the eyes. Dante Coppola wasn't pulling his hit on her anytime soon, and now that he knew where she was, she had a target on her back. The FBI would offer her protection, if she was willing to deal, but they couldn't make her accept their help. No, that would take persuasion. And that was where Vincent came in.

He smiled as he opened the diner's door. A bell chimed overhead, announcing his arrival. It was old-fashioned and kitschy, and he liked it. As he stepped inside, he finally admitted to himself that he'd been anticipating this meeting with Avery Coppola since he'd first seen her photo nearly a year ago. He was excited, and when his gaze zeroed in on her behind the diner's counter, his chest tightened because he knew… This was going to be fun. Lots and lots of fun.